Doil Pettyjohn was an entertainment mogul; the P.T. Barnum of northern Alabama. A man with his finger on the throbbing jugular of the amusement hungry farmers and tradesmen, and their kin, that peopled this remote section of old Dixie. The seat of his empire lay at a crossroads where two county roads intersected a state highway. Pettyjohn's Monkey Ranch, it was called. A combination zoo, theatre, gas station, grocery store, and bootlegging operation. It was by far, the busiest hub in the county. Approaching from any direction, you were treated to Doil's version of the 'Burma Shave' ad campaign;

SEE THE MONKEY——————RIDE THE
SWING——————WHILE HE'S
PLAYIN'——————-WITH HIS THING————
——-AT PETTYJOHN'S.'

From another approach it read:

MEANEST GATOR——————-IN THE
WORLD——————-EATS
PREACHERS——————-AND LITTLE GIRLS'.

Some were better, some worse, but whether you stopped out of curiosity, or outrage, you still stopped, and that was the whole point of the exercise. Doil Pettyjohn had an innate, grass roots sense of the motivational factors that separate men, and or women, from their purses. It's what made him a legend, and earned him powerful friends, as well as a few powerful enemies. I loved Doil Pettyjohn as one would love a nere-do-well uncle.

The ranch itself sat a couple of hundred feet or so off the road, separated from it by a dirt parking lot, where hormone ragin' farm teens 'scratched off', and cut 'dados' in their daddy's trucks, keeping the whole place cloudy, and covered with a choking layer of dust. There was one big oak tree at the back of the lot, next to the eight foot tall plank fence that was salvaged, or stolen, from neighbor's barns and outbuildings, (outhouses, judging from the smell), that separated those in the parking area from marauding animals and reptiles. Under the spreading oak branches was a cage with a dozen or so mangy, mail-order monkeys, that had obviously been driven to insanity by the constant harassment of children and thrill-seeking hillbillies, and Doil's belief that alcohol makes monkeys more entertaining. Adjacent to the monkeys, was a small fenced petting area, that contained a foul smelling goat, crudely tethered to a concrete block, and a one-eyed, pot-bellied pig named Cecil, whose blind eye bore mute testimony to the entertainment value of the drunk monkeys. This free section of the ranch had always been a favorite of the local children, and they even had a call and response, inspired by their fond remembrances of afternoons spent tormenting the animals.

"DID YA'FEED THA'MONKEYS? YEAH, WE FED EM' TO THA'GA-TER" was chanted by little girls as they jumped rope. When the county was finally able to build a central school to replace all the community schoolhouses, the Gater' was unanimously voted as team mascot, and the chant became the favorite of the crowds at the ball games. The cheerleaders snapped their fingers under their elbows in the same rhythm they had practiced since they were small. Such was the influence of show bidness'.

The plank fence was decorated from one end to the other with crudely drawn renderings of snakes and gators, and the occasional movie poster, filched from the local theatre, depicting Steve Reeves as Tarzan, his heavily muscled torso hanging from a vine with a knife in his teeth, and 'The Creature From The Black Lagoon', rising from the murky water in the moonlight, draped with seaweed. My favorite, and the favorite of all who stood before it, was the poster that hung beside the gate to the reptile show. It showed 'Sinbad the Sailor' in a death struggle with the Cyclops on the beach; a chilling preview of what adventures one might have for the mere pittance of a dollar. It was the essence of free-market capitalism.

Once inside, you found yourself in a chicken-wire safety enclosure for protection from marauding reptiles. Nervously surveying this forbidden world, your eyes would be drawn to a stagnant pond, about twenty yards away, covered in bright green scum, with what appeared to be a large, rotting log floating peacefully on the surface. To the left of the pond, and much nearer the safety wire, was an old chicken coop, that rattled and buzzed ominously, as Doil Pettyjohn, the consummate showman, a vision from a pygmy's nightmare, stepped into view, and whacked the wall with his riding crop. Dressed in army surplus desert gear, complete with canteen and survival knife, and topped by a pith helmet, at three hundred forty-six pounds, he looked like Rommel's pastry chef. He would move closer, and executing that odd, one-two hop to attention made famous by the British Army, salute the audience with his crop. The monologue remained pretty much the same, having been refined through trial and error, and the fact that those adventurers who came back to the show time and time again, were not generally the type to be dissuaded, or upset by stale material. They seemed to enjoy the predictability of it all.

"Private Pettyjohn, Alabama Reptile Wranglers repawtin' fa'duty!" It was, after all, show bidness'.

"Tha' CHICKEN-WIRE is ya'onliest' protection! Stay behind it at ALL times!"

Anxiety levels rose considerably at this point, in that 'chicken wire' was to protection, what Wallace was to civil rights. Now you have to understand, as Doil did, that in the south, and especially in the 'Celtic' blood region that stretched from northeastern Alabama, up through the Appalachians, shows of male bravado were expected and encouraged; a genetic tradition stretching all the way back to the clannish tribes of Scotland and Ireland, where boastfulness, and affinity for strong drink were considered virtues. In homage to that noble tradition, Doil would always start the show with a rather non-threatening species, to allow the more vocal of the tribesmen to establish their manliness for all of the ladies in the audience.

Marching to the coop, he would reach into a small cage that stood just ouside the door, and extract a life-form of some sort, his bulk blocking the view, and concealing the identity of the beast. With delicate step, cupping the creature in gloved hands, he would come close to the enclosure, causing women to shrink back, thus creating the ILLUSION, that the men were moving forward, to face the danger, as their genetic make-up would dictate. In his most dramatic voice, he would announce,

"Horny toad!"

This always elicited a squeal or two from the nervous women, who as a general rule, were not big fans of any member of the toad family, be it horny or not. They did, however, usually overcome their squeamishness, and look at it closely, it not being native to the state, and most of them never having actually seen one. To the men, however, this was a subliminal signal to open the testosterone flood gates, and start the pissing contest between themselves, and Doil and his puny creatures, with off-hand remarks like,

"I thought is' was sposed' ta' be some dangerous shit." and

"How'd ya' know e'was horny? De' try ta' mount ya'?

Sometimes, the banter went beyond good natured ribbing, and one or more would say some pretty cruel things to Doil, having fortified themselves with spirits, questionong Doil's courage, or lack there-of, and attempting to establish male dominance from the INSIDE of the safety enclosure. These unfortunates, who were usually the biggest chicken-shits in the lot, unwittingly became players in this carefully considered drama.

Doil would casually return the small toad to his cage, and disappear into the curiously singing coop, momentarily to re-appear with the biggest, angriest rattlesnake that God ever put a gut in. Six feet of writhing muscle, as big around as a man's fore-arm, followed by thirteen rattles and a button, all shakin' like a Cuban rhythm section, with a head as big as a spade. He would stride directly to his antagonists, holding the hissing demon in outstretched arms, it's mouth wide open, revealing a pair of two inch daggers, dripping with death, and giving way to a huge, pink gullet, big enough to swallow a cat. This horrific display sent everyone, including the swaggering mannish-boys, to the rear of the enclosure, trembling with fright.

It was at this moment in the performance, that Doil took complete control of the audience. The heckling would stop, and all would give him their rapt attention, right on cue. The terrified, yet curious crowd watched in silent awe as he milked this monster by allowing him to bury his fangs in a piece of an inner tube stretched over a fruit jar, and gnawin' it like a pit bull, squirt enough poison in that jar to mix a martini. No one dared question Doil's courage after that. With their un-divided attention, he launched into a soliloqouy about the need to preserve these magnificent creatures, with their unparralled ability to control the rat population, which was equally as terrifying, or maybe even more-so, than the snakes, repulsing the enraptured audience with the symptoms of the 'plague'.

The real reason he encouraged restraint in the disposal of rattlesnakes, is that he had a thriving side business selling these nasty ankle-biters to several area churches, allowing the faithful to put that faith to the ultimate test. Several whose faith was not all it could have been had succumbed to wounds from these venom pistols, but he viewed these as casualties of show bidness', the same result as a tragic movie stunt. Besides, he always demanded payment up front, just in case.

By this point, Doil has worked himself up into an emotional frenzy, his adrenaline pumping, sweating as though he were attempting to balance a checkbook, psyched for the climax to this reptilian orgy. He disappears into the coop to re-deposit the snake, and after a few tense moments, he emerges courageously, like Robert Lee from his field tent; the 'Beau Ideal' of southern manhood, surveying the battleground, and holding by the ankles, between his chubby fingers, a limp, and lifeless, dominicker chicken, wings widespread. He walks slowly toward the silent crowd, measuring every step, milking each one for dramatic effect.

"If I don't come back," and he slowly glances toward the scummy pond,

"If I don't come back, ya'll remember what ya' seen here taday," and he reverently makes the sign of the cross from pith helmet to each patched pocket, as he turns and walks as slowly as a bridegroom, toward the putrid-pool. The transformation from mere roadside reptile show, to a battle between good and evil, the supremacy of Homo

Sapiens, the cosmic struggle between believers and non-believers, was the genius of Doil Pettyjohn.

No one is breathing. The air is dead calm. No birds singing, no crickets chirping, no katy-dids diddling. There is only the sound of the sweat as it drops on your boots, and the incessant screeching of drunk monkeys. He stops, ten yards or so from the water, as the immense 'log' turns slowly toward him, as if it were a compass needle, and Doil was 'magnetic north'.

You can hear hearts pounding now, louder and louder. The sun seems to get hotter. The air grows so thick and heavy, that you can't pull it into your lungs, and you become light-headed. Ever so slowly, Doil raises the chicken above his head, and waves it back and forth, like the priest in a bloody voo-doo ritual. The pounding hearts become so loud that they sound like native drums! Were it not for the stalwarts, whose fear of being labelled as cowards, was greater than their fear of the un-known, the entire audience would flee for their very lives. Just at that instant, as Doil has delivered us up to be sacrificed, the gates of the underworld spring open, and up and out charges a vision of hell that 's burned on my memory like a Polaroid. Fourteen feet of ground-pounding demon, gigantic mouth open, baring row after row of flesh-ripping teeth. The vile, gaping maw of hell; spewing mud, brimstone, and pond scum, and heading straight for Doil. Women are screaming, babies are crying, a couple of people are reciting the Lord's Prayer. Grown men are covering their eyes. Bodies begin to fall, overcome by the sheer terror of it all. The beast leapt, and with one bone crushing snap of it's horrible jaws, it snatched the chicken from Doil's hand, and crashed to the ground, causing the earth under our feet to tremble! Blood, guts, and feathers sprayed over Doil's legs. Three mighty chomps, and the carcass disappeared down the monster's gullet. Doil dared

not move a muscle. Almost as quickly as it had come, the filthy beast turned, and sank out of sight under the disgusting bacterial crust of the pond. For several excruciating minutes, no one spoke. Those who had feinted came slowly back to life. First one bird, and then another began to sing. The crickets picked up their chirping. A cool breeze began to blow from the direction of the pond. The huddled audience was overcome by a nauseating smell. It was Doil.——————————————————-
He had shit himself.

2

Northeast Alabama is farm country. Not massive plantation acreage with porticoed mansions, but small family operations, clustered in quaint communities with colorful names, like Needmore, Little New York, and Duck Springs. Most of these informal communities had a small school, and some, if not all, had a gymnasium of some sort, or at least a designated area, for the kids to play basketball, which was, and still is, a poor man's sport. Although, if you dared to call one of these proud southerners poor, you would surely get your ass kicked, and probably more than once.

Basketball requires no expensive equipment, just a ball and a hoop. It's also the only sport in which underwear constitutes a uniform, although for the girls, in most cases, this was not practical. There was, however, one piece of equipment, though not necessarily essential for participation, that was the burning desire of every country ball player. Possession ensuring that men envy, and women desire you: the most coveted shoes in the history of sport: Converse All-Stars. To own a pair would elevate even a mediocre player to professional status. Young men had been known to have followed the example of Sargeant York, and work two, or even three jobs, to save enough money to purchase their version of 'bottomland'; the legendary canvas and rubber 'ruby slippers'. A pair of 'high tops' cost thirteen dollars and change. Out of the reach of almost everyone. Into this arena of competitiveness, longing, and poverty, strode Doil Pettyjohn; budding entertainment mogul.

A couple of years earlier, he had purchased a dozen or so Mexican burros at a livestock auction, because it was, and still is, the belief in northern Alabama, that donkeys will discourage coyotes from taking up residence on your place, and Doil had a lot to protect, what with the petting zoo, and the drunk monkeys, and so forth. The drawback with this plan, however, became painfully evident the first winter, when the fuzzy little bastards nearly ate him out of house and ranch.

Now Doil grew up poor, on the principle of 'earning your keep', and he resolved to turn the burros into living slot machines of sorts, feeding oats to one slot, while money dribbled out another. A true artist has vision, and he gathers up the materials at hand, and creates a thing of beauty. In his mind's eye, he can see the resulting masterpiece.

Genius is the only word to describe Doil Pettyjohn's vision of hillbillies playing basketball while riding on the backs of burros. Had he lived in biblical times, he would surely have been considered a prophet, worthy of inclusion in the King James edition of 'Believe It Or Not'. He had succeeded in a goal, thought un-attainable, and first attempted by a northerner, name of Lincoln. He had taken a sport, where height was a distinct advantage, and MADE EVERYONE EQUAL! IT WAS GROUNDBREAKING; REVOLUTIONARY! THE WILT CHAMBERLAINS OF THE WORLD NOW HAD NO ADVANTAGE OVER THE BOB COUSEYS, BECAUSE THEY WERE ALL RIDING ON THE BACKS OF JACK-ASSES! A LEVEL PLAYING

FIELD, WHERE DESIRE AND ABILITY DETERMINED THE OUTCOME OF THE CONTEST! SO SIMPLE AND, AND YET SO BEAUTIFUL! THE CONCEPT WAS STAGGERING! THE PROPHET ENDEAVORED TO DELIVER HIS MESSAGE TO THE MASSES! THUS WAS BORN; DOIL PETTYJOHN'S DONKEY BASKETBALL!

The rules were simple. You had to pass and shoot while on a donkey's back. No penalties for traveling, or double-dribbling, (you were'nt even required to dribble), no three-second rule. Fouls could be called on players, but not donkeys, and free throws had to be shot from the mounted position, providing you could get the mount to co-operate. The teams consisted of volunteers from the audience, usually the tougher boys from the county high school team, and former country ball-players who were, at one time, community big-shots due to their legendary court prowess, trying to re-gain some stature with the ladies.

Added to this were always a few drunks, and individuals with a highly developed sense of their 'Celtic' heritage, who would do anything on a dare, including this. Doil even provided safety equipment in the form of old surplus flight helmets from the Army/Navy store, but no self-respecting southerner is gonna' wear a helmet to ride a donkey, or anything else that travels on four legs.

This was a time when you did'nt sue a man for allowing you to make a fool of yourself in public, but just to be on the safe side, and on the outside chance that a yankee might slip under the radar, Doil had all the volunteers 'make their mark' on a release, stating that if you got killed, or addled to the point of vegetability, that he would'nt have to raise your younguns', or put up with your ugly-ass wife. Exceptions could be made in the case of the wife, for obvious reasons.

The teams would play until one or the other scored ten points, which took quite a while, as you can imagine, and then ten more eager volunteers would take over. This went on until everyone who had signed up was given the opportunity to have his or her brains kicked out by a rampaging donkey. Although recreational opportunities were limited, and spectacles such as this were almost sure to draw a large crowd, insuring that he would have a steady supply of athletic types willing to risk life and limb, was a primary concern. To that end, Doil, with an un-canny ability to guage public wants and desires, offered as the grand prize for high scorer, a gift certificate redeemable at the nearest sporting goods retailer, for a pair of CONVERSE HIGH TOP, CHUCK TAYLOR SIGNATURE, ALL STAR BASKETBALL SHOES, WITH AN EXTRA PAIR OF LACES.

Always eager to help others promote their own enterprise, and offset overhead of his own, he offered limited sponsorships to small bidness' concerns in each community, allowing them free association with the extravaganza, in return for donations of goods, and or services, as prizes for sportsmanship, most valuable player, and so on. The advertising potential was immense. The rumor even circulated that Martha White Flour had offered their sponsorship, in conjunction with the Grand Ole' Opry, and that Little Jimmy Dickens himself was to emcee the games, but Doil had flatly refused, fearing corporate take-over, and the games being moved to Nashville, away from the loyal, and loving fans that had made the sport great. A moving story, guaranteed to bring in even more loyal and hungry fans, originated by Doil himself, master of show bidness' promotion.

Every legendary figure had a sidekick, and Doil was no exeception. The Lone Ranger had 'Tonto', The Cisco Kid had 'Pancho', 'Country Boy' Eddie had 'Happy' Hal

Burns, and Doil Pettyjohn had Waddell Strickland. A raw boned, big-eared plowboy who was as tough as a pine-knot, and as loyal as a puppy.

They had entered into a bidness' arrangement a few years earlier, distilling whisky 'on the halves'. Doil supplied the sugar and corn, which he purchased as feed additives for the varied, and exotic animals at the ranch, (who knew that monkeys require five hundred pounds of sugar every few weeks), and Waddell tended the fire, and stirred the mash. Marketed through the rear of the monkey ranch, it was a lucrative arrangement for them both. They became fast friends. Waddell was fascinated by Doil's uncanny ability to ferret out the show bidness' buck, and Doil profoundly dependent on Waddell's unwavering loyalty. It was a team destined to make it's greasy mark on entertainment.

The most respected, and at the same time, the most reviled man in the county, depending on who you asked, was the Reverend Ocie Dalrymple. Everyone knew his story. In his younger days, he skulked around the county like a stray dog, runnin' whores, drinkin' likker', and disrespectin' his momma. He was an un-welcome visitor at every function.

"Drop o' sweat offn' at' sumbitch ud' cure T.B.", it was said of him.

His most striking feature, as a young man at least, was his flaming hair. They called him 'Booger Red'. Now Red had undergone an amazing transformation in his twenties. According to his own testimony, he was delivered on a Sunday morning in his trailer, after several days of drinking Doil and Waddell's vile, and disgusting corn likker'; (bought on the credit; a point that he conveniently omitted.) As the story goes, he was wallowing in his own filth, un-bathed, and un-shaven, un-fit for society, too drunk to dress, when, without warning, The Ernest Angley Hour mysteriously appeared on his soon to be repossessed television set. Ernest was on fire, wiggling his bony finger at the camera, and urging the sick and shut-in, as well as the hard-core, whisky swillin' sinners in the viewing audience to place their hands on their T.V. sets, and receive an 'over the airwaves' dose of his famous 'palm to the forhead' smash, the sure cure for everything from hair loss to hemorroids. Booger Red was mortified, not willing, or ready to hear the truth, and attempted to change the channel to 'Mutual Of Omaha's Wild Kingdom', and the gospel of nature, quietly and non-threateningly preached by Marlin Perkins.

As he placed his hand on the set to steady himself, the heavens parted, and a bolt of lightning shot from the tip of the All-Mighty's index finger, straight to the antenna that fed moving pictures to the screen, rolled down it like a yo-yo, and exploded the picture tube. Booger Red, the unrepentant sinner, stuck fast to the heavenly charged set, felt the fillings in his teeth melt, before everything faded to black. He was unconscious for two, maybe three days, during which time he was given tours of heaven, and various other celestial points of interest, by an angel, who, given the specific details of his appearance, gait, and mode of speech, sounded, to me at least, an awful lot like Walter Brennan in 'The Real McCoys'. Just prior to his awakening, the angelic Granpaw' McCoy had charged him with the salvation, and moral leadership of a three county area of northern Alabama, which he reluctantly accepted, protesting his un-worthiness.

When he awoke, his hair had turned snow white, and was blown straight back, just like Charlton Heston's after his chat with 'the burning bush', though whether from conversing with an angel, or the effect of fifty thousand volts passing through him like a dose of salts through a widder' woman, one can only speculate. Whatever you may conclude, there's no doubt that this experience sobered him up, and set him on the path of self-righteousness, his salvation delivered by a nineteen inch Sylvania. The Lord, indeed, moves in mysterious ways.

In a few short years, with the help of some spectacular, but medically un-verified healings, and that amazing 'Moses on the mount' hair-do, the Reverend Dalrymple had gathered unto himself the biggest flock in the county. He had become a very powerful figure in the community, especially with the ladies, since he remained un-married, and in the tradition of true show bidness' theology, had taken to wearing fancy, tailored suits, and expensive jewelry, and having his show-stopping hair-do maintained at a beauty shop. All of this was graciously paid for by his grateful followers and lusting female fans.

In the years since his miraculous conversion from skirt-chasing drunk to tee-totalling celibate, no one had seen the Reverend with a woman outside the context of his religious duties. This alleged 'no-nookie' vow that all assumed had come with the office, had a curious effect on the women. They openly fawned and flirted, and danced around him like a herd of nymphs, freely offering themselves as objects for fantasy, yet secure in the belief that they were completely safe in doing so, due to his rigid moral discipline.

Even more curious was the fact that this free fantasy exchange was witnessed by the curiously silent husbands. It was all very 'Freudian'. Those who had known the Very Reverend Booger Red since childhood, knew that he was 'wettin' his beak' somewhere, but were not interested enough to waste time figurin' out where.

Then suddenly, after a two week mission trip to Memphis, the Reverend Booger returned with a wife, and not just your average matronly clergy groupie, but a bleach blonde, red-lipped bombshell with a body like butter, and a chest to rival the bumper guards on a 'Coupe De Ville'. Thrust into this bland, and colorless throng, she stuck out like a sore thumb. Wyvanelle was her given name, and the women grudgingly accepted her, because she was chosen by their charismatic fantasy partner, but they did'nt like it, and behind her back they whispered that a Christian woman would'nt bleach her hair like Marilyn Monroe, and wear brassieres that lifted and separated her massive bosom.

The men, on the other hand were characteristically silent on the matter, but curiously, male church attendance rose by thirty-four percent in the weeks following her arrival, causing those of us who were crass enough to express it, that if Hugh Hefner had called the Playboy Mansion a church, this would be a nation of religious fanatics.

It did'nt take long for the good women of the church to start ingratiating themselves with Wyvanelle, including her in their every night of the week committee meetings, ice cream suppers, and the like, to allow them to stay in close proximity with the preacher. She was just another hurdle on the road to Heaven. Before the year was out, The Reverend and Msres' Dalrymple were the 'golden' couple of the county, considered a-listers' for every important function or event. As fate would have it, the Preacher received a call one night from the basketball coach/principal at the Walnut Grove community school. Looking up at his voluptuous wife, in her leather corset and 'bat-girl' mask, he asked,

"Honey, have you ever heard of donkey basketball?" Show bidness' worlds were on a collision course.

Doil had cut a deal with the principal/coach for a 75/25 split on the gate to get the gym. With Doil handling the gate receipts, it usually ended up at more like a 90/10 split, but Waddell always made sure that the coach/

principal received a full half-gallon of sweet mash for all his trouble. This went a long way in over-coming bookkeeping errors. Doil had gotten a shoe shop to make little donkey 'booties' with rubber soles, to keep the hooves from ruining the gym floor, because doing any kind of damage to a gym floor was an instant ass-whoopin'. He even had diapers made out of 'guanner' sacks, to keep the donkey apples off the court.

The entire community of Walnut Grove was buzzin' on the night of the game. People were coming from as far away as Joppa and Lick Skillet to cheer their favorite players. The Reverend Dalrymple and his buxom bride were the 'special' guests of the coach/principal. This was 'big time' show bidness'. As the bleachers began to fill, Waddell took all the volunteer players out to the horse trailer for gaming instructions, a short talk on sportsmanship, and the Pettyjohn pre-game ritual of passing around several fruit jars of sour mash to loosen everyone up. It's a known fact that a drunk is less likely to be seriously injured in an accident, including those involving donkeys, than a sober person. Alcohol tends to make impending doom seem like high adventure.

One of the volunteer players that night was an ol' boy that all the locals called Wormy, because all that knew him, figured that he was. He'd have been lucky to weigh a hundred pounds soaking wet, and was a strange looking young man. He was all hands; little bitty head, little bitty feet, and enormous hands. If he had'nt gotten wormy as a kid, and grown into those hands, he would surely have been a giant. It is one of the great mysteries of sport, why Wormy, who as far back as anyone could remember, had never participated in a sport of any kind, chose tonight to lay claim to his manhood.

"Here's to tha' first time", he said as he raised a jar to his lips.

"First time onna' donkey?" asked one of the other players.

"An' tha' first time I ever hadda'drink", he said, as he turned up the jar, and took a long, thick gulp, that very nearly brought him to his knees. Waddell knew that it was gonna' be an extra-special night.

By game time it was standing room only. The heat was stifling, and most of the women were fanning themselves with carboard fans on wooden handles that bore a beautiful picture of Jesus riding his donkey into Jerusalem on Palm Sunday on one side, and 'HOLY GHOST FUNERAL CHAPEL, DOGTOWN, ALABAMA, SUPPORTS DONKEY BASKETBALL' on the other. The Reverend and his wife were seated at the place reserved for dignitaries at mid-court, front row. She was fanning furiously, as the support required to uphold a bosom such as hers was quite a burden in hot weather. Her cotton dress was starting to soak with sweat, and cling to the dramatic arch of her breasts. We pretended not to notice, she being the preacher's wife and all, but it seemed the more that dress clung, the hotter it got in that gym.

The donkeys and players were ushered in, led by Doil himself, dressed nattily in a referee's uniform, and wearing a big, silver whistle around his neck. He strode to mid-court, with the intention of making a brief speech, since he never let the opportunity pass to be in the spotlight, but before he could open his mouth, from way up in the stands, a nasally voice cried out,

"Hey Doil ! Are those your legs r' are you ridin' a chicken?"

The gym erupted with laughter, and Doil attempted to shout his message over the hoopin' and hollerin', but no one heard a word he said. The ruckus finally died down enough for him to introduce the Reverend Booger, whose commanding presence brought instant silence to the anxious crowd. The Preacher, resplendent in seersucker, and sporting a pair of white bucs', took center court, and in that booming Burt Lancaster voice, delivered the invocation. He blessed the brave volunteers, prayed for the safety of the donkeys and the president, and asked blanket forgiveness for the un-specified sins of the audience. He made no mention of Doil. Everyone was moved; Wyvanelle was beaming, and sweating. Wormy was having trouble standing up. Doil blew a shrill burst on the big whistle and yelled,

"God-a-mighty, les' play some ball!"

The teams had divided themselves into shirts, and skins, to make it easier to identify team-mates, and simplify body identification. Instead of the traditional tip-off, possession was decided by the flip of a coin. The 'skins' won the toss. The players mounted, Doil handed the ball to the nearest half-naked hillbilly, and blew a long, shrill blast on the whistle. Chaos erupted:

The pudgy little donkeys that had seemed so docile up to now, looked like the a-string broncs at the Calgary Stampede. Bodies were flying in every direction. Men were screaming, donkeys braying, the sound was deafening. Several people in the stands were throwing up from the combined effects of un-controllable laughter, and intense heat. Kicking, riderless donkeys were going everywhere. A few of the bigger men were actually mounted, but looked for all the world as if they were riding jackhammers. The whole crowd was on it's feet, all but those collapsed from laughter and or heat exhaustion. The entire gym was at a fever pitch, except for Wormy. The whiskey had wrecked his perspective, and he was standing alone at mid-court, oblivious to the carnage happening all around him. A few in the crowd started to chant

"Wormy, Wormy,Wormy,Wormy", and soon everyone joined in. I was sure I'd heard the same chant by some lost tribe in a Tarzan movie. It was mesmerizing. It began to seep into Wormy's alcohol soaked brain, softly at first, and then louder and louder, until the mystical chanting awoke Wormy's man-spirit. Adrenaline started to flow into his limbs. He could feel hair sprouting on his chest. Testosterone quivers overtook him.

Eyeing a donkey across the court, that was standing stock still, and staring, I swear to you, at the preacher's wife, Wormy started to run toward it. Slowly at first, but as the adrenaline flooded his legs, they started to pump furiously. By the time he reached the donkey, he was runnin' flat out. In the most graceful 'Gene Autry' move ever seen outside the theatre, he jumped, planted his hands on the donkey's rump, and was about to execute a flawless rear mount, when disaster struck. The first rule of donkey etiquette; never put your hands on, or near, the donkey's ass.

While Wormy was still in leap-frog position, about a foot above, the donkey bucked for all it was worth to get those big hands off his rump. The momentum achieved in that one foot of empty space between donkey and man was roughly the same as that realized by a rocket launch. Wormy was catapulted, at blinding speed, straight at the stands, directly at the Preacher's divinely proportioned wife. She did'nt even have time to scream. His huge, outstretched hands hit her first, and he grabbed blindly, hoping for anything to slow himself. As she fell backwards into the bleachers, his big, knobby knuckled hands grabbed the underwire on her brassiere, which was as large as the handlebars on a 'Huffy', and the downward force of his fall yanked her sturdy support garment straight down, ripping open the sweat soaked cotton dress, and releasing those jaw-dropping twins. An old man, too overcome with the heat, and unable to stand, was sitting beside her, and he attempted to break her fall, but as he leaned in, one of the twins swung in a wide arc, and slapped him square in the face, popping out his upper partial, and it chattered on the bleachers like a baseball card in bicycle spokes. As she threw her arms back, desperately trying to catch herself, her hand struck the Reverend on or about the scrotal area, and sent him crashing to the court, gasping for air, and clutching his babys like a mother monkey.

And poor ol' Wormy: His tiny little head had come to rest dead in Wyvanelle's crotch, and the instant that his tiny little nose struck the pubic mound, she had clamped those muscular thighs together like a venus fly-trap, holding him fast.

At that instant, time stood still. The heavens opened, and illuminated a tableaux worthy of Michaelangelo. A once in a lifetime vision that is burned, even to this day, on my memory like an x-ray. Wyvanelle on her back, her cotton dress ripped all the way to the back of Wormy's tiny head. Her milk-white flesh was as moist as a pound cake, her outstretched arms revealing pink pits, shaved as slick as a mole. As beautiful a sight as I have ever seen. And then, like puppies opening their eyes for the first time, we all saw it at once. Hearts almost stopped beating. A peace enveloped us like a mother's love, for there, just above the the back of Wormy's tiny little skull, tattooed in the most beautiful calligraphy ever to grace parchment or flesh, were the words 'THE BURNING BUSH'. The silence was deafening. Even the donkeys grew quiet.

"Hallelujah", I whispered.

Here and there others joined me, and whispered the same. It was a very spiritual moment, some might say, a revelation. All of us, the men at least, felt at that moment, that all was right with the world. All except Wormy, whose tiny head was being mashed like a zit. Suddenly, the Preacher had him by his tiny little feet, yanking as hard as he could, but Wyvanelle was overcome and would'nt, or could'nt, let him go. Instantly, the gym erupted in laughter, even louder than before. Gasping for breath, eyes filled with tears, someone finally regained their composure enough to yell,

"Stick a match to his ass preacher! It works on ticks!"

This last and final insult sent the Raging Holy Man over the edge. He emitted a gutteral, primal cry, that shocked Wyvanelle to her senses, and he yanked with all his might, just as she relaxed her death grip on Wormy's sweaty little head. The boy came flying out backwards, legs wide apart, the Preacher still holding his ankles, and his bony little ass caught the good reverend square in the nose. They both tumbled backwards onto the gym floor, with Wormy coming to rest, sitting bolt upright on Red's face. Doil raced over and stood the little feller' up. Underneath, the minister lay semi-conscious, with blood trickling over each jaw. He came back to life as Doil led the wobbly, sweat-soaked, sore-assed community hero away. As they stepped over the Preacher, Doil leaned down to him, and in a very quiet voice said,

"Now that, by God, is show bidness'."

3

Seven Bridges liked to think of herself as a movie star. She had a few small roles in big-budget movies on her resume', but the reality was, that she never had the chops for the big dramatic roles, or the screen-filling beauty of someone like Lana Turner. She had banged around the industry for years, moving from b-movies, to soft porn. In Hollywood, as in many other show bidness' arenas, dare I say it, run by men, acting ability is directly proportional to one's degree of EXPECTED undress. Likewise, the length of one's film career is in direct proportion to the combined effects of age and gravity on one's 'skills'.

Seven's abilities usually insured that she would be as nekkid' as a jay-bird within fifteen minutes of the opening credits. This is not to say that she was not a striking woman. She was quite exotic, with very dark, Mediterranean features, piercing black eyes, and an enormous mouth, with inviting, bee-stung lips.

She had legally changed her name to Seven Bridges while still in high school, reasoning that being named after a popular song would give her instant name recognition, and feeling that her real name, Mildred Tarwater, might be an impediment to her far-flung, and grandiose ambitions. Her years in Hollywood had left her lonely, and un-fulfilled, and she was desperate to establish herself as something more than a 'nipple extra', before it was too late.

Through her association, and subsequent romance with a rather militant lesbian, who was in the forefront of a fledgling animal rights movement, incorporated as 'ACTRESSES' NETWORK OF ANIMAL LIBERATION', but soon to be known worldwide by it's acronym, 'A.N.A.L.', she had hatched a scheme to make a documentary film that would become the rallying cry for the movement, make her a household name, and the darling of all the other 'nipple extras' who sought a vehicle to establish their legitimacy.

The obvious place to film such a documentary was the American south, where frightening 'Dixiecrats' hunted rabbit and squirrell, devouring them freely, and whole families considered an afternoon of fishing to be entertainment. The boiling spring of animal abuse was rumored to be northeastern Alabama, and the high plateaus and deep valleys of the Tennessee river basin, where half-blood Irish/Cherokee savages still took whitetail deer and wild turkey with the bow and arrow, and the black-powder gun, consuming the flesh, and decorating their lodges with the heads and beards.

She sold everything she owned, and with the proceeds, and meager financial backing from a few interested razor-free, hairy-legged women, she bought an old Suburban, hired a cameraman, and rented the equipment needed for such a production. Just like Lewis and Clark, they headed into the vast, un-charted hinter-lands of old Dixie, un-sure of what they'd find, but dedicated to the proposition of capturing on film, the barbaric practices of these un-civilized, backwoods people.

4

Waddell Strickland had an old collie that roamed the fields and forests, following every kid in the county on their adventures through this un-tamed land, warning them away from dangerous dug wells, empty mine shafts, venomous reptiles, and rain swollen creeks. Waddell had named the dog 'Sputnik'; not after the first Russian space capsule, but after 'Sputnik' Monroe, of Memphis Tennessee, World's Greatest Wrestler. All the kids called 'Sputnik' 'Lassie', for obvious reasons.

A collie's long, thick coat is a marvelous depository for the transient seed pods, and passerby grabbing vegetable matter of the southern woodlands. Once a week or so, Waddell would give every kid that was willing, fifty cents and a grape Ne-Hi to pull the cockleburs off 'Sputnik/Lassie', and put them in a gallon pickle jar. That old dog could pick up a hell of a lot of cockleburs in a week. Sometimes, the jar was nearly full. With a marketing scheme straight from the Pettyjohn playbook, he would allow them to age in the jar until they were all a uniform brown in color, and then place thirty or forty of them in neat little rows on a pie-pan, and slip it under a hundred watt bulb in an old cricket box at the monkey ranch, below a hand lettered sign that read PORKYPINE' EGGS. Unsuspecting 'Yankee' tourists eagerly forked over the very reasonable price of a buck a'piece for the spiny 'eggs', and took them home to New's York and Jersey to wait impatiently for them to hatch. An innocent act of southern retribution that would play a pivotal role in the as yet un-written history of animal activism.

Seven's shocking tell-all about the brutal nature of the southern psyche had been a dismal failure up to this point. They had managed to film a family butchering a hog in Arkansas, which spoke more of hardy pioneer survival than wanton abuse of animal resource, and in Mississippi, they wasted a whole day filming an old black farmer, clearin' pine stumps with a fine pair of red mules, that he was as proud of as his own children. As they made their way into the Tennessee Valley, they had very little to report to their 'long in the toenail' investors, and no indications, judging from the lush scenery, and picturesque farms, that they would fare any better here, though it was rumored throughout the 'civilized' sections of the nation, that indeed this area was inhabited by ghouls. It was late in the afternoon when they approached quite literally, the first signs of what they were seeking.

CECIL THE PIG———WANTED TO CRY———
——-WHEN WADDELL'S
MONKEY——————-POKED OUT HIS EYE ——
——-AT PETTYJOHN'S.

She stared at the cameraman in utter dis-belief.

"Did that say what I think it said?"

"That can't be real. Just somebody pulling a prank."

Seven became very serious, and in a condescending monotone said,

"And Tarzan was only a myth until white explorers heard his plaintive cry in the jungle."

"Uh huh."

The cameraman, whose name was Steve, already suspected that his employer was a tad loopy, and this confirmed his worst fears. Too many years in show bidness' had blurred the line between real life, and 'reel' life, but he played along, because in truth, he needed this film to work as much as she did. He too, was a victim of Hollywood's in-difference. He had spent years trying to get 'in the clique' with the big production companies, with no success. A film school graduate, he had hopes of becoming an award winning director, but the high point of his career thus far, was directing a mayonnaise commercial. He had a basic, working knowledge of how to operate a camera, and a burning desire to make a name for himself, if not as a director, as perhaps a photojournalist. He had lobbied hard for this job, and being the more desparate, and the more experienced, he was unanimously chosen from a field of two, and became cameraman, assistant director, roadie, and chauffeur. He slowed to a crawl as they approached the next series of signs.

PET THE GOAT——BUY SOME GAS——LOVE A DONKEY?——-KISS MY ASS!——-PETTYJOHN'S RANCH—— IS JUST AHEAD——WE GOT MILK——
AND LOAFA' BREAD!

All doubt about it being a prank evaporated as they rounded the bend and got their first glimpse of the 'Empire'.

"Pull in" she said.

He eased the suburban into the corner of the lot and stopped. Dust was hanging head –high in the heavy, humid air. Through the choking haze they could see the tall plank fence with it's gaudy decoration, the colors muted by successive layers of dirt and tree sap. The big oak, with it's sheltering branches, looked like an oasis in the shimmering

Alabama heat. On the far end of the compound, it was evident that commerce was being carried on. A gas pump rung like a mantle clock, one ring per gallon, and here and there, sweaty men in dirty over-alls leaned over the sides of pickup trucks, peering in, their elbows resting on the hot metal. They would punctuate their observation with periodic turns to spit mouthfuls of disgusting, tar colored spewtum, like black Texas grasshoppers, and return to their perusal, wiping their chins with their sleeves.

A few were seated under the shade of an awning that stretched from the front of the grocery and mercantile section to the gas pumps, and appeared to be dragging knives down the entire length of twigs and branches, the long, curling, cut away strips piled up around their feet like day-old spaghetti.

Stretching all the way to the road, on either side of the compound, was a ramshackle fence made entirely of signs, some plywood, some tin, that advertised and announced every form of human endeavor, time-saving service, or retail opportunity to be experienced in this remote portion of the state. It gave the illusion, that the compound formed the centerfield wall in a grassless baseball stadium. As Seven read her way from the road to the compound, the dust settled somewhat, and she spotted the cage. From their position, at approximately the visitor's dugout, she could'nt quite make-out the contents.

"Pull closer."

"Are you sure? These people look dangerous to me. There's a gun hanging in the window of that truck!"

"Of course I'm sure! This whole thing is an act, like the cowboys at a movie ranch. These are probably all stunt people. Nobody dresses like extras from 'The Grapes of Wrath'."

"They look real to me! And the one's on the bench all have knives!"

"I'm the one signing your check, and I said to get closer! I want to see what's in that cage!"

Steve nervously guided the truck across the dusty lot, and stopped under the shade of the tree. Swirling dust still occluded their vision, but it settled quickly, and they were greeted by screaming monkeys that bounced from hog wire wall to wall of the filthy cage, throwing orange peels and pecan hulls, stopping intermittently to expose their genitals, and give anyone within range, a golden shower. Fortunately, the only victim was Cecil, the one-eyed pig, who squealed loudly, and hurried to the far side of his pen to roll in the dirt, the hot monkey urine apparently burning his back like an acid bath. The filmmakers sat in stunned silence, while the incessant monkey screaming grew louder and louder. Steve, who looked as though he were shell-shocked, mumbled,

"Please tell me that I'm dreaming."

Seven, far from being in shock, had a look of steely determination.

"Get the camera ready."

It took Steve a moment to respond.

"What?"

"I said get the camera ready!"

"But what about——"

"Do it!"

As he went about gathering equipment and loading the camera, Seven, with a handkerchief held over her nose, cautiously slipped through the front gate to scout the location. Inside, a small, covered walkway led a few feet to a cinder block building with a rusty metal door. The walkway was lined on either side, with used tires, buried upright, halfway in the ground, slick tread to slick tread, and painted white. Several pink plastic flamingos were scattered about in the weeds, along with a dry bird bath, and an old timey' rotary blade push mower with a broken handle.

She knocked very gently on the rusty door, and leaned close to listen for footsteps, or sounds of activity. Hearing none, she cracked the door gently, and slipped in like a cat burglar. The small, low ceilinged building was hot, damp, and dark, with a smell that was organically putrid. She bumped into a table just inside, and stood motionless for a moment, waiting for her eyes to adjust to the limited light, and hoping that she had'nt alerted the savages. Slowly, the blinding Alabama sunlight melted from her vision, and she got her first glimpse of the inner sanctum of what she viewed as Pettyjohn's 'Gulag'. The table that she was leaning against was the admission station, which consisted of a cigar box, and a crudely stenciled sign that read;

ADMISSION $1.OO AMERICAN
WAIST HIGH AND UNDER –50 CENTS
NURSING BABIES ADMITTED FREE!
NOT RESPONSIBLE FOR SOILED DRAWERS!

"Disgusting pig", she murmured, as she slowly turned to survey the barbarous shrine.

Against the wall to her right were several, obviously home-made wire cages that stood on un-painted two-by-four legs, dimly lit by one naked light bulb that hung like a plumb-bob from the ceiling. As she silently edged her way toward it, she noticed that the cages were separated from the viewing area by a length of bright yellow ski-rope, that was tied to a step-ladder on the one end, and a saw horse on the other. She squinted at the hand lettered signs that hung below each cage as she slowly walked the length of the barricade, occasionally detecting movement, or the glint of an eyeball; groundhog, wood rat, weasel, possum, chicken snake, rat snake, copperhead:

"Copperhead?" she whispered," What the hell is a copperhead?"

She leaned as far as the rope would allow, trying to get a glimpse of the un-familiar creature, when out of the hay that was piled in the far corner of the cage, a huge open mouth, with a pair of fangs to rival Dracula, came shooting directly at her face, and hung itself in the wire, in a desparate attempt to chew it's way through and get at her. She felt the scream rising in her throat, but she choked it back, as she stumbled backwards, in abject terror. She stood, trembling; sweating so hard that she could'nt be sure if her clothing was soaked with sweat, or the contents of her bladder.

When she had re-gained her composure enough to move, she took a deep breath, turned to creep out, and came face to face with Waddell's cricket box. She froze, unable to move a muscle, the fear of another reptile attack sticking her fast to the floor. She held her breath, expecting any minute to be consumed by the tortured property of a hillbilly slaver. When she could hold her breath no longer, resigned to her fate, she lifted her head, and read the words,

"PORKYPINE EGGS, $1.00 APIECE"

Instantly, all her fear dissipated, replaced by righteous indignation and smoldering female anger. It was bad enough to capture, and display these helpless creatures, allowing them to be ogled and prodded, and driven insane, but to rob a mother of her eggs, while she patiently waited for babies that would never appear, was not only a blow against the animal kingdom, but a blow against motherhood, a blow against mankind! No longer concerned with the consequences of exposure, she stormed out, banging the rusty door against the wall. As she blew through the front gate, an unseen hand quietly closed the door behind her.

Steve had the camera perched on his shoulder, and was busy filming the loudly bitching, violently urinating monkeys when the sweat-soaked actress appeared. Anrgy and pre-occupied, she stalked by the cage, well within range, and was pelted, spat upon, and showered for her insolence. The action-packed drama began to un-fold before the camera lens. Both of them sensed that they were caught up in a film of monumental social importance; she so driven, that she ignored the primate insults, and walking directly into the shot, launched into an impromptu monologue that was as scathing as a movie review. She made vague reference to the weasels and rats, the lunatic monkeys needing little, if any verbage, having presented their case quite convincingly on their own. The bleeding heart of this im-passioned cinematic milestone was the 'porkypine eggs'. The defining example of cavalier southern savagery. The conclusion of her melo-dramatic delivery was the the command to,

"Follow me!"

She led the cameraman, and thus the viewing audience in a wide arc around the deafening 'piss olympics', and through the gate, filming as they went. When she tried to open the rusty door, that she did'nt remember closing, much to her surprise, she found it locked. Indignant, and emboldened by her moral crusade, she began to bang loudly with her fist, yelling for the as yet unseen perpetrators to

"Open this damn door!"

The sound of shuffling feet and squeaking wheels became apparent behind the locked door, growing louder and louder, and a moment of silence ensued before the knob started to rattle and shake, as if the unseen hand were having trouble un-locking it.

Seven's steely resolve was beginning to weaken, as she pondered the possibility that the opened door might have her staring down the barrel of a gun, in the hands of a deranged hillbilly entrepreneur. Steve drew a tight shot of the rattling knob, and prepared to bolt, if and when weaponry was presented. There was a distinctive click, as the lock finally disengaged, and the knob made a quick quarter turn to the left. They held their breath, valiantly fighting the urge to run screaming from the compound. As the door slowly opened, they both started to hyper-ventilate. The camera started to shake as oxygen deprivation took it's toll on the camerman. At the halfway point, the door jerked open violently, and they felt the oddly familiar warmth of lost bladder control, as they abandoned themselves to their martyrdom. As their eyes came into sharp focus milliseconds later, it was not down the barrells of a shotgun, but into the wide eyes of a loudly bitching chimpanzee, wearing a house frock, and holding onto a mop handle that protruded from a rolling bucket with a wringer attachment.

They both stood dumbfounded, as the chimp ranted and raved, shaking her long, monkey fist at them, and making all manner of animated monkey faces, as if they had interrupted her housework. Then, with a dis-gruntled snort, she turned, and holding the hem of her frock over her head with one hand, and waving the other in the air for balance, waddled toward the back of the building, and disappeared through a door that Seven had not noticed on her previous intrusion.

A little shaken, but none the worse, they filmed their way inside. Someone, possibly the chimp, had turned on a series of fluorescent fixtures, and the previously dank room was now blindingly bright, perfect for filming. Steve made full use of every camera angle, getting some interesting shots of writhing snakes, and hissing possums. Waddell's 'cricket box' was examined from inside out. Seven even removed one of the 'eggs', and cupping it in her hands, delivered the finest performance of her life, culminating with huge 'horse tears' streaming down her face.

Curiously, no one had appeared thus far to stop, or even question them, but so impassioned were they at this point, they did'nt seem to notice. She stood and pointed toward the mysterious door where the chimp had made her exit. Steve was shaking his head 'no', behind the still running camera, but she was on fire, and would'nt be dissuaded. She walked over and knocked loudly. When she received no answer, she impulsively grabbed the handle, and opened the door to the seat of power in this entertainment empire.

They stood in stunned silence, as the chimp, just inside the door, started screaming, and turning flips off the arm of an ornate victorian couch. On the wall, directly in front of them, hung the head of a razorback hog, sporting 'Ray-Bans'. Six inch tusks curled menacingly around the snout, just behind a huge cigar that protruded from it's mouth. On either side of the severed head hung crossed spears on fake zebra hides, and below it all sat the mighty Khan, the greatest showman in northern Alabama, Doil Pettyjohn himself.

He was resplendent in a Shriner's fez, and leopard print shirt, shooing the flies from his face with a flywhisk made from donkey-tail hairs affixed to a sawed-off hoe handle, and gnawing on a turkey-leg. He rose, as regally as the Bishop of Namibia, and held the partially-eaten leg out to her as he continued to swat flies.

"Eat yet?"

Infuriated at this indignant display, she marched to his desk and tenderly placed a 'porkypine egg' in front of him on the polished wood.

"Would you care to explain that?"

Doil slowly shook his head back and forth, and with a demonic grin on his face, he raised the turkey leg high over his head, and smashed the cocklebur with it, laughing like a hyena. Seven swooned, and Steve had to stop filming, and grab her before she fell. The chimp grabbed a glass of water, and taking a mouthful, sprayed it in her face, reviving her instantly.

"You heartless bastard!" she screamed, as Steve led her out of the office.

"I'll be back! Do you hear me! I'll be back!"

5

Arvin Kilgore was a chicken-fighter. Some say, the greatest chicken-fighter who ever lived. He was considered the 'Bear Bryant' of the sport. His chickens came right up the middle; nothin' fancy, just consistency. He knew how to win. It was all he knew how to do. Outside the fighting arena, he was as useless as tits on a boar hog. A momma's boy, raised on cornflakes and beer, Arv was a hundred and ten pounds of pure, hillbilly hell. He spent his days drinking, and gunpowdering chickens to ensure their agressiveness, and his nights, before and after chicken fights, swaggering around the local Dairy Queen, in the hope that his reputation as a sporting type might garner favor with the ladies. Thus far, this romantic plan had been a total failure.

Elsie Freeman was a simple girl, with simple tastes. She had worked at the Dairy Queen since she was old enough to quit school, and longed for the day when she could quit that too. She lived alone on her daddy's old place in the country. Her momma had run off with a Rosebud Salve salesman when Elsie was but a toddler, and her daddy had died of consumption, alcohol related, a couple of years back. Her spartan lifestyle had taken quite a toll on her mental condition. She cared, not a fritter, for politics, religion, sports, or humanitarian causes.

In fact, the one and only thing that Elsie Freeman ever gave a shit about, was Conway Twitty; but more than giving a shit, she worshipped him, spending endless hours fantasizing about the day that he would drive up to the Dairy Queen, climb out of his convertible, and serenade her through the 'order' window. Then, with all the 'snotty' local girls watching, green with envy, he would pull her through that window by her wrists, and sweep her up, her arms around his neck, her head resting on his manly chest, and carry her like a bride to the waiting convertible, where she would take her place in the seat as close to him as she could squeeze.

As they drove away together, she would toss her milk soured red apron, that was covered with chocolate sauce and gooey nut syrup into the air, and it would flutter to the highway, like Marlo Thomas's beret. Simple dreams for a simple girl. When Conway failed to answer her two hundred or so, sexually charged letters, and refused close to a thousand collect calls, all the spark went out of Elsie. She merely existed, taking up valuable space. Her co-workers attempted to cheer her up with good natured banter, like,

"How bout'che' Elsie?"

But the only response that she ever gave was,

"I don't give a shit about nothin'."

She was as charming as a bed-sore.

Arvin Kilgore, never having been accused of setting his sights too high, set them on Elsie Freeman. Desparation and dis-enchantment; the hallmarks of a great romance.

The flirtation started innocently enough, with Arv purchasing 'Dilly Bars' from her, and slowly attempting to open a faltering, romantic dialogue. By the time she had sold more 'Dilly Bars' than anyone in the history of the franchise, Arv's beleaguering charm had coaxed her out, to sit silently with him at the picnic table during her breaks.

Arv, ever the romantic, wanted more from this relationship than a platonic, heavily scrutinized courtship, divided into ten minute intervals every two hours. It did'nt take him long to re-locate himself, and his fighting stable to the old Freeman place with his new-found love interest. He asked, and she said,

"I don't give a shit." That was about it.

We saw less and less of Arv, and sometime later, Elsie became heavy with child, and just stopped coming to work; a small part, it seemed, of her dream realized. Arv and Elsie disappeared from the social fabric of the Dairy Queen, and did'nt even leave a hole, their contribution being so minute.

Arv continued his domination of the sport that he was so reknowned for, requiring that he operate in ever widening circles to bring fresh blood, as it were, into the arena, and avoid the inevitable ass kickin', as he continued to fleece the local gamers. He would leave on extended chicken-fighting trips, and be gone for weeks. Eventually, he disappeared all-together. Some speculated that he had exhasusted the profitability of the area, and had simply been forced to re-locate due to financial constraints, but others claimed that he had run off with the reverend 'Booger's' wife, and they were operating a 'Kentucky Fried Chicken' franchise in Biloxie, Mississippi. Our interest in the matter was so miniscule, that we never bothered to confirm, one way or the other.

Elsie became more and more reclusive, and as the delivery hour drew near, sightings became rare. Weeks turned into months, and she dropped out of minds like an anniversary date. I can only recall seeing the kid once, when she rode her 'mo-ped' to town to try and peddle an old pocket watch; the only thing ol' man Freeman had left behind that had any intrinsic value, other than the home-place. The 'mo-ped' was equipped with a big metal basket, and she had it lined with straw, and an old quilt, like a make-shift, mobile manger. I was standing only a few feet away when she lifted the kid out, and went into the hardware store to try and unload the timepiece.

He was un-remarkable, as kids go, and had a shock of red hair that ran the length of his head, listing to one side, like an off-kilter mohawk. Around each nostril, was a green snot ring, that made him appear to have a pair of lime life-savers stuck on the end of his nose, as did almost every other ragged little kid in northern Alabama at that time. He was wearing one of those old timey' cloth diapers, a 'dingey' brown in color, that hung like a damp hammock from two gigantic safety pins, and from downwind, smelled like the shit-house door on a shrimp-boat. He was precious. That was the last time anyone had seen him.

Although we did'nt know it at the time, and those who suspected were'nt the type to get involved, Elsie was retreating further and further from reality. Conway's heart breaking rejection, compounded by Arv's departure, and the post-partum pressure of single mother-hood, had caused the never very vocal, depressed young mother to become mute, not having uttered a word to the kid during the critical months when he should have been coached in the use of primitive language skills. When Arv left, he had taken the television set, and Elsie had smashed the radio in a fit of frustration, so the kid never heard the spoken word. They lived so far out, and the place was so overgrown, that those who did venture by would'nt stop, owing to the sheer filth of the place.

Every morning, after he was fed, such as it was, from a huge stockpile of canned goods, pickled eggs, and the like, that a few Samaritan neighbors would leave by the mail box on return trips from town, she would turn him out, to grow like a weed in the garden.

He was alone, for all intents and purposes, his only playmates, role models, if you will, were yard chickens that were the by-product of Arv's departed fighting stable. He followed them around, did what they did, and eventually, on his own primitive level, he developed non-verbal communication skills, and began to think of himself as one of them, as did they of him.

I had read stories, and seen supposed film footage of kids raised by wolves and monkeys, and of a teenage girl raised by wild dogs in an abandoned tenement, that scurried around on her hands and knees, and barked and growled like a schnauzer, but gave little credence to such show-bidness' hucksterism, until I came face to face with Elsie's kid again.

Several years had passed, and someone at he county school board happened to remember that Elsie Freeman had a child, although he had'nt been seen in years, that had never been registered for school. Elsie had been seen briefly, from time to time, over the ensuing years, but never with the child, and no one could recall seeing her at all for a year or more. The school board made a call to the Sheriff's department, as was the custom in these matters, and the Sheriff called on a part-time deputy to check it out, not willing to have a full-timer tied up with the school's truancy problems, which in these parts, were legion. The part-timer that lived the closest to the old Freeman home-place, was Waddell Strickland.

One might think it odd that a man, neck deep in the illegal liquor trade, would be a badge-toting, part time law enforcement official, but that was the beauty of Doil Pettyjohn's 'special' arrangement with the department. In the event that Waddell was pulled over during the course of commerce in another county, all he had to do was flash his badge, and the attendant 'Barney Fyffe' style picture of himself in uniform, and the questioning officer would immediately embrace him like a missing lodge brother. An extremely helpful arrangement for those whose work does'nt exactly follow the letter of the law. The only demand that the sheriff put on the relationship, was that Waddell was sometimes called on to do some light housework, such as this. I happened to be at Waddell's, doing some light housework myself, when the call came in. Being a close, personal friend, and also very curious by nature, I inquired as to the possibility of going along, and Waddell was agreeable, thankful for the company.

The old Freeman homeplace was about eight miles west of Waddell's, up a winding, one lane pig trail, in a place that the locals had dubbed 'penitentiary holler', due to the fact that most of the inhabitants spent more time in the penitentiary, than in the holler'. The dirt road was so narrow, that if you met another truck, you would both have to get halfway in the ditch to pass, but meeting another was rare, as many that came in, never came back out. The ditch-banks were littered with the un-mistakable signs of alcohol consumption; broken glass, rusty cans, and wounds on roadside trees at bumper level, in successive layers, with healed over patches that rose twenty feet in the air or more, as if the trees had been a part of some mysterious, native scarification ritual. It was the kind of place that felt dangerous.

The drive up to the old Freeman place was so overgrown and full of broken glass, that we had to park in the ditch and walk the quarter mile through the woods to the house. It sat in a clearing that old man Freeman had hacked out of the woods twenty or thirty years prior. It was never a beautiful place, but it was sound and dry when he built it, and that's all that was necessary. The past several years of neglect had turned it into a shit-hole. What was once a dirt yard that Elsie's momma had swept diligently, and kept devoid of even a single blade of grass, was now a sage patch, choked with head-high summer cedars and 'poke salat', and littered with all manner of drums and pens, the remnants of Arvin Kilgore's legendary fighting stable. Most had been overturned by curious coons and coyotes, and were now home to huge red wasps and hornets. Scattered throughout, were the hulls of rusting, junked cars, grills grinning ominously through the weed patch.

As we emerged from the woods, we spotted Elsie, sitting on the ramshackle front porch in a rocking chair, rocking with absolute conviction, like a kid saddle-breaking a hobby horse.

"Elsie!" Waddell yelled, but she only rocked harder, seemingly oblivious to our presence.

"ELSIE FREEMAN!" ———Still no response.

"I bleve' Elsies' come un-stuck," he observed.

"Reckon?" was all I could say.

"You don't see a kid wanderin' around up there do ya'?"

"I don't see nothin' but snake bit." I answered.

"Reckon?"

We stood at the edge of the woods for quite a while, hoping against hope to catch a glimpse of the kid without having to confront his furiously rocking momma, neither of us eager to enter the no-man's land that stretched like the fields at Gettysburg, between ourselves, and the old Freeman home-place.

"We gotta' findat' kid. Les' split up."

"Ain't no damn way! Sorry."

Waddell gave me a sympathetic nod, and we headed, single-file, and very slowly toward the porch. As we neared, we got our first close-up view of rockin' Elsie Freeman, and while pitiful, it was also disgusting.

She was filthy. Her shoulder length hair was greasy and matted, and here and there, a few little downy chicken feathers were stuck like big snowflakes. Out of her grimy house-frock, stuck two appallingly hairy, un-shaven legs, culminating in the most horrendous pair of feet ever to carry man or beast. They were swollen and cracked around the heels, her long bony toes twisting in every direction, and out of each grew a lumpy yellow toe-nail that curved ominously, like the talons on a great horned owl. Both feet were completely en-crusted with dried chicken shit. She stared directly at us, with a wide-eyed, angry expression, like a cat just before it attacks. She never spoke, and never stopped rocking. We stood, transfixed by her un-blinking stare. Finally, Waddell freed himself from her hypnotic spell.

"Goddam' Elsie, you look like the Sasquatch!"

I elbowed him hard in the ribs.

"Are you nuts? If she hooks you with onea' them toe-nails, it'll be worsen' a komodo dragon bite. Damn wound'll fester up an' poison ya' fore' we can get back to tha' truck. She may be crazy, but she probley' aint' deaf!"

She just kept right on, rocking and staring.

"You might be right," Waddell answered, rubbing his ribs. "Les' check tha' house."

"YOU check it. I'm goin' aroun' back. Gimme' ya' billy-stick."

"We better stick ta'gether. It'd be easier for her ta' pick us off one at a time."

I knew he was right. We eased past Elsie, and into the house. Seeing Elsie up close should have prepared us for what lay ahead, but sometimes, reality is much more frightening than imagination.

"Put ya' hanky ova' ya' nose. They's diseases in here that aint' even got names yet."

Stepping into that house was like entering a fundamentalist preacher's vision of hell. The funk very nearly brought us both to our knees. It was hot, oppressively hot, and sweat began to drip from the end of our noses, and soak our clothes. Filthier places may exist on earth, but it's highly un-likely. Chickens roamed freely through the house, roosting, and defecating on everything. The floors were slick from it. The air was thick with tiny, unknown particles that glittered, and danced in the sunlight, waiting for the opportunity to dive into your lungs, and grow into the 'Skyfosa', or the 'Spuckets', or some as-yet un-named, filth be-gotten malady. In the front room, a goat stood, casually chewing on a tattered, dusty curtain, totally oblivious to our presence. We passed through quickly, trying not to slide down on the shit-slick floor, and burst out the back door, gulping in the un-contaminated air, and mopping the sweat from our faces. It was at that instant, both at the same time, that we saw him.

"Well, kiss my ass," Waddell whispered. I was, for once in my life, speechless.

He was small for his age, and just as nekkid' as the day he was born. He was about twenty yards away, in a bare spot on the ground, outside of the badly leaning barn, and he, along with a half-dozen or so yard chickens, were scratching around in the dirt, intently searching for hidden seeds, and roly-polys, and the like. He was standing erect, looking straight down, and clucking contentedly, along with his companions.

"Tha' kid's turned chicken."

"Aw,'get tha' hell outta' here!"

"Well, look at im'!"

As much as common sense told me that what I was seeing was not possible, I had to admit, at least on face value, that he was right. The kid turned slightly, as he dug at the ground with his toe, and from our vantage point, the shock of red hair that grew sideways on his head, now looked exactly like a rooster's comb.

"I'll be damned. Gotney' idea how ta' catch im'?"

"We'll run em' inna' barn. Maybe we can hem im' up."

Waddell placed his hand on my shoulder, and gave me

a very serious look. I prepared myself for the 'police bidness, don't feel obligated to help' speech.

"Hickey, do ya' know how I know for certain at' kid's turned chicken?"

"No;——— How?"

"CAUSE I CAN SEE HIS PECKER! GET IM'!"

We took off at a dead run toward the kid and his cohorts. Startled, they all ran in zig-zag patterns, as poultry will do, with a great deal of squawking and shrieking, into the hall of the barn.

"You stay out here an' watch the door in case e' give's me tha' slip!" Waddell called out, as he melted into the long shadows of the barn. A cloud of dust rolled out the barn door, and there was a great deal of commotion, and the sound of falling lumber before it suddenly fell quiet.

"Hey,——— HEY!————you okay in ere'?"

I was starting to get a little anxious, not hearing from Waddell, and expecting at any moment for Elsie to hook me in the back with those talons, and peel me like a ripe banana. Slowly, from the swirling dust and shadows, two figures began to emerge, one carrying the other. As Waddell stepped into the sunlight, with the little nekkid' kid sitting on his arm, he flashed me that buck-toothed, plowboy grin. The kid, instead of struggling to escape, was holding Waddell's badge, turning it over and over in his hands, and directing reflected sunbeams onto Waddell's stubbly chin.

"Well I'll be damned, I guess this proves it."

"Whassat'?"

"That chickens and children are fascinated by shiny objects."

"Or handsome men in uniform," Waddell observed.

"Yeah, that too. What are we gonna' do with im'?"

"Take im' ta' Doil's for processin'."

"What about Elsie?"

"We'll come back and get er'."

"An' how we gonna' do that?"

"You gotta' portable tape player doncha'?"

"Yeah."

"Bring a Conway Twitty tape;————-and an 'Air-wick'."

We made our way around the house, with Waddell carrying the kid, and me running interference from wild dogs, snakes, and Elsie. As we passed the porch, she glanced our way, but never stopped rocking. Waddell called out to her.

"Elsie, we gonna hep' ya'. Me an' Ol' Hickey here gonna' take ya' boy back ta' town an get im' seen about, an' we gon' come back fa' you. Comprende'?"

She stared at us with those piercing, unblinking eyes as we retraced our steps across the sage patch. She never stopped her determined rocking. I stopped, just as we cleared the porch, and saw tears making ruts down Elsie's dirty cheeks. I nodded to her, but got no response.

The little nekkid' kid squatted on the seat between myself and Waddell. Away from his avian companions, he seemed much more like a regular kid, other than the fact that he could'nt speak, and clucked like a yard-bird.

"I wonder if e's hungry?"

"Why doncha' ask im'?"

"Hey kid! You hungry?"

The kid looked up at me, and made a low clucking noise, and went back to fiddling with Waddell's badge.

"He did'nt say."

"I'll stop at tha' 'San-Ann', an' get im' sumpn'."

"Like what?"

"Candy corn. What else would ya' feed a kid a kid that thinks he's a chicken."

6

Doil Pettyjohn prided himself as an avid student of all things 'show bidness', but especially film. He had in his possession, every 'Photoplay' magazine that had ever been issued, and had rarely missed screenings of new titles, sometimes traveling as far away as Birmingham to catch those that were sure, due to content, never to be shown at a theatre that fell under the jurisdiction of the keeper of the county morals, Reverend Booger.

Some would eventually make their way to the drive-in, but Doil considered that to be a very poor venue for the study, and enjoyment of film, and he felt that one could only appreciate the cinematic pleasures of Bardot, or Jane Russell, in the absence of honking horns, grunting farm girls, and girdles airing on antenna masts. It was one of the great showman's vaulted ambitions to be a matinee' idol himself, in the mold of John Agar, or perhaps Ernest Borgnine. He had recognized Seven Bridges the moment he laid eyes on her, and though he considered her acting abilities to be marginal, and only made palatable by her nudity, he saw in her the opportunity to further his cinematic desires, or at the very least, realize nationwide endorsement for the 'empire', already in place.

He was humped over his desk, pecking with one finger on an old 'Remington' typewriter, slowly churning out a script for his starring role in Seven's blistering expose'. Thus far, the only thing he had managed to type was his name, in lower case letters. The creative process was interrupted by a loud knock at the door.

'Shit, she's toughern'I thought. WHO ISIT'?"

'IT'S ME, WADDELL. I GOT YA' A SURPRISE!" He knew Doil loved surprises.

'WELL————COME ON IN!"

The door opened slowly, and Waddell pushed the stark naked, filthy little urchin inside.

"God-a-mighty son! You fagot' ta' put ya' panties on nis' moanin' did'n ya'?"

The kid made some barely audible clucking noises as he examined, with great curiosity, everything in the office, from cigarette butts, to a bowling ball.

"Whad ya' say boy? Speak up!"

Doil gave Waddell, who had stepped just inside the door, a questioning look, and held his palms up, as if to say,

"What tha' hell?"

Waddell just flashed him that big plowboy grin, and held his index finger to his lips. When the odd little kid spotted the 'razorback' hog-head, he wandered around behind the desk, right up next to Doil, to get a closer look at this pig with his head stuck through the wall. Doil leaned back in the the wooden, swiveling desk chair, as far as his enormous bulk would allow, and said,

"Damn if you ain't a strange lookin' lil' bird", as he reached out and touched the cock's-comb of red hair on the little one's head. Instantly, the kid jumped as though he'd brushed up against an electric fence, and let out an ear-splitting,

"BRAAAAAAAWK!" that sent Doil crashing backwards to the floor, pawing the air as he fell, and banging his big 'melon' head on the block wall. From Waddell's point of view, on his knees, laughter sucking the oxygen from his brain, the only part of Doil that was now visible was the soles of his 'chukka' boots, sticking up behind the desk, un-moving.

"Hoddam kid, what tha' hell's wrong wi' you? WADDELL! Bring yo' happy ass ova' heah' an' hep' me up!"

Still chuckling, he helped the struggling, over-weight showman to his feet.

"If this is yo' idea ova' joke, it aint' too damn funny," he said, as he rubbed the rapidly rising 'goose egg' on the back of his head.

"It aint' no joke; tha' kid thinks he's a chicken."

"Oh bullshit! Who put ya' up ta' this kid?"

Waddell stepped forward and dropped a few candy corns on the corner of the desk, and Doil watched in amazement, as the boy rushed over and grabbed them up, munching, and clucking, almost inaudibly, to himself.

"Who IS this kid?"

"Belongs ta' Elsie Freeman. We figger' Arv Kilgore's his daddy."

"Well, there ya' have it. Ya' don't reckon Arv's been gunpowderin' HIM do ya'?"

"Could have. He gassed a coupla' times onna' way ova' here, an' damn near swinged tha' hair outta' mine an Ol' Hickeys' nose."

"Betta' not smoke around im' fa' a day r' two. Where's is' momma?"

"Out at tha' homeplace. She's purty' bad off."

"Anybody seen Arv?"

"Sumbitch took offa' while back."

"You n' Ol' Hickey here go an' get Elsie an' bring er' back here."

Doil was grinning like a possum.

"We fid'n ta' make show bidness' histry'!"

As we started out the door, he said,

"An' leave me a handfulla' at' candy corn."

7

Every municipality, and backwater community has a watering hole where deals are struck, and alliances are formed, whether clandestinely, or brazenly open to public scrutiny. A hub, not only of commerce, but a haven from the storms of life; where a person might escape the pressures of rural existence for an hour, or a week, if need be.

Where he could get his belly full of good home cooking and bonded whiskey, and if over-served, retire to a comfortable room, complete with queen bed, 'Magic-Finger' massage, bolted down t.v., and a sparkling toilet, inspected and insured with a sanitary paper ribbon. The 'Shady Lawn' motel, with it's free standing 'Restaurant and Lounge', was just such a place. Nestled just across the line in a 'wet' county, bordered west, north and east, by the Reverend Dalrymple's three county 'Dry' protectorate, it was a favorite of bidness' travelers, and those whose religious principles were deeply rooted in the doctrine of 'Out of Town Rules'.

Mildred Tarwater, a.k.a. Seven Bridges, and her hired man Steve, sought refuge there, after their harrowing encounter with the south's greatest showman. After securing lodging, they had commandeered a booth at the 'Restaruant and Lounge', and the actress was in the process of draining the third in a series of poorly mixed cocktails, in an effort to calm her shattered nerves. Steve found it ironic that a woman who had been surrounded by snakes, and pompous hucksters her entire professional career, should be rattled by the same when confronted in a different context, but all things being equal, he wisely kept his opinions to himself, and allowed her the freedom to revel in her performance, if only for a captive audience of one.

"This Pettyjohn has got to be stopped!", she slurred, as she tapped the bottom of her glass on the 'Formica', and wiggled it at the bartender, before continuing with her painfully dramatic soliloquy, real tears beginning to lightly puddle in the corners of her eyes. Steve, having knocked back a few cocktails of his own, was moved by her apparent sincerety, and he surprised himself, when he too felt a tear trickle down his cheek, paying no heed to the fact that there was enough cigarette smoke hanging in the un-vented atmosphere to approximate a house fire.

"Those beautiful creatures are being caged like,——— - LIKE ANIMALS! MOTHER PORCUPINES ARE HAVING THEIR NESTS RAIDED, THEIR EGGS STOLEN, TO SERVE A BARBARIC , BACKWOODS TOURIST TRADE! IT MAKES ME SICK TO MY TUMMY!"

She would stab the smoky air with her bony finger to punctuate each atrocity, and pause dramatically to run her hand through her sweat-soaked hair.

Steve, occupying the sole seat on the 'amen' pew, and quickly losing his presence of mind, nodded his woozy' agreement. As he stood, albeit with some difficulty, to retrieve the two fresh cocktails that sat on the bar, his eyes were drawn to a brightly colored poster that hung on the wall, above the double row of liquor bottles. It was one of those old-timey, block lettered, pole-hangers that were used all over the deep south, to great effect, by 'The Grand

Ole' Opry', and all the big 'chittlin' circuit rhythm and blues outfits, like James Brown and the Famous Flames, and Otis Redding, and Poo Nanny and the Stormers. He stood at the bar, and placed his palm over one eye, to overcome the effects of alcohol induced double-vision, and began to read softly to himself.

THE GREATEST SHOW ON EARTH
DOIL PETTYJOHN PRODUCTIONS PRESENTS
FOR ONE NIGHT ONLY
DOIL PETTYJOHN'S DONKEY BASKETBALL!
FEATURING
WADDELL STRICKLAND'S WORLD FAMOUS
PILE DRIVIN' ASS!
FRIDAY NIGHT, MAY 9TH,
MOUNT HEBRON SCHOOL GYMNASIUM
TIP OFF AT 6.OO P.M.
FIRST ASS BUSTED AT 6.01!
CONVERSE ALL-STARS FOR HIGH SCORER!
ADMISSION $1 DOLLAR U.S.
NURSIN' BABIES ADMITTED FREE !!!!!!!!!!!!!!!

He motioned for the bartender.

"Do you mind if I see that poster over here?"

"I don't give a shit," he said, as he took it down and handed it to Steve, who carried it to the table and placed it in front the actress turned activist. She read it very slowly, committing to memory every word, and slammed her palms on the table.

"We've got that son-of-a-bitch now!"

8

Doil sat quietly at his desk for almost an hour, and watched this odd child's every move, the wheels in his head turning like the gears in a swiss watch. As the kid wandered around the office, delicately balancing on his toes and the balls of his nasty little feet, his head would bob forward with each carefully considered step. His thoughtful, gentle clucking, had a profound effect on the childless, entertainment mogul. The kid reminded him of the pet chicken he had, when he was but a kid himself. He picked up the phone, and quietly dialed his home number.

"Betty-Fay, you need ta' get down here. I gotta' surprise fa' ya'!", and he hung up, and continued to stare with wonder, at the kid.

Betty-Fay Pettyjohn was a humorless, holiness woman, who had'nt cut her hair in over a decade, and had it piled on the top of her head in a curious, spherical arrangement, the trademark of the faith. She wore no make-up, declaring it to be the exclusive province of whores and clowns. Her uniform was drab and sexless, the dresses tightened around her neck like a whiplash collar, hemlined at her crew-socked ankles. Her shoes were sensible. There was something forbidding about these holiness women, many of them married to known 'hard-tails', and many of them former 'hard-tails' themselves. They all looked alike, and you got the eerie feeling that they would'nt have a problem blowing your head off, if the situation, or a higher power called for it. That she put up with Doil Pettyjohn made her all the more mysterious. Reptile show, snake-handling; it made for some very dark rumors; the kind that are whispered around campfires late at night.

She marched into Doil's office, and straight up to his desk, focusing her eyes on Doil, and nothing else. Very direct, these holiness women.

"This better be good! I left several of the sisters at the house workin' on tha' preacher's quilt."

Doil just sat there grinning, and pointed to the corner, past her left arm.

"Oh, fa' heaven's sake," she muttered, as she gave Doil a disgusted look. A look that he had seen constantly for over a decade, and was quite accustomed to. She wheeled in the direction of the corner, and froze like a statue, one hand over her open mouth, unable to speak, or to look away. Finally, she took a few non-threatening steps toward the kid, and gently stroked his 'comb'. He looked up at her with tender green eyes, and lovingly clucked a few times. She knelt, put her arms around him, and pulled his nekkid' little body to her bosom. He let out a couple of muffled,

"Braawks", and stood motionless, his face buried in breast and sack-cloth.

"Dammit' Betty-Fay, don't smother tha' boy!"

"Whose child is this Doil? Have my prayers finally been answered?"

"Was ya' prayin' fa' a 'Rhode Island Red'?

"Don't be a fool, if thas' possible."

"He's Elsie Freeman's kid, but she had a wheel ta' run off, an' it looks like tha' chickens been raisin' im'."

"Whos' is' babys daddy?"

"Best we can figger' it's Arv Kilgore."

"A worthless sinner, and drunkard!"

"But a helluva' chicken fighter. Listen; why doncha' take is' boy ova' ta' tha' house an'see can ya'clean im' up. He gon' need a place ta' stay fa'while, least till we see ta' his mamma."

She stood, with the child still clutched in her arms, and left the office without saying a word. As she reached the door, she glanced back at Doil, and just for a fleeting instant, he imagined that she smiled at him. Then she was gone.

9

Not at all thrilled with the prospect of wrestling with Elsie Freeman, we drove back to Waddell's place to mentally prepare ourselves for the task at hand. As he gathered wardrobe, I scrounged through my car, and found a well worn, but functional eight track copy of 'Conway Twitty's Golden Greats'. I had, through a credit arrangement with a local pawnbroker, procured one of the only portable tape players in the area, making me quite popular, and an oft' invited guest at functions where electricity could'nt be had; Barn dances, submarine races, and the like, and I loaded it into Waddell's truck.

He located a pair of coveralls that belonged to his sister, who, though raw-boned herself, did not have quite the physical stature of her brother, making a tolerable fit for me, although I surmised from the smell, that she wore them to pump out the cess pool.

After donning his own, he produced a flat of pints containing 'first run', or as Doil referred to it, 'Special Reserve', and we cracked open a jar, and took seats at the kitchen table, following the time-honored tradition of 'Nerve Steadying'.

"To Doil Pettyjohn — Greater men may have lived, but I doubt it!" toasted Waddell, as he took a long pull on the jar, and passed it to me, shaking his head to counter-act the dizziness.

"To Elsie Freeman, salt o' tha' earth!"

I took a mouthful, gargled it like 'Listerine' and swallowed, almost losing it through my nose, as it blistered my tonsils on the way down. I pushed the container back across the table to Waddell's waiting hand.

"To tha' kid that thinks' he's a chicken!" and back to me.

"I hear ya' cluckin', but I cain't find ya' nest!" I eloquently offered, even as the rising fumes gave me occasion to swoon.

Not to be outdone, I raised the flagon and swallowed hard, the crystal clear whiskey dripping from my chin.

"Whadda'we drink to now?" He asked as he pulled the glass from my hand.

"To Arv Kilgore!" I said.

"I aint' drinkin' ta' that son-uva'-bitch!"

"By God, you're right; he is a son-uva'-bitch!"

"To son's-a-bitches!"

"Amen!" He said as he clumsily attempted to stand. I responded in kind, with a clumsy attempt of my own, and raised the empty chalice in the air.

"To chicken-fightin' sons-a-bitches!"

"HALLEULAH! LES' GO GET AT' BOY'S MOMMA! Grab at' flat on ya' way out."

"We liable ta' get drunk!"

"Reckon?"

The return trip was a good deal more exiteing, what with the truck careening from ditch bank to ditch bank, dodging abandoned automobiles, tree trunks, and so forth. This time, we drove straight up the over-grown drive to the house, running down saplings, crushing bottles, cans, and humble forest creatures beneath the tires of Waddell's truck.

Elsie was still out front, and though I had serious doubts about Waddell's ability to get us stopped before we took out the porch, She evidently had complete confidence in him, because she never blinked, and never stopped rocking. We sat for several minutes in complete silence, attempting to formulate a plan of action that would be consistent with the high standards of conduct preached, and practiced by representatives of the Pettyjohn empire. That being next to impossible in our rapidly advancing state of inebriation, Waddell opted for the alternative.

Crack tha' lid on one'm jars."

With very slow, and deliberate movements, so as not to spook our charge, I unscrewed the lid on a fresh offering, and as inconspicuously as possible, under these conditions, took a long swallow, and slid it across the seat cover to the brains of the im-pending operation. He studied her carefully, as he raised it to his lips, and deftly poured an ounce or two down the front of his coveralls.

"Shit!"

"You a little nervous?"

"A little; you?"

"Maybe a little; hell, maybe a lot."

"We can do this."

"Reckon?"

"I reckon we got to! Ease out tha' door, real quiet-like, and get them tin-snips outta' tha' tool box."

I froze, with my hand on the door handle.

"Tin snips? What tha' hell are we gonna do with tin snips?"

"You gon' cut er' toenails fore we put er' inna' truck."

"Whoa now, hey, uh uh! You know I gotta' deal bout' women's feet, an' aint' no damn way I'm touchin' hers. They nasty."

"Well hell, we cain't let er' in here without cuttin' em'. She's liable ta' go ta' kickin', an'gut tha' wires out from under tha' dash. You don' wanna' be out here with er' broke down after dark, do ya'?"

"I DON'T WANNA' TOUCH HER DAMN NASTY FEET!"

"Well, you gon' haf'to, cause I got tha' arthritis in my hands when I'se in tha' army, an' I caint' squeeze hard enough ta' pull a wet string outuv' a cat's ass.

"You a damn lie! You ain't ever been in tha' army."

"Army doctor told me if I ever squeezed down on anything too hard, they liable to ball up permanent, an' I'd hafta' learn ta' eat with my feet."

"At's tha' biggest crock-o'-shit you ever told."

"CROSS MY HEART N' HOPE TA' DIE! Listen; won't be nothin' to it. Set at' eight track onna' hood, an' cue tha' tape up ta' 'Hello Darlin'. Ever time she hears it, she melts like a pair o' wax lips."

"Arthritis my achin' ass," I mumbled as I slipped out, and fumbled quietly in the tool box for the snips. Once located, I placed them in the pocket of the reeking coveralls, and gently lifted the portable player from the bed, and placed it on the hood, facing in the general direction of the frantically rocking, casualty of circumstance.

"Can you get out, or do I need ta' open tha' door for ya'?"

As he climbed out, grinning broadly, I punched the 'play ' button, and we waited, for what seemed like minutes, for Conway's rich voice to speak to Elsie from the shiny silver box.

"Hello Darlin, it's been a loooonngg tiiiiiiiiiime," came booming out of the speakers. The rocking stopped. Birds fell silent, and the crickets stopped chirping. A cool, gusty breeze began to blow through the trees, picking a feather or two from Elsie's matted hair, and they danced above her like pixies, before blowing off the porch. She sat stone still, her expression beginning to soften somewhat. We hesitantly mounted the stairs, and circled her like a pair of buzzards. Tears had rutted Elsie's grimey cheeks, and spotted her ragged dress.

"Now what?" I whispered nervously.

"I aint' gotta' clue!"

"Well, you got about fifteen seconds before is' song's over ta' figger' it out!"

"Shhhit", he mumbled under his breath, and he pulled a familiar container from the oversized pocket of his coveralls, unscrewed the lid, and took a drink. Conway's voice faded away, and I held my breath, anticipating a physically violent intervention. Then, something amazing happened. Elsie looked up at Waddell, tears pooled in the corners of her eyes, and held out her hand.

"Ya' want a little horn Elsie?" He handed her the jar.

"Unh unh," I grunted through clenched teeth, but it was too late. She took a long, luxuriant pull on the whiskey, and even though she was filthy, and crusted with chicken feces, I have to admit, I found her manner with the makeshift snifter mildly erotic, as though the corn likker' had awakened all five senses at once, and flooded her dormant pleasure receptors. However any connection with eroticism instantly disappeared for me, as Conway began to sing "Lay You Down', and Elsie, after having taken another man-sized drink, turned and looked directly into my eyes, and raked her tongue over her skinny, chapped lips.

"Oh wait, whoa. Aint' no damn way!"

"I think she likes ya', Hickey."

"Reckon?"

She finally looked away, and taking another sip, she closed her eyes, and began to rock, and nod her head with the music. She seemed to be totally relaxed, but as Waddell attempted to take the jar from her hand, she opened one eye, and with her free hand, very gently pushed him away.

"You keep it then, we got some more."

He looked over at me and cocked his head toward the truck. I shook my head, refusing to no avail, as he just stepped off the porch and got it himself. He offered me the first drink, and cognizant that the time was drawing near, when I would be called upon to draw the tin snips that were hidden in my cover-alls, I accepted, and drank reverently, like a kamikaze pilot, as Waddell nodded his glowing approval. He leaned over, near Elsie's ear, and spoke softly to her as she rocked and drank.

"You're foundered Elsie, an' Ol' Hickey here's gonna trim ya' hooves."

She opened her eyes and stared at Waddell, and then shifted her gaze to me. Still, she had not spoken. I handed the jar to him, as I slowly pulled the snips from my pocket. He took a hard pull and wiped his mouth on the sleeve of his cover-alls.

"It's all gon' be good girl. Hickey here's gotta' thing bout' women's feet. Likes ta' paint toenails an' whatnot. Hell, he's probley' tha' best damn toenail man in tha' county, maybe ebn' tha' whole state!"

If looks could actually kill, Waddell Strickland would have ceased his drunken existence after that speech. I turned, and with my back to Elsie, stradding her knees, I reached down, and lifted one of her disgustingly filthy feet to the point where I could lock my legs around her hairy leg at mid-calf, and choked back the urge to puke. My blood ran cold, as I felt her other foot come to rest on the cheek of my tender butt, and give it a warning tweak with her 'owl-talon' nails. I knew that if I made one false move, or caused her the least bit of dis-comfort, she would bury those claws, and rip it off like a pop-top.

I started to sweat profusely. The perspiration mingled with my 'Vaseline' hair tonic, and became toxic, as it flowed into my eyes, burning like tear gas. I drug the sleeve of my filthy cover-alls across them in a vain effort to clear my vision, and glanced over my shoulder to guage Elsie's demeanor, just as she raised the glass to her lips again, and narrowed her eyes. What if I misjudge, blinded by sweat and confused by the crusty chicken shit, and cut off a toe? I swallowed hard, placed the jaws of the snips just past where I could only hope that her pinky toe stopped, and squeezed down hard on the handles. A crusted, yellow toenail ricocheted off the hood of the truck. One down; nine to go.

As I made my way slowly from toe to toe, the stress, and increasing exertion over-whelmed me, and I threw up, barely missing the 'paw', that I held between my knees. I forged ahead, and cleared the first foot. So far, so good, but my strength was starting to fail me, and I felt as though I was walking up a mountain backwards.

"You doin' some purty' work now," gushed Waddell, and I snatched the jar from his hand, and turned it up, my need for alcohol so great, that I drank it like water, emptying the container, and handed it back in silence, the deranged look on my face causing him to back away.

Elsie had allowed her foot to drop from my butt after I completed the first without mishap, and as I reached for it, I stole another glance back at her. She was smiling. Fortified by alcohol, and with the finish line looming in the distance, I summoned the strength to carry on.

The operation continued without incident, but by the eighth toe, the short respite that had allowed me to continue was but a memory, and I was rapidly fading, unsure if I could complete the task before losing consciousness. Drawing on my last reserves, I finally made it to the last hurdle; the big toe on her right foot. Though, to call it a mere hurdle, would be akin to referring to Mount Everest as a steep hill. It was enormous. As long as her thumb, and as wide as a shoe horn, with a nail so thick, that it looked like a 'Frito'.

I took a few deep breaths, and grasped the snips with both hands, squeezing with all I had. They would'nt budge. I was beginning to see spots before my eyes, and I knew instinctively, that I only had one more push left in me, and if the last one had'nt made a dent, this was not even apt to do as well. A defeatist attitude began to creep it's way into my consciousness, withering my resolve. Waddell stepped forward, seeing that we might well lose this contest, and spoke softly, and re-assuringly, as he massaged my shoulders.

"You can do it, Hickey, I know ya'; bettern' ya' know ya'sef'. You're standin' at tha' crossroads. From right here, you can triumph, and go on ta' live up ta' ya' potential, never facin' a hurdle too high; never wonderin' what if? Or you can give up, an' spend tha' rest uv' ya' miserable life knowin' that you was whipped by a goddam' toenail."

He patted me on the shoulder, and stepped back.

I looked deep inside myself, to my center. The place where youth springs eternal, and courage lies at the ready. The place where resides the 'man spirit'.

As I gripped the snips and started to push, the veins in my temples began to swell and throb, as well as those on my hands and arms. Sweat running in rivulets down my face, I started to tremble from the in-human exertion, and still, the toenail held.

'SNIP, DAMN YOU, SNIP!" I cried.

As the last molecule of strength ebbed from my arms, and victory started to slip slowly away, Elsie raised her other foot, and as deftly as a surgeon, stuck her freshly clipped big toe, square in the crack of my trembling ass. I yelled, as a rush of raw power shot through me, and the jaws of the snips slammed together with a piercing 'clack'. The severed 'Frito' shot across the porch at blinding speed, caught Waddell right between the eyes, and sent him stumbling backwards off the porch.

I dropped to my knees, sobbing like a heart-broken teenager, soaked with sweat, too exhausted, and too sick from exertion to remain standing. I could hear Waddell moaning from somewhere off the porch, but I was powerless to help him. Suddenly, I heard a muffled laugh, and I slowly turned to see Elsie trembling. A chuckle, like the low rumbling of a volcano, was pushing its way up her throat. It erupted into an open belly laugh. She laughed so hard that she gagged, and then started all over again. Huge tears of pure joy made fresh ruts in her dirty face. She laughed until she was completely exhausted, and slumped in the rocker like a discarded sock monkey. Waddell had climbed back to the porch, and was rubbing the 'goose egg' that the flying toenail had produced on his forehead.

"Elsie, welcome back," He said, as he helped me to my feet.

"You gon' hafta' clean up a little fore ya'get in my truck, gal'. You gotta' hose pipe out here anywhere?"

She did'nt answer, just sat there chuckling softly to herself, and taking the occasional dainty sip from the magic jar.

"Hickey, see if chuckles here's gotta' outside 'spickit'. They's probley' a hose pipe in tha' barn. I got sumpn' she can wear inna' truck."

I located a water 'spickit' sticking up in the yard, with a hose already attached, and I threw the end over a low-hanging china-berry branch behind the house, producing a make-shift shower. Waddell dug around under the truck seat, and fished out a pair of semi-clean, 'Liberty' over-alls, and an undershirt that he maintained as 'emergency' replacements in the event that alcohol consumption, or diet related gastric disturbances might render the clothes on his back embarrassingly un-wearable. In the glove box, he kept a shaving razor, that he used to touch himself up prior to ballgames, and out of the tool box, he fished a can of 'Go-Jo' hand cleaner.

"Elsie, we aint' got'ney bar soap, or shampoo, an' I aint' sa' sure that they'd work anyhow. What we do have, is 'Go-Jo', which fa' my money, is the finest grease remover on tha' market, an' a razor with a fairly fresh blade, to trim tha wool offn' ya' legs. If at' won't do it, I got a gas-powered weed-eater in tha' truck. Ol'Hickey here, who did such an outstandin' job on ya' toenails, has throwed a hose pipe over a tree limb behind tha' house, and even as I speak, fresh cool water is showerin' down, as refreshin' as a spring rain. Take ese' 'Libertys', an' is' under-shirt as ya'go, an' see can ya' make ya'sef' presentable.

Elsie uttered the first words she had spoken in years.

"Waddell Strickland,—KISS MY ASS!"

At which point, she doubled over with laughter. It truly is the best medicine, because as she stood up, she left all the pain of this place lying on the porch around that old rocker, and with a big smile, stepped forward to accept the folded clothes with the hand cleaner, and the razor on top, just like she was receiving army issue.

"Yall' aint' gonna' watch me, are ya'?"

"Why hell no!" we both answered at once.

She threw back her head and laughed, stumbled off the porch, and around the house.

10

Over at the Pettyjohn place, Betty-Fay had the kid soaking in the tub, while she read him bible stories, one after the other. He had fallen fast asleep almost as soon as he hit the water, and she was holding his head with one hand, as she turned the pages with the other, figuring that he could receive salvation through osmosis, if no other way. She finished her last story and sat by the tub, holding that tiny head with the bright red 'comb', and she thought to herself,

"If the preacher and me had a child, he would probley' have looked just like this one."

She became all dreamy and moist. Betty-Fay, like a lot of these very pious women, had a severe crush on the Reverend Booger Red. She blathered on about him all the time. It's a curious phenomenon, that many an unscrupulous minister plays to full advantage, and Red was certainly no exception. As long as he could keep the women in his flock fixated on himself, he could ask for, and get most anything he wanted by making it known to them, who would see that he got whatever it was, by making their husbands miserable till he did. Since he preached that your gifts would pay your way into heaven, the men went along with it, as a sort of celestial insurance policy, premiums due. The more payments on the preacher's Cadillac, the bigger the double-wide in heaven; show bidness' as theology.

As she sat, fantasizing about a front row pew full of red-headed kids, and the jealous, yet admiring looks of a host of holiness women, her course became clear.

"Wake up baby."

The kid slowly opened his eyes, and answered with a questioning,

"Cluck?"

"We gotta get you dressed an' call tha' preacher."

She stood and stretched her arms as far as she could toward the ceiling, her palms facing up, ready to receive a fly ball from heaven.

"We gonna' get you saved!" she yelled, and she began to speak in tongues like an auctioneer with a speech impediment. Little Conway slowly, and purposefully, sank into the tub, attempting to hide in the water.

11

Since the ballgame fiasco, the Reverend Dalrymple had been keeping a rather low profile; low for him, at any rate. He had denounced Wyvanelle, and run her off, tearfully proclaiming that he knew nothing of those infamous tattoos, and that he had never even gazed at her nakedness, for it was un-Christian to do so. He even went so far as to say that they had only consummated the marriage once, on their wedding night, only in accordance to popular custom, and that was done through the rear of flannel 'footie' pajamas that he had purchased for her as a wedding gift, to avoid temptations of the flesh.

In the righteous spirit of true 'show bidness' theology, the adoring women of the congregation bought this carefully considered fabrication, and directed the full force of their blame on his wife, whom they all had spotted as a 'Jezebel' from the moment she arrived, or so they said. The man with the mighty hair-do and the Burt Lancaster pipes became more Godly than ever to them, adding pity to his ever increasing list of hormonal strings to pull.

The men, of course, knew the real truth, but to their credit, and wanting in no way to be involved in cooking, washing, and cleaning, said nothing.

The Preacher was asleep in his office when the call came. Betty-Fay spilled the whole story, adding her own spin to the tale; demonic possession, which she was sure would bring her hero running, and allow her to spend some quality prayer time with him.

The Preacher was always titillated by calls from his 'girls', as he like to think of them, but now, none moreso than Betty-Fay Pettyjohn. He figured that he owed Doil one for costing him Wyvanelle, who had performed salacious acts with him that had yet to be named, and he had no intention of 'turning the other cheek'.

He listened intently, and in his mind's eye, he could see book deals, and radio, and possibly even a television ministry, but mostly what he could see was a shitload of money, and the collapse of the Pettyjohn Supremacy. He could'nt have been more tickled with a feather 'up is' arse'. As he hung up the phone, he whispered a muffled,

"Halleujah!"

12

Waddell Strickland, myself, and Elsie Freeman were now, by all legally accepted forms of measurement, officially shit-faced. Waddell and I lay on the hood of his truck, waiting for Elsie, who was behind the house singing 'It's Only Make Believe' at the top of her lungs, to hopefully split her crust, and step out a new woman, leaving her hull under the china-berry tree like a 'July fly'.

"Dammit' Elsie, hurry up! Me n' Ol' Hickey's gon' get snake bit."

She only sang louder, making the most of her re-discovered vocal abilities. Somewhere down on the bluff, a pack of beagles took up the catchy hook, and were singing along with a mournful wail. Waddell mumbled something that I could'nt quite understand.

"Whadyu' say?"

"I said, Elsie wad'nt too bad lookin' an' ol' gal when we was in school."

I just lay there, looking up at the clouds, offering no reply. Poor ol' Waddell, bless his heart, was no Troy Donahue, and had never had much luck with the women. I held my tongue as long as I could, but as it always does, alcohol nullified common sense.

"Waddell, if you fixin' ta' tell me that youre' havin' feelins' for Elsie Freeman, I suggest at' you start sippin' onat' bottle o' 'Sal Hepatica' right now, cause when you sober up, you gon' be one sick sonuva'bitch."

He rolled over, and without so much as a word, pushed me off the hood, and I landed butt-first, in the top of a big fire-ant bed. Much like Wormy, the corn likker had wrecked my perspective, and I sat there, in a fatal moment of in-decision, while hundreds of angry ants charged into my over-alls. By the time the brain said "jump", the ass was covered.

"AAAAAAAAAAAAAAAHHHHHHHHHHHHHH-HHH!" I screamed, as I scrambled, trying to get my footing.

"Whatha' hell's wrong wiyu'?"

"AAAAAAAAAAAAAAAHHHHHHHHHHHHHH-HHHH!"

I screamed again, as I tore off the over-alls. Waddell sat straight up and stared in open mouthed wonder, as I ripped away clothing till I was nekkid' as a new-born, slapping myself on the ass, and jumpin' like Jackie Chan. As Waddell broke into hysterical laughter at this personally embarrassing turn of events, I remembered the water hose that hung in the china-berry tree, and tore around the house, headed straight for the cooling water, and nekkid' Elsie Freeman. She saw me coming, but to her dis-credit, instead of running away, which is the normal response when one sees a drunken, screaming, naked man charging at breakneck speed straight for you, she stayed right there, under the cold, running water, watching and waiting.

"I knowed' youd' come," she purred through her big, yellow teeth.

I ran up, spun around, and exposed my lilly-white, ant covered butt to the cold water, and sex-starved Elsie Freeman, and yelled,

"SLAP IT, SLAP IT!!!"

"I will baby! Momma whup' is' bad boy if at's whatcha' want," and she reared back, and popped me on the ass with the palm of her big 'field-hand', as hard as she could, causing my hips to lurch forward, and driving the ants deep into my pale, stinging flesh.

"SON-UVA-BITCH!" I cried, "DO IT AGAIN!"

"You like at' baby? Want momma talk dirty while she whup is' nasty boy?"

This time, she slapped my poor, burnin' butt so hard, that she damn near broke my hip, and sent me crashing face first into the fresh mud. In the distance, I could hear the sounds of wretching, as Waddell had laughed so hard, he had begun to puke.

"Okay, okay, thas'enough!"

The fire ant stings were still burning as though my backside was covered with bits of glowing charcoal, but I was unable, and un-willing to take another slap from Elsie's big hand, no matter what the benefit. I wiped the mud from my tortured brow, and turned around to face Elsie, nekkid' as a jay bird, and leering at me with a mysterious half-smile, like a sasquatch 'Venus di Milo'.

"You wanna' spank me now baby?"

She stepped under the water, letting it run through her stringy hair. I started to cry; a whimper at first, and then full-blown bawlin' like a baby. I'd close my eyes and it would subside somewhat, but when I opened them, and saw Elsie, writhing under the water hose, it would start all over again. I staggered away from the tree, rubbing my wounded pride, with the hundred or so fire ant stings, and the two huge, bloody red handprints. Behind me, I heard Elsie take up another chorus of 'It's Only Make Believe.'

13

Doil Pettyjohn had made up his mind that he was going to keep this kid. It would not only give Betty-Fay the child that she craved, but all of Doil's show bidness' dreams, and aspirations could be realized as well. He'd have to come to some kind of agreement with Elsie Freeman, but that should'nt be too hard. Hell, he would adopt her too, if need be. Then, there were the authorities, who were embodied in the sheriff, who already had a 'special arrangement' with Doil, but a man whom Doil did not consider completely trustworthy, as he had indicated to myself and Waddell many times,

"I would'nt trust the sheriff in the shit-house with a muzzle," whatever that means. Doil determined to make the way easy with the law first, and called to arrange a sit-down.

Cecil Dowd had been sheriff for three terms. He was a 'puscle-gutted', bald, duck-footed man, whose hands were always cold and clammy; the sure sign of a snake. He had very little education, and no law enforcement training at all. Before being elected sheriff, he ran a twelve room motel about five miles up the highway toward Tennessee, where a man could cash a paycheck, buy a little likker', and rent female companionship, and a semi-clean room by the hour. He was the ideal candidate.

County sheriffs are not elected for their ability to enforce the law. They are elected for their open-minded discretion in not en-forcing it. Cecil was the most open-minded sheriff in recent memory. They met at Doil's office, away from prying eyes.

"Come on in Cecil, howsya' mammanem'?"

"Why, you heard sumpn'?"

Cecil was none too bright, and the new-found lawman in him made him ever suspicious.

"Naw, naw, just aint' seen em' in a while is all."

"Whadyu' want Doil?"

Cecil cut straight to the bone.

"That bidness' with the school board."

"Yeah, what about it?"

"You sent Waddell out to tha' ol' Freeman homeplace ta' look for at' kid uv' Elsie's."

"Yeah?"

"Well, he found im'."

"Yeah, well, ise' slow r' sumpn'?"

"He's a chicken."

The sheriff sat in silence for a few moments.

"He's a chicken, ya' say?"

"Well, he thinks e' is; caint' talk, just clucks."

Cecil sat stone still, staring at Doil like a pig staring at a wristwatch, his small brain trying to absorb this information. Finally, he spoke.

"Aint'at' Arv kilgore's kid?"

"Probley."

"Where's tha' kid now?"

"Betty-Fay got im' overt' tha' house cleanin' im' up. Boy was nasty."

"Where's is' mamma?"

"I sent Waddell an' Ol'Hickey out to get er'. She come un-glued."

"Damn Arv Kilgore," Cecil muttered, "He aint' worth tha' powder it'd take ta' blow is' head off, but at' sumbitch' is a hell uva' chicken-fighter."

"I'll go along wi'ya' there, Sherriff."

"Well,———— les' go see bout' tha' kid."

14

Betty-Fay got the kid out of the tub, scrubbed him dry with a towel until she turned him pink, and then dusted him all over with 'Avon After-Bath' powder on a big powder puff, which made him sneeze several times, the first sounds she'd heard him make that did'nt sound like poultry.

"Honey, we gotta' find you somethin' to wear. Ya' caint' be runnin' round' nekkid'. It aint' Christian."

When they were keepin' company, Doil had won her a stuffed monkey in a blue sailor suit, by knocking down weighted milk bottles with a lop-sided softball, at the carnival. She had kept it all these years, the way women with kids keep baby booties. She un-dressed the monkey, and held the suit up to the kid's powdery, pink body.

"This'll be perfect, till we can buy you some new clothes," she said proudly.

The kid looked down at the dusty sailor suit, dumbfounded. She kept a couple of big dolls in the closet for her nieces'amusement, when and if they ever showed up, and she pulled a pair of cotton panties with a butterfly print from a ragged doll, and slipped them on Conway. He started to cluck nervously as she dressed him in the sailor suit, and grew panicky when she bobby-pinned the white sailor's cap, cocked jauntily to the side, next to his 'comb'.

He dared not move though, reasoning that the huge mound on Betty-Fay's head might well be a hornet's nest, of which he was familiar, and any sudden movement might prove fatal. Though she might dress him as one, he was certainly no dummy. Betty-Fay stepped back and admired her work.

"Oh honey, you look so handsome in your uniform; just like Popeye."

She took his hand and led him to an old full length mirror, that swiveled on a big wooden stand. It was the first time that he had seen his own reflection, since Elsie had smashed all the mirrors at the homeplace after Arv left, and he was totally perplexed. He stood for several minutes staring at the strange image in the mirror. He gently touched it, and traced the face with his finger, pulling back several times, as the strange creature in the glass did the same. He touched his nose, and put his finger in his ear, and the image followed suit. Suddenly, a light flashed on in his head, and he realized that the image in the glass was his own. A look of terror came over him as he grabbed at his face, searching for his beak, and rubbed his hands over his arms, amazed that he could find no feathers. His mind reeling, he began to cluck and brawk' in a terrible way, and he turned and buried his face in Betty-Fay's colorless house frock.

"It's awright baby, Mom-Betty gon' take care o' you now."

She heard the slam of car doors, and heavy footsteps comin' across the porch.

"You stay in here honey, Mom-Betty be right back."

The kid watched her walk out, and close the door behind her. He slowly turned to face the mirror, and stood there staring at his freshly manufactured image. The tongue peeked out slowly at first, then darted in and out, circling the mouth, and attempting to touch the end of the 'beak'. The fingers went into the corners of his mouth, and he pulled sideways, exposing his tiny teeth, as he cocked his head from side to side. Soon, the entire body was involved, and he bounced and shook, thououghly amusing himself, almost as if he were a normal little kid.

"Betty-Fay, where's at' young'un?" Doil bellowed, as he and the sheriff stomped into the kitchen. Betty-Fay came stalking down the hall, with her holiness hackles up.

"Shhhhhh! don't be sa' loud. He's in tha' back bedroom, an' he's a little upset right now. Whatr'you doin' here Cecil?"

"I need to see the youngun' Betty-Fay."

"Not now."

"I just need to ast' im' a couple a' questions."

"I said not now! He caint' talk anyway, and I doubt he can understand what we're sayin'. Furthermore, I bleve' that child to be demonized!"

"Aw, good God-a-mighty Betty-Fay."

"Don't you use at' language inis' house Doil Pettyjohn!"

"Well at least letim' lookit' tha' boy."

"He can peek through tha' door, but thas' it."

Doil pointed to the door, and Cecil tip-toed over and cracked it open, wide enough to poke his bald head in. The kid was still standing in front of the mirror, shaking his tailfeathers. He never knew Cecil was anywhere around. The sheriff stared intently for a few moments, and then curiosity got the best of him.

"Hey," he whispered.

The kid spun around, and seeing the body-less, lumpy bald head, he let out a "Brrraaaaawk", that nearly busted Cecil's eardrums.

It was hard to say who was more frightened, the kid, or Cecil. Not knowing which way to run, the kid just stood there, 'brawking', louder and louder, and as Cecil stood, humped over, with his head poked through the door, Betty-Fay crow-hopped across the kitchen floor, and with grace and power reminiscent of Lou 'The Toe' Groza, planted a sensible shoe square in Cecil's fat ass. The impact knocked him through the door, and it swung open and banged against the wall, as Cecil plopped onto the hardwood, his belly spreading out like biscuit dough, before the first of his chins bounced off the floor like an under-inflated basketball. Conway started running wildly, in zig-zag patterns, around the bedroom, losing the bobby-pinned sailor hat, just as he disappeared thru the curtain that served as the closet door. Doil ran over, and struggled to get the obviously addled sheriff to his feet.

"I saw a chicken in a sailor suit!" he mumbled over and over.

"Jew' seeit'? A Goddam' chicken inna' sailor suit!"

"Nice goin'," Doil said to Betty-Fay as he put the sherriff's arm over his shoulder, and helped him out the door.

"A chicken inna' Goddam' sailor suit," he kept muttering.

As Doil drove him away, Betty-Fay stood in the open door and began to sing 'The Battle Hymn of The Republic' at the top of her lungs, and was still singing as they faded out of sight.

15

By the time I had waddled back to the truck, the corn liquor, and the immensity of the situation had proved too much for Waddell, and he had passed out, cold as a stone.

I gently stood on his lifeless body and reached into the truck seat for the semester-sized can of 'Bruton Snuff' that he kept stuffed between the cushions, and adjusted the door mirror to a spot where I could examine the horrific condition of my throbbing backside. With my head cocked precariously over my shoulder, as I stood on Waddell's butt, I took pinch after pinch of the sweet powder, moistened it in my mouth, and very gently applied the gooey, brown paste to every sting that I could see. Before long, my entire butt was crusted, and took on the appearance of a big chocolate cake. There are those who scoff at such un-conventional hillbilly remedies, but there is no finer poultice in the world, and it did'nt take long for the snuff to begin to ease my suffering, and I crawled into the truck seat, and fell fast asleep. I don't know how long I was out, but I awoke to a vaguely familiar voice cooing',

"Mmmm-mmmm' I love me some chocolate cake."

"Sheit!", I cried, and slithered out the driver's door, careful not to let anything disturb the balmy icing on my tail, and covering my credentials with a yellowed copy of the local advertiser that I had snatched from the floor-board on the way out. I looked back through the open door, and there stood Elsie, scrubbed and somewhat combed, and wearing the over-alls that Waddell had provided. The breeze carried the distinct odor of 'Go-Jo' past my nose. Elsie had officially re-joined the race.

"By God Elsie, you look nice."

Which she did, comparatively.

Waddell had come to, and was sitting on the ground, holding his head.

"I feel like I been eat by a wolf, and shit over a cliff."

There was half a fruit jar of mash sitting on the ground beside him, and he picked it up, took a long slug, and wiped his mouth on his sleeve before leaning back on his elbows.

"Issat' yew' Elsie? Damn girl, you clean up purty' good! Commere' an' get yew' a taste, an' lemme' take a look".

Elsie walked around the truck, and stopped in front of him, doing a pirouette, of sorts, slowly turning, with one hand above her head, her armpit red, and polka-dotted with tiny drops of blood from its' cold water shave.

"See there, you look damn near like you did when we was in school."

A big smile came across Elsie's face, revealing her yellowed teeth.

"Well damn near", Waddell said under his breath, as he rose to his feet, and offered the jar to Elsie.

"Where's my boy Waddell?"

"We took im'over to Doil's place. He'll take care of im' till we get there."

"To Doil Pettyjohn," Elsie toasted, and took a hard pull before handing off to Waddell.

"I'll drink to that man!"

Waddell took a horn of his own.

"Jesus", I thought,"Here we go again."

Waddell was caught up in the tender moment, and had forgotten about me. When he turned and caught a glimpse, a big smile of recognition lit his face. He walked over, the liquor in his outstretched hand, and cocked his head sideways, reading the headlines that concealed my hastily covered private playground.

"Looky here, Garvis Kittle grows record watermelon; pitcher' on page two. Turn it over Hickey, so's we can"———

"Gimmee at' damn jar" I snarled, interrupting his comedic delivery. He and Elsie started laughing like two drunk hyenas. I took an angry swallow, draining the last drop, and tossed the empty container into the weeds.

"I caint' siddown'," I whispered.

Waddell peeped around to have a look.

"Damn, yo'ass looks like a———"

"Chocklit' cake? Yea, so I heard. This aint' funny dammit, it's killin' me."

"Aw-right, take it easy." he said, and he picked an old tire up off the ground, bounced it around a few times to remove standing water and mosquitos, and pitched it up in the truck bed.

"Belly down onnat' n' we'll get tha'hell out from here."

"That aint' gon' be cumptable' worth a shit!"

"Maybe Elsie'll letcha' lay acrost' her lap!"

"I don't see it happnin'."

"Then crawl yo' crusty ass in an' lay down."

"Please go slow."

"Relax, boy, you inna' hands uva' pro-fessional!"

He crawled in, and fired up the truck.

"Comeon' Elsie, an' we'll take ya' ta' yer' kid. Whasat' boy's name anyhow?"

"Conway," she said, as she climbed in the truck.

"Conway Twitty Freeman."

She punched the play button on the portable eight track that Waddell had pitched in the seat. As the truck lurched forward over the un-even ground, I held on to the tire for dear life, and as Conway sang 'Lyin' Here With Linda On My Mind', we headed for Pettyjohn's Monkey Ranch, and our questionable place in entertainment history.

16

Now everyone who had seen the kid thus far, assumed that he must be severely mentally challenged. After all, he ran around nekkid' as a new born, and had the communication skills of a layin' hen. Nothing could have been further from the truth.

The kid was actually extremely bright, some might even say, genius. Sure, he looked and acted strange, but his semi-feral lifestyle had allowed his human sensibilities to develop in some very unusual ways.

He could read emotions like a lie detector, animal or human. An amazing ability that allowed him to cut through layers of bluff and bullshit, and read a person's intentions, and nature, almost immediately. That mysterious sensation that we call a 'gut' feeling, was a highly developed science in this kid. One of the more amazing of his gifts, was his uncanny ability to communicate with non-humans. This became shockingly clear to Betty-Fay after she had coaxed him out of hiding with some candy corn. She led him to the kitchen table, and sat him in a chair.

"Honey, we gotta' get you somethin' ta' eat besides candy. Ever' tooth in ya' head's gon' rot out."

He sat there quietly, staring at Betty-Fay. He sensed that she was lonely, and probably not the sharpest pencil in the box, but he sensed goodness in her, and that she meant him no harm.

"Hey, I know somethin' you might like,"

She disappeared into another room, and returned with an ornate bird cage containing a brilliant yellow parakeet , hanging onto his violently swinging perch for all he was worth.

Conway eyed Betty-Fay curiously, and made some strange, low, clucking sounds. Immediately, the parakeet began to answer, and a lively conversation ensued. Betty-Fay stood in mute witness, her senses completely overwhelmed, unable to fathom the possibility. As the kid reached over and opened the cage door, she reached out her hand, as if to say stop, but she was unable to mouth a word, being too frightened, and too fascinated. She watched in wonder as the little, yellow bird hopped through the open door, and strode purposefully over to the kid, chattering incessantly the whole way.

The boy began to answer in the same chattering, chirping dialect, and they carried on, face to face, for five minutes or so. Betty-Fay felt feint. Deeper possibilities than she was taught to accept were un-folding before her very eyes. There was no room in her old brain for this. She did'nt even notice the knocking at the door that grew louder and louder. She would have never have heard it at all, but the kid stopped chattering, and looked over his shoulder toward the door, trying to locate the source of the banging. Betty-Fay regained her senses enough to answer the knock.

As she opened the door, the sunlight beamed in around a towering figure, seemingly illuminating him, and she felt her heart leap, for she knew, although she could'nt see his face for the glare from his solar halo, that it was the very Reverend Dalrymple. She instinctively grabbed his hand and kissed it, as though he were the Pope, as she pulled him inside and closed the door.

"Sister, are you all right?"

That big, Burt Lancaster voice covered her like a warm quilt.

"I'm glad you're here," she whispered, almost like a little girl.

"Where is the child sister?"

She led him by the hand toward the kitchen.

Conway and the parakeet had resumed their noisy conversation as soon as Betty-Fay left the room, and they could be heard chattering wildly as she and the preacher approached the kitchen. The preacher stopped, and pulled her back.

"Let me go in alone, sister."

She dutifully stepped aside, and waited outside the door.

The Preacher did not enter the kitchen, however, but stood in the shadows, observing the surreal scene for several seconds. Betty-Fay was overcome by possibilities that she could'nt comprehend. The Preacher comprehended the possibilities perfectly. He strode manfully into the kitchen, like a real movie Moses. The heavy footsteps startled the kid, and he immediately stopped chattering, and spun around in his seat. Terror filled his face as the over-cologned minister, with his electric hair-do, placed his hand on the kid's shoulder. Conway squirmed and jerked, trying to break free from the icy grip, but to no avail.

He had sensed this charlatan's intentions instantly. He could feel no compassion, no goodness, no intelligence. All he felt from this man was self-serving desire, and the heavy-handed will of an ego-maniac. He was terrified, and rightly so.

"The hour of your deliverance is drawing nigh, when the demons that torment thee shall be cast into the lake of fire!"

He spoke in that 'Cotton Mather' dialect that was, and still is, so popular with fans of the clergy.

Now up until this moment, the child had never experienced torment. A peculiarly human device that is not practiced in the animal world, exept by maybe spiders, and although he seemingly had no clue as to what this man was saying, every keen sense that he had was telling him that he was about to receive his education, whether he wanted it or not.

17

Doil and the sheriff were just climbing out of the car, when Waddell slid the truck into the gravel parking lot at the monkey ranch. Doil was grinning from ear to ear as he approached the truck, threw his chubby hands on the top, and leaned in.

"How boutche' Elsie? You lookin' good girl!"

Butter would'nt melt in Doil's mouth.

"Still fulla' shit, aint' ya' Doil? Where's my boy?"

"He's overt' tha' house wi' tha' ol' lady. She's fixin' ta' clean im' up an' make im' some dinner."

"Bless er' heart. Whas' at' puscle-gutted' bastard doin' here?"

She nodded toward Cecil, whose popularity with management was not shared by those in the labor force.

"I ast' im' here sos' we could have a sit-down Elsie."

"Sit down about what?"

She rolled her bloodshot eye toward Doil. He stepped back, threw out his chest, opened his arms wide, and announced,

"The future, Elsie, the future. Fame an' fortune, T.V. an' movies, grits an' gravy!"

He opened her door, and proffered his hand to help her out; Sir Walter Raliegh in khacki.

"Les' all go inside n' talk about it, jewont' to?"

She had yet to accept the offer of his pudgy hand.

"Gotney' thing ta' eat inere'?"

"We'll rustle up sumpn.' Yall' go on in, make yasef' at home."

She slid out of the truck without taking his hand. An awkward moment for anyone, except Doil.

"Where's Ol' Hickey Waddell, I thoughte' went wiya'?"

Waddell pumped his thumb toward the truck bed. Doil peered over the rail at my sun-blistered body, and my swollen, snuff-crusted butt, as I continued to lie face down on the recap.

"God-aw-mighty son, yo' ass looks like"—-

"Choklit' cake?" Waddell and I answered in unison.

"Naw, a burnt match. Climb on outta' there an' les' see can we get ya' fixed up."

He walked over to his car, reached into the backseat through the open window, grabbed an old overcoat, and pitched it to me.

"An' on yer way in, go through tha' store n' grab a stick o' baloney, some loafa' bread, n' a jar o' salve. At's' a good boy."

He disappeared through the plank fence.

I squatted in the truck bed, and slipped on the overcoat, carefully trying to avoid contact with my swollen, aching butt. Being, if nothing else, obedient, I hobbled into the general store side of the Pettyjohn complex, and proceeded to do my assigned duty.

I did'nt say a word to Shirley, the cashier, as I entered, just stabbed the air with my index finger in the general direction of Doil's office.

Shirley was as irritating as head lice, and asked a million questions a minute, although she rarely waited for, or understood, any of the answers.

"Hey Hickey, whachall' up to? Aint' at' unca' Doil's car coat? You spectin' some bad weather? Why you walkin' sa' funny? Are you nekkid' under there? Where's yer' close'?"

Still a little drunk, and in quite a bit of pain, I was in no mood for this in-coherent cross-examination. Once out of Shirley's line of vision, I reached into the meat counter and grabbed a big red stick of baloney, placed it vertically against my belly, and closed the overcoat, while I held it by the lower end, my hand on the outside of the coat, as if I were holding my stomach due to some gastric disturbance. I turned and headed toward the checkout, grabbing a loafa' 'Merita', and a jar of 'Bama' mayonnaise, the 'salve' that Doil was referring to, with my free hand. I dropped the bread and the jar on the counter in front of Shirley, and wordlessly cocked my head toward the office, as she bombarded me with her incessant nosiness.

"Yall' been drinkin'? Whossat' woman wi' Waddell? Issat is' girlfriend? Yall' gon' make some manase' samwiches'?"

She chattered away like one of Doil's damn monkeys, the whole time staring wide-eyed at my bare chest, wantonly curious. I knew that it was killing her not knowing if I was nekkid' or not, under that coat. I never uttered a word, and paid her no attention at all.

Finally, her extreme nosiness overcame her faltering judgement, and she impulsively reached over the counter, and yanked open the coat. A shrill scream gushed from her throat, as eighteen inches of bright red, stick baloney fell straight at her, like a falling tree from a woodsman's axe, barely missing her chin, and crashing onto the counter, crushing under its' throbbing bulk, a four inch section of the loafa' bread. Her hand slid the full length of the firm, slick baloney, as her eyes rolled back in her head, and she feinted dead away, collapsing in a shuddering heap in the space behind the checkout counter.

This had made the pain in my ass a little easier to bear, and I gathered up the groceries and headed for the office, leaving Shirley at the mercy of her sub-conscious fantasies.

I'll add a footnote here, that to Shirley, and that nosy 'flock o' guineas' that she ran with, I ceased, on this day, to be called Ol' Hickey, and forevermore was known in their admiring whispers as 'Hammerloaf'.

As I entered Doil's office, I noticed yet another jar of mother's milk was making it's way around, and Elsie seemed to have one of her own. It became obvious, to me at least, that the plan was to keep Elsie greased, to make her more agreeable to Doil's grandiose scheme.

"Comeon' in Hickey, an' make Elsie a couple'a samwiches'," Doil said, as he pitched me his 'pig sticker',

"An' fix me a big un'."

I stepped over to the card table that served as Doil's liquor cabinet, and with my back to the others, cut myself a half-inch hunk of baloney and devoured it before starting my catering duties, as I felt the immediate need to offset the day's alcohol consumption with a belly full of pig noses and duck beaks. Waddell stumbled over, and I cut off a big hunk, and handed it to him.

"I've knowed Elsie since we was kids," he mumbled, between chews on the cold baloney. He wiped his mouth on the back of his hand.

I was touched by the tenderness in this drunken plow-boy, and although my suspicion was, that if sober, he would think better of it, I had a thousand aching ant stings to remind me to keep my opinion guarded, so I only nodded in acknowledgement. Behind me, I could hear Doil keeping up the small talk, trying to keep Elsie relaxed.

Ol' Doil was cagey, and had some pretty highly developed senses of his own. He instinctively knew what the church practitioners had known since the beginning, that breaking bread with someone was a very intimate act. He had an old, faded print of 'The Last Supper' hanging on the wall behind his desk, and had told Waddell and myself, on numerous occasions during Sunday services, that if you really want to get next to somebody, share a meal with em'.

"It's the clostest' you can get without holdin' hands."

I never knew what he meant until now, as I watched him work. It was like going to school. I walked over, handed Elsie two clumsily prepared sandwiches on a brown paper sack, and handed the third to Doil, dripping a big gob of 'salve' on his desk as I passed it over.

"Eat up Elsie," said Doil, as he raised a fruit jar and toasted,

"To you an' yer' boy."

Elsie gnawed on the baloney, and raised her jar in the air.

"Now you jus' relax hon', an' eatem' samwiches', an' I'll call tha' ol' lady an' get her ta' bring yo' boy ova' here. By tha' way, whassat' youngun's name, anyhow?"

It took Elsie several seconds to answer, as her mouth was completely full of the sweet baloney. She washed it down with a long pull from her jar.

"Conways is' name; Conway Twitty Freeman."

"Well, bless is' heart," he said, as he dialed the number.

The phone rang several times before Betty-Fay grudgingly picked it up.

"What," she said tersely.

"Whas' goin' on ova' there?' asked Doil, but before she could answer, he heard the low rumble of a man's voice in the background, and instantly his demeanor changed from amiable host, to battle hardened warrior.

"Holy shit," he yelled as he slammed the phone into the receiver.

"Everbody up! Les' go! Bring em' samwiches' wi' ya' Elsie!"

He was a blur of motion. For a fat guy, he could really move in a crisis. Put me a little in the mind of Churchill.

"What tha' hells' wrong?" asked Cecil, for whose small mind events were un-folding much too fast.

"Booger Red's at tha' house wi' tha' boy! We gotta' get there NOW! Me n' Elsie'll ride wi' you inna' po-lece' car. Waddell, you n' Ol' Hickey foller' us in my car!"

He was barking like a Parris Island drill instructor. As we scrambled to our assigned rides, he yelled to the Sherriff;

"Turn on at' Goddam' sireen', Cecil, and put tha' hammer down! We gotta' save at' boy!"

Doil turned to Elsie, who was beginning to look panic stricken.

"Elsie, I aint' got but a minute ta' lay this out faya'. Bottom line is, you got tha' opportunity here ta' be richer than ya' ever thought possible. You n' ya' boy would never hafta' worry bout nothin' for tha' rest uv'ya' life. Yall'ud' be as famous as Elvis n' Gladys. But if at' suva' bitch Red gets is' hooks in at' boy, everthing'll go right in tha' pocket of his' I-talian' suit, and you'll end up as a side-show inna' tent revival in Po-dunk, Alabama, scroungin' fa' crumbs offn' his table!"

Doil made a powerful case against the Preacher. Elsie started to tear up.

"I don't know what ta' do. I aint' been much uva' momma to im'."

"I'll handle it if you'll trust me to Elsie. I promise they won't take ya' boy away from ya',n' I'll take care uvya' both from now on, but ya' gotta' trust me, n' go along wi' what I say, no matter what."

"I do' wanna' lose my boy, Doil. He's all I got."

"Trust me", said Doil.

He extended his right hand. Elsie timidly reached out and shook it, and the deal was done.

As they approached Doil's house, they saw the Preacher's Cadillac backing down the drive, and in the passenger seat, they could see a little, white sailor's cap sticking up.

"Block im' in!" yelled Doil, and Cecil slid the screaming police cruiser sideways across the mouth of the drive. Doil signalled to Waddell to cut him off by dragging his finger across his throat, and that's what he did, completely blocking any route of escape.

"Now what?" asked Cecil, totally unprepared for action such as this.

"Arrest at'suva' bitch!" said Doil.

"Arrest im' fa' what?"

"Kidnappin!" he growled.

"Are you kiddin?"

"I'm serious as a damn heart attack! Do it!"

As the sheriff mentally prepared himself to arrest the preacher, Elsie sprang from the criuser, ran up to the Cadillac, snatched open the door, and caught little Conway as he dove into her arms. At that moment, I thought I saw the glint of a tear in Waddell's eye.

18

Runt Weaver was the only attorney in the community. He grew up dirt poor as a sharecroppers son, but he was bright and ambitious, and had vowed early on to find a way outta' them damn fields. He worked hard and studied hard, and had graduated at the head of his class of twenty-seven members at the county high school, of which Doil Pettyjohn was a member; that is until his sixteenth birthday, when he quit to devote himself full-time to show bidness'.

Runt had received a small scholarship to the nearby community college, and Doil, always having had a soft spot for Runt, let him work at the monkey ranch, allowing him to arrange his schedule around his classes. Doil and Runt became fast friends, and when the time came for Runt to finish his under-graduate degree at the state university, Doil made sure he had a decent place to live, and food money, sending him a check every month. After graduation, he even lived with the Pettyjohns, working at the ranch in the daytime, and commuting to the Birmingham School of Law at night. Runt Weaver owed a lot to Doil Pettyjohn. When Doil called, he dropped everything. They were proud of each other. They were friends.

The minute that little Conway was safe in Elsie's arms, Doil had waddled his way to the house, brushing aside a loudly bitching Betty-Fay, and called Runt. He laid out the whole story, right up to the point where Cecil was, at that instant, in the process of arresting Booger Red.

"He can't do that Doil!"

"Caint' do what?"

"He can't arrest Red for kidnapping. It'll open a can o' worms that we'll never get the lid on. Go get Cecil and put him on the phone, and whatever you do, do not let him cuff that Preacher!"

Doil dropped the phone and charged out the door, very nearly knocking down his wife, who was now standing just outside the door singing 'Onward Christian Soldiers' in a high falsetto, and goose-stepping in place, to the rhythm of the tune. Doil need'nt have rushed so, because the sherriff's resolve had withered under volley, after furious volley from the Preacher's mouth, and what greeted Doil was a scene reminiscent of 'The Ten Commandments', where Cecil, like a calf-worshipping child of Israel, was receiving the full brunt of Moses' fury, cowering beneath him, waiting for the tablets, or the Preacher's huge Bible, to come smashing down on his head.

"Telephone Sheriff," announced an out of breath Doil, as he lumbered up to the pathetic scene.

Cecil did'nt take the time to ask who, or what. He instantly took off toward the house, putting as much distance as possible between himself, and the brimstone spewing Preacher. Doil put the 'stink eye' on Booger Red. A long few seconds passed before he spoke.

"Unless you came ta' pay tha' money you owe me, I suggest you get ya' sorry ass off my place."

"I came at the request of your wife, and in concern for the soul of that evil-infected child, and maybe save him from you and your circus from hell."

"Well Halleulah! I guess at' means you DID'NT come to pay."

"I refuse to pay for that radiator flushed, rot-gut that you corrupted me with, and continure' to corrupt the good people of this county with."

"It wad'nt run in no damn radiator, and you did'nt consider it rot-gut long as you could buy it on tha' credit. Ats' tha' way I remember it."

He opened the door on the preacher's Cadillac.

"Now get tha' hell offa' my place."

Red got behind the wheel and closed the door. As he cranked up, he rolled the window down about halfway.

"I will save that boy. My voice will be heard, and he shall be delivered."

Doil did'nt say a word. He held his fist about a foot from the window, and with an un-mistakable gesture of defiance, un-rolled his chubby, middle finger, and pumped it once, with great passion, right in the Preacher's face. Both fully understood the implication. The talking was over, and from this moment on, any exchanges would be with knuckles. He glared at Doil, who stood like a statue, with his finger outstretched, and bowing to his 'call', rolled up the window. Doil motioned for me to move the sheriff's car, and as I backed the cruiser away, the Reverend shot out of the driveway, and disappeared over the hill. I climbed out, and walked over to Doil, who was staring at the empty road.

"Reckon he'll come back?"

"Like a bad check son,—— like a bad check."

19

The Reverend Booger was not one to trifle with. Although his stature had diminished somewhat since the debacle at the donkey ball game, he had played the sympathy card, and actually turned turned the whole thing to his advantage. He was well on his way back to pre-game eminence, eager to expand his base, and itching to 'break one off' in Doil Pettyjohn. He had almost single-handedly kept the county dry in at least three wet-dry referendums over the past few years, fashioning himself as the mouthpiece, as well as the hair-piece, of the religious right. In an effort to enforce the Preacher's allegedly rigid sense of morality through legislation, this remote section, along with much of the rural bible belt, was a place where it was illegal to sell or transport alcohol, possess it in public, or have more in your home than you can easily swallow before they kick down your door. It was a practice as outdated as public floggings, and though the Preacher and his judgemental flock would never admit it, it was one that made this county one of the poorer in the state.

Other than the Reverend, the person who realized the greatest windfall from this archaic law, was Doil Pettyjohn, who anonymously poured vast sums of money into Red's temperance movement. It was a host/parasite situation that applied both ways, to the mutual benefit of both.

The current situation, however, was a horse of a different color. If the Preacher got the upper hand in the struggle over Elsie and her amazing child, Doil would end up as a footnote in the crusading minister's resume'. He would have to move fast, while he still controlled the ball. Come Sunday, the Preacher would terrify his congreation with lurid tales of demonic possession, organized criminal activity, alcohol consumption, animal sacrifice, and any other pagan parlor game that he could connect, even in the most remote terms, to the Pettyjohn organization, with two goals in mind; both of which would elevate The Very Reverend Dalrymple to the level of the Apostle Paul, the greatest preacher in the history of the church. Those being the deliverance and salvation of the demonically possessed child of Elsie Freeman, and the damnation, and possible crusifixtion, of the greatest home-grown showman since 'Country Boy Eddie.'

Sincere in his belief, and dedicated to the proposition that all men in show bidness' were NOT created equal, Doil started issuing orders to his troops like a field marshal.

"Cecil, Drive Waddell an' Ol' Hickey back to tha' ranch. Waddell, you do tha' three o'clock show. Hickey, you work tha' back door. It's Saddey'; people be lined upta' buy likker. Elsie, you an' tha' boy ride backta' tha' house wi' me."

He opened the back door on his car, and waited for them to climb in. Conway sat in his momma's lap, with his head leaned against her breast, as she gently rocked back and forth, her arms wrapped around him, softly humming the tune to 'Louisiana Woman, Mississippi Man', as Doil chauffered them up the long, dirt drive to the house. He parked in the yard near the front porch, jumped out and snatched open the door, but when he saw that the boy was fast asleep in his rocking momma's arms, he whispered,

"Yall' come in when ya' get ready," and he left the door standing open, and disappeared into the house. Plopping down at the kitchen table, he yelled for Betty-Fay.

She stalked in, still fuming over what she considered the interference of Doil and the Sherriff in the performance of her 'Holy Orders'. Doil pushed out a chair on the opposite side of the table with his foot.

"Have a seat," he said, very calmly.

"No I'm not gonna' have a seat!" she hissed, and launched into a tirade that very nearly peeled the paint off the walls. She shouted and stomped, shuddered, shook her fist at Doil, raised her palms to the ceiling, broke into tongues a time or two, and had what we commonly refer to as a 'fit', that lasted for over five minutes. When she started to wind down, sweat streaming down her un-powdered face, and her 'ecumenical bee-hive' listing dangerously to the side, Doil, in that same calm, controlled voice, said,

"You bout' through?"

She fell silent.

"Then siddown'."

Betty-Fay felt justified. She had cleaned her off a spot, and had a spell, which made her weak kneed' and giddy, almost like she'd just had sanctioned sex, which I suppose, in some perverse way, she had. Flushed with her climax, she did as she was told.

"We gon' take Elsie n' er' boy in, an' we gonna' watch out for em'."

She leaned forward and opened her mouth to speak, but he raised his hand, palm toward her, and she understood implicitly, to sit back, and shut up. She did'nt understand every thing about their relationship, but she had an in-born understanding of the concept of the 'Alpha Male', and being Doil's wife gave her the freedom to pursue her curious ambitions without fear of actually having to provide herself with food and shelter. It was the price she chose to pay.

"At' boy belongs ta' Elsie, an' she'll make tha' decisions about what he'll do an' won't do, an' who he'll see or not see." Which was not entirely true, but for the purpose of keeping the preacher away, it would suffice for now.

"An' don't you say a word ta' her about is' 'Foghorn Leghorn' demon nonsense at' you an' Booger Red dreamed up."

At that instant, the spring on the screen door squeaked, and it slammed shut, and Doil rose to go into the living room, where he knew his new children would be waiting.

"Member what I say!"

Betty-Fay signified her compliance with a nod, but unbeknownst to her husband, her fingers were crossed, her hand hidden in the folds of her 'cassock'.

20

Biloxie, Mississippi is brutal in summertime. The sun's so hot, and the humidity so high, that even breathing is a sweaty effort. This whole section of coastline had been virtually wiped out by a brutal gulf hurricane, and though these hard-bitten, tough as nails Mississippians were sweatin' their asses off building it back, highway 90, the coast road, was still littered with decayed heaps of live oak, couch cushions, splintered lumber and, here and there, an old range or refrigerator, as mute testament that a family had once lived there.

On the beach side of the road, shattered pilings poked up at odd angles out of the sand, like skeletal fingers trying to dig their way back to the blistering sunshine. The storm surge had been so strong, that it had washed corpses from their mausoleums, and they had floated and bobbed like fishing corks, making it virtually impossible to distinguish those killed by the storm, and those already deceased when it hit.

Wyvanelle's father had spit in the face of mother nature, and had wound up in a makeshift morgue, not far from the beach. He had finally been identified by a local cop who recognized the tattoo of a catfish on his fore-arm, underneath the words 'bottom feeder'. He had been, according to all who knew him, a lard-can son of a bitch, that could'nt be killed without the aid of a silver bullet, and or a wooden stake, though the raging storm proved that to be a bit of an exaggeration.

He had worked the oil fields all his life, lastly on the huge platforms scattered around the gulf, living on the rig for two weeks, and in the local jails for two weeks, month after month, for drinking and fighting, or generally being a public pain in the ass. He had not seen, or tried to locate his only child in close to twenty years, since his wife, God rest her soul, had died, some thought by his own hand. He was never charged.

Somehow, the authorities tracked her down, shacked up with Arvin Kilgore in Gulfport, and requested that she come and claim the body. It was during this process, that the Reverend Dalrymple had become privy to her where-a-bouts'.

As it turned out, her scandalous father had quite a pension piled up, as well as a healthy life insurance policy, that named her as beneficiary. She was'nt quite as upset about having to bury the old son of a bitch when she found that out.

She had used a portion of the money, following Arv's advice, who knew nothing about anything except poultry, to purchase a Kentucky Fried Chicken franchise in Biloxie, which was generating money hand over fist, owing to the fact that construction crews from all over the country had converged on the Mississippi gulf coast to rebuild the shattered economy, and there were very few places left to eat. Wyvanelle discovered that she had a God-given gift for free enterprise, and was parlaying her earnings into buying more franchises.

Arv, in the meantime, had taken the ancient, and gentlemanly 'sport' of cock-fighting to a new level. The whole area was swamped with laborers, pockets bulging with money, and not a damn thing to spend it on. Chicken fighting became as big as football, and the 'kingfish' of the sport was Arvin Kilgore. He had gone inland a few miles and built an arena with bleachers and a roof, parking for two hundred, and a snack bar with chicken supplied by the K.F.C. The law even looked the other way, because as long as these men were at the chicken fights, they were'nt in town fighting with each other. Arv and Wyvanelle were getting rich.

21

The Preacher was boilin' by the time he got back to the church office. He had once again been humiliated by Doil Pettyjohn, who, in his mind, had thwarted his sexual ambitions with Wyvanelle, and was now doing the same to his religious ambitions with the kid. He was by God, bound and determined not to let it happen, even it it meant stepping outside the law, which he did'nt think applied to him anyway. He picked up the phone, and dialed the operator.

"Can I help you?"

"Infamation'."

"What state?"

"Missippi'."

"What city?"

"Biluxie', fa' God's sake."

"Don't get smart or I'll disconnect!"

A few moments later, a very nasally voice with a 'thick as peanut butta' delta accent answered.

"Did yew' wont' a bizness' numbah' ara' residence numbah'?"

"Business numbah', er' number; Kentucky Fried Chicken."

"You all hold on, an' I'll connect ya', an' haveuh' wundafull' day."

The phone rang a dozen times or more before she could stop to answer it.

"K.F.C.," she pleasantly chirped.

"Wyvanelle?"

That big, Burt Lancaster voice rolled out of the earpiece, and covered her like a shroud, and though it was ninety plus in the shade, little chill bumps popped up on her arms. She was silent for a few seconds, and when she finally spoke, it was'nt in the vengeful tone that you would expect from one who had been humiliated and cast aside. Money had dulled the memories, and made them a little less painful. She was very calm, and matter-of-fact.

"Well, well; startin' to miss ya' spankins' Preacher?"

"I don't want any bitterness between us, Wyvanelle."

"We both know what you wanted between us, and since THAT aint' ever gonna' happen again, what in the hell are you callin' me for? And how did you know where ta' find me?"

"I got a call when they found your father, but that's not why I'm callin'. That boy of Elsie Freeman's; they're sayin' Arvin Kilgore's his daddy."

"Yeah, so?"

"So you knew about it?"

"Course I knew about it. He's been sendin' er' money all along."

"Are you sure about that?"

"The only thing I'm REALLY sure about is you bein' a prick."

"Be that as it may," and he proceeded to lay out the whole disturbing tale, stacking the deck in his favor whenever possible.

He knew that Wyvanelle detested Doil Pettyjohn for causing her fall from grace, and that she, like himself, was aching to get a shot at him. He concluded his delivery with a very dramatic concern for the child's immortal soul, and his pivotal role in the salvation process.

"And other than a kid that clucks like a chicken, what exactly would we realize outta' this arrangement?"

"A twenty-five percent share of the expanded ministry, quite possibly to include television, delivered to the 'Conway Twitty Freeman Foundation', that would be administered by yourself, and Kilgore."

"She named tha' kid Conway Twitty? I don't know, this whole deal smells like a fish ta' me, but I'll talk it over with Arv, and we'll get back to ya'," and she hung up.

"Make it quick," he said, into the empty line.

He leaned back in his chair, and locked his fingers behind his hair-do.

"What a woman," he whispered,"what a woman."

22

Betty-Fay's expression softened when Elsie and little Conway entered the kitchen, the kid holding on to the hammer loop on Elsie's over-sized 'Libertys'. The holiness diva knelt in front of him, and wiped the sleep from the corners of his eyes with the hem of her very un-attractive skirt. He leaned his head until it rested on his momma's thigh.

"This is a precious boy", said Betty-Fay, as she looked up at Elsie.

"I know."

She stood and took Elsie by the hand.

"Come on honey, I'm gonna' run ya' a hot tub a' water, and find ya' somethin' ta' wear. The baby can curl up on my bedn' take him a nap. He's had a rough day."

"Ain't we all", answered Elsie, and they disappeared into another part of the house.

Doil had watched in a fatherly silence, and as they headed down the hallway, he called;

"I got some bidness' ta'tend to, but I'll be back after a while. Yall' get some rest. We got plannin' ta' do," and he left.

Pettyjohn's Monkey Ranch was the busiest place in the county on Saturday afternoon. Shirley was pumpin' gas, dippin' minners', and ringin' up sacks full of potted meat, hoop cheese, and sody' crackers. There was always a popsicle dripping carload or two in the parking lot, poking cigarette butts, and empty peanut hulls through the wire to the monkeys, as they impatiently waited for the world famous reptile show to commence, and, there was the celebrated 'back door'.

Doil had, through special arrangement with the county commissioner in his district, gotten a 'gubment' road crew to cut a dirt drive across his corner situated acreage, from one county road to the other, right past the back door of the ranch, close enough to create a 'drive-through'. He had even installed a sliding window to accommodate those who wished to remain in their cars, guarding their anonymity, usually for religious purposes. That dirt drive was the most heavily traveled road in the county, and Saturday was the busiest traffic day.

Cecil had dropped Waddell and myself off, Waddell had donned Doil's pith helmet, and I had managed to scrounge a wadded-up shirt, and a pair of sansa-belts' out of the rolling wardrobe in the trunk of my car. In the bathroom, I found a bottle of blue medicine that Doil used to treat wounded ranch 'attractions'. I carefully cleaned the the snuff crust off my butt with a shop rag, and watching over my shoulder in the medicine cabinet mirror, painted my entire backside a shimmering shade of blue, before standing my post at the drive thru. It was'nt long before I was busiern'a one-legged man in an ass kickin' contest.

Doil blew in, still flushed with his momentary victory over the Preacher.

"How's bidness Hickey?"

"Bout' sellin' it fastern' you can run it off."

"Do bidness', do bidness'," he sang, to the tune of 'Corina-Corina', and did an impromptu twist routine behind the sales window. He was quite graceful for a fat man.

I was about to go to the store-room for another flat of pints, when there was a loud knock on the back door. I thought it odd, since I had'nt heard a vehicle, or seen any dust. I looked out the sliding window, and there, sitting on the door-step, was Wormy, who, unable to deal with the shame and embarrassment of his performance at the ball-game on his first night of inebriation, and finally finding something that he was good at, had become just another community drunk.

"Wormy, what tha' hell do you wont'?"

He was sot drunk, and his head floated from side to side, like the 'bobble-head' dog that decorated my hat rack, as he desperately tried to locate the source of the voice calling his name.

"Woooooooorrrrrrrmmyyyy" I called, trying to produce a facsimile of the booming voice of the Almighty.

"WWWWWWOOOOOOOOOORRRRRRRRR MMMMMMMMYYYY", I intoned, louder and deeper. He spat angrily, a curiously southern male response to being threatened, but most of the spittle dripped in slow motion off the fuzzy stubble on his chin. He stumbled to his feet, looking frantically in every direction, for what I was sure he thought was the voice of the Lord.

"What Goddammmmmit'?", he yelled.

This un-characteristic, sacrilegious response caught me completely off-guard, and I fell in a shuddering heap, laughing too hard to catch my breath, and continue the ruse. I heard Doil fall against the wall, and slide to the floor, his gasping lungs making squeaking noises, like a catfish struggling on the bank of a pond. After a few minutes of hysterical, nearly suffocating guffawing, I was finally able to drag myself to the door.

"Gimmee a drank'!" he barked, the instant it opened.

"I don't bleve' you need a drink", I said, barely able to mouth the words, and choking back the laughter.

"Tha hell you say, where's at' Doil?"

"Hang on a minute", I said, as I tried to pull the still-sputtering showman to his feet.

He finally made it up, and wiping the tears from his eyes with his dirty hanky, he stepped to the open door.

"What tha' hell you wont' Wormy?"

"Gimme' a damn drank'."

"Gotny' money?"

"Got sumpn' better!"

He dug in his filthy shirt pocket and produced a clumsily folded page, torn from a back issue of 'Field and Stream'. With great difficulty, he un-folded it, and attempted to hold it with one hand, and point to the creased image with the other, but in his sodden condition, his finger always slid past the image, off the page, and into empty air. It was a picture of a squirrel.

"Now gimme'a fuggin' drank'!", he demanded, as we again sunk into hysterical laughter.

"Are yall' sumbitches' laughin' at me?" he yelled, as he dropped the page, and staggered toward us.

"Doil, I'll knock yore' goddam' teeth out!"

"Doil fell hard against the door jamb, both arms holding his bouncing belly, and with the last bit of bit of breath he could muster before the laughter sucked the oxygen from his brain, he managed to turn to me and falteringly say,

"Hickey,——if it aint'—- too much trouble,——— run over to tha' office—- and get my teeth!", and he flashed me a toothless grin as he fell in a trembling heap.

I felt the warmth run all the way to my socks, as I lost all control of my bodily functions, the laughter numbing me to the point of complete in-continence. I could only watch through tear–filled eyes, as Wormy clumsily climbed over Doil's heaving bulk, and helped himself to two pints of mash; all he could carry. He slithered out, and disappeared down the road.

"My God" I thought. "I love this place!"

I heard footsteps coming from the ranch side, and the sound of the door creaking open, as Waddell stalked in, having heard the commotion over the din of the drunk monkeys.

"Damn boys, what happemed' here? Yall' git' robbed?"

"Yeah", I mumbled, still unable to stand, and now fully cognizant of the fact that I'd soiled my 'sansa-belts'.

"Did ya' know em'? Which way'd dey' go? asked Waddell frantically, as he grabbed the sawed-off double-barrell that hung under the drive-thru window, broke it open, and crammed two shiny red Winchester 'double oughts' into the open breech.

"Wormy," whispered Doil, who was still crumpled in the doorway.

His huge body began to quiver, and I could hear a new type of hissing noise as he tried to choke back the laughter.

"He went that-a-way!" I heard him spew, as he tried to point his wildly bouncing, un-controllable finger toward the dirt drive.

"Wormy? Yall' got robbed by Wormy?"

As the cackling started all over again, we could hear horns blowing outside, the traffic having backed up during this daring daytime caper. Waddell pulled the sweat-soaked mogul to his feet, poked his head out the door and shouted,

"Hang on jist' a minute ya' impatient bastards".

"Yall' gon' make it?" he said, flashing us that toothy, plowboy grin.

"Man I gotta go" I said, now feeling quite embarrassed by my obvious lack of control. Doil was still chuckling as he waddled out of the room.

"I'll see you boys later. I gotta' get Runt over to tha' house an' take care o' some bidness'."

At the instant that Doil disappeared into the hallway, a dis-embodied hand reached through the open window, holding a five dollar bill between the thumb and fore-finger. Waddell snatched the greenback away, and holding the 'Addams Family' imposter by the knuckle-side, he placed a pint fruit jar with a shiny new lid against the palm. The bony fingers closed tightly around it, and disappeared out the window.

"Thank you Thing," he said as he stuffed the five into the cigar box.

I took off my shirt, tied it around my waist, and headed off in search of dry duds.

23

Elsie soaked in the hot water for half an hour. It had been a long time since she'd felt really clean. She scrubbed her hair with a handful of 'Prell', and then scrubbed it again, sliding under the water and holding her breath, as she moved her head from side to side, feeling the slow pull of the water, like waves massaging her scalp. That's the way Doil found her. He had blown in the back door, and headed straight for the bathroom, having had to pee since before he left the ranch. His pants were unzipped, and he was digging through his 'boxers' when he spotted her.

"Sheit!"

He reached into the tub, grabbed a fistful of her gently swaying tendrils, and yanked her head up, and out of the water. Terrified, she swallowed a mouthful of sudsy water, and was choking and kicking, struggling with the un-seen force that had her by the hair, stretching her neck like a rubber band. Doil, in a momentary panic, and lapse of common sense, thought she was drowning, and was holding her nose, attempting to administer mouth to mouth, as his Boy Scout training would dictate. Betty-Fay heard the commotion, and burst in, just in time to see Doil clamp his big mouth onto Elsie's, while she did the 'crappie flop' in the tub, sending water and soap-suds sloshing and spraying in every direction.

"Doil!" screamed Betty-Fay, and it startled him so, that he dropped Elsie back into the tub, very nearly causing her real drowning, and spun around to face his wife.

When she saw the un-zipped trousers, and the terrified look on his face, she naturally assumed the worst, and snatched up the commode brush, and proceeded to beat him about the head and shoulders, reciting one of the ten commandments between each blow, and hanging on 'THOU SHALT NOT COMMIT ADULTERY', like a skipping record.

"Oh! Wait a damn minute! Hold it!" He pleaded, as the bristles pierced his flesh like a hundred tattoo needles, causing tiny, red droplets to appear on his ears and shine through his 'flat-top'.

He stumbled out, rubbing his stinging head, as Betty-Fay grabbed up a towel and wrapped it around the still sputtering Elsie, and helped her from the tub.

"Come on honey. I'll keep these heathens offa' you," Betty-Fay whispered, as she led her to the bedroom. Doil and Betty never had any children, and now it appeared, they were gonna' have two; if fatherhood did'nt kill Doil first.

24

Arv had a busy weekend, over-seeing chicken fights and drinking, since Friday night. It was now Sunday morning, and he was dragging in with a paper sack full of money, and a two 'Stanback' hangover.

Wyvanelle was up, with a fresh pot of 'Luzianne' waiting for him.

"You look like shit, Kilgore."

"Good ta' see you too" he mumbled, as she handed him a cup of the thick, black coffee and chicory.

"Siddown' for a minute, we need to talk" she said, in a very businesslike manner. After two days of drinking, with no sleep, her words stuck him like an ice pick.

"I did'nt know she us' only sebumteen'," he mumbled under his breath, his sub-conscious verbally searching through the list of offences that might have gotten him painted into this corner.

"What was that?"

"I said you the best lookin' woman I eva' seen."

He was proud of himself, in his condition, for that quick recovery.

"Now whadyu' wanna' talk about? I gotta' get me some shut-eye."

"Your son."

"My son? Well, awright'en', hell yea' we can talk about my son, if at's' whatcha' wanna' talk about, les' getter' said."

He felt his entire body relax. He assumed that he'd been caught for any, or all, of a number of in-discretions, and the realization that he was'nt going to have to produce alibis, and fake sincereity, made him almost chatty. The problem that presented itself now was, that he was so shallow, self-absorbed, and whiskey-sodden, that he'd forgotten about allegedly fathering an actual child, although he liked to brag that he had younguns' scattered all over Alabama, which was an obvious lie,

intended to buttress his reputation as a 'sporting rake'.

"Now, which son is at'?"

"Just how damn many have you got?"

"Jus' at' one I guess."

"You guess? You remember me tellin' you that tha' word was out around tha' community before we left, that you'd 'knocked up' that pitiful-lookin' Freeman girl you were shackin'with? I told you to send her money all along, cause even if she was'nt, you lefter' in a lurch, stuck in tha' middle o' nowhere. Well come to find out, she WAS pregnant, and she had tha' baby; a little boy. You have been sendin' that money; right?"

"Why hell yea I been sendin it!"

He was lyin' his ass off.

"Ever' damn month. Whas' the problem?"

"I got a call from tha' Preacher about your boy."

"What Preacher?"

"Tha' one I useta' be married to!"

Whas' at' son uva' bitch got ta' do wi' my boy?"

She recounted the whole story, as told to her by Booger Red, up to, and including the promised percentage in the ministry, television rights, and the foundation.

"Lemme' see if I got is' straight. I gotta' son by a crazy woman, an' he's possessed by a poultry demon?"

Arv's whisky soaked brain was struggling to grasp this concept.

"Red thinks your evil, chicken fightin' ways, brought all this on; awakened the demon, and so forth."

Arv pulled a pack of Luckys' from his rolled-up shirt sleeve, tapped it on his finger a couple of times, and when the filterless 'ready-rolls' appeared, he pulled one from the pack, and sat there rolling it between his thumb and fore-finger.

"I aint' had enough ta' drink ta' believe at' bullshit!"

He packed the lucky on the table, stuck it in the corner of his mouth, and producing a 'Fire Chief' from a box that lay on the kitchen table, he struck it with his thumbnail. He held it away from his face long enough for the sulfur to burn away, before lighting up, and inhaling deeply, slowly blowing the smoke out his nose, like a pulley had seized in his brain, and the belt was burning.

"I don't buy it either, but somethings goin' on up there, and if tha' kid does act like Red says he does, there's a helluva' lot o' money to be made, and we need to be the ones' makin' it. Think about it; a kid that can't talk, but clucks like a chicken as the mascot for K.F.C.. It's perfect! We can petition tha' court to have Elsie declared an un-fit mother, and we'll get custody. She obviously is'nt fit, or he'd be playin' ball instead of scratchin' for worms, but we gotta' move fast. Doil Pettyjohn is tryin' to adopt em' both, and if we don't hurry, he'll have a whole damn circus built around YOUR kid."

"What about tha' deal with the Preacher?"

"We'll string him along, as long as we need him, and then do unto to him, what he plans to do unto to us."

"Whas' at'"

"Screw him!"

"Whas' is' name anyway?"
"Whose name?"
"My boy."
"Conway Twitty Freeman."
"Figgers'."
"How?"
"Elsie didn't give a shit bout' nothin' but Conway Twitty."

25

Runt Weaver had been patiently knocking at the door for five minutes, when a disheveled Doil appeared, his forehead and neck festooned with tiny red dots. Runt broke into a wide grin.

"She get you with tha' commode brush again?"

"Yeah, Good thing she don't clean at' commode with a butcher knife. Come on in. Want some coffee? Smells like a fresh pot."

"No I'm good" he answered, as he pulled a yellow legal pad from his briefcase.

"Now what is it that we're doin?"

"Me and Betty-Fay wont' to adopt," Doil announced proudly.

Runt looked over the top of his glasses, and arched his eyebrows.

"You want to adopt this kid that can't talk? What does his mother say about that?"

"Her too."

"Her too what?"

"We wanna' adopt em' both."

The counselor's arched eyebrows now dropped into a deep furrow, and he leaned back in his chair, tapping his lips with the tip of his pen.

"That might be a tough sell. Have you even mentioned this to Betty-Fay?"

"She'll sign off on it."

"The judge'll have to sign off on it too. Lotta legal hoops to jump through."

"You can handle it," Doil said proudly.

"I got faith in ya'."

Runt just smiled. He loved Doil Pettyjohn.

"Well, get em' all in here and let's start the paperwork."

Doil walked to the hallway door.

"Betty-Fayyyyy, yall'come in here and talk ta' Runt."

The sound of shuffling feet could be heard from down the hall, and in a moment Betty-Fay and Elsie appeared. Runt rose from his chair as they entered the room. He had impeccable manners. He stepped forward, and kissed Betty-Fay on the cheek. She blushed. He extended his hand to Elsie.

"I'm Samuel Weaver Miss Freeman. It's my great pleasure to meet you."

Elsie timidly extended her hand, and nodded in response. She had never met anyone so elegant. Betty-Fay had dressed her in one of her sex-less sack-cloths, and had put her hair up in a high-holiness twist, which made them look like the poster women for some Victorian temperance movement.

"Now where is this amazing child?", asked the counselor.

Elsie stepped aside, and there, holding the hem of her dress, with sleep still in his eyes, was Conway Twitty Freeman. He slowly looked up at the counselor, and the sleep hang-over disappeared instantly, as he stared in amazement. Runt squatted before him, and very quietly said,

"Hello son, my name is Samuel."

Conway was transfixed. He had not made a sound. Looking into his un-blinking eyes, the counselor could see the wheels in his tiny head spinning. There was no fear. Conway's fine-tuned senses told him that this was an extraordinary being, the likes of which he'd never seen, burning with intelligence and purpose. Conway was hypnotized by his presence. Very deliberately, and with no hesitation, the kid reached up and touched the counselor's face. He rubbed his cheek with the tips of his fingers, and traced his lips. He felt his hair, and then he examined his own hand, as if he were searching for tell-tale signs of grease-paint. They smiled at each other.

"You the first black man he's ever seen," said Elsie, very quietly.

"Well this is a first for us both, because I've never met anyone quite like him before either."

They continued to smile at each other, each seeming to sense the other's intelligence. Doil stepped up behind the kid and said;

"Cute ain't e'?" and reached down and touched him on the head.

The kid jumped, and let out a deafening "Brrraawk!"

that startled Doil out of his paternal 'hominess', and he jumped backwards, the cup of steaming coffee in his other hand sloshing out onto his chest.

"Oooowww dammit!"

He ran to the sink, turned on the water, and splashed handfuls onto his burning flesh.

"You gotta cutat' out boy! You killin' me!"

The counselor, trying not to laugh, said

"Lets all sit down at the table and try to put this to paper."

To everyone's amazement, Conway waited for everyone to take a seat, and then he climbed up in Runt's lap, staring intently, and absorbing every word he said.

26

Sunday mornings were a time of quiet reflection around here. Families were scrubbed, hair plastered, suits bought from Sears 'on the credit', and most of em' headed to hear the plan to purchase their 'salvation' from the burning pits of hell, from the fieriest, most ambitious, and most well paid salesman in the county, Booger Dalrymple.

It was in this spirit of reflection, that several of us congregated every Sunday morning in Doil's office at the ranch, to share our thoughts and feelings, reflect on the past week's events, drink, bet on ballgames, gossip like old women, and generally enjoy the fellowship of kindred spirits. It was a church of sorts, with Doil as the purveyor of wisdom and alcohol, much like an Episcopal priest.

We had a few stalwarts who never missed a service; me, Waddell, ol' man Dooley, who ran the local gin, Raymond 'Puzz' Colquitt, feed and fertilize merchant, Lemuel 'Dooder' Pankey, of 'Dooder's Honey Wagon' fame, and Clayton 'Stump' Otinger, semi-pro barrel racer, and president of the saddle club. There were those who attended sporadically, like attorney Samuel 'Runt' Weaver, and those who only showed up on high feast days (when we decided to cook a pig in the ground), like 'puscle-gutted' sheriff, Cecil Dowd.

On this particular Sunday morning, we were waiting anxiously for word of what the Reverend 'Booger' had said from the pulpit, concerning Elsie and little Conway. Attendance was particularly good in anticipation of the coming 'shit-storm' that Doil expected would commence after the Preacher's sermon. Doil was in a reflective, yet receptive mood after the sacrament had made it's way around a few times, and I, being emboldened by the same, decided to inquire as to Doil's insights on the developing conditions.

"Ya' know", I said,"You're developin' some purty' serious enemies outside ese' walls."

"Tha' Preacher?" he asked, as he took a long pull on the sacramental jar.

"Well yeah. He rants and raves about ya' from the pulpit nearly ever' Sunday"

I answered rather sheepishly,

"An' e' tells everbody' who'll listen at' you're a boil on tha' butt o' tha' community."

Doil gave me a bemused smirk.

"Let me enlighten ya' bout' the high and mighty Reverend. His 'Holiness' still owes me money from buyin' likker on tha' credit; a lotta' damn money. I should'a knowed' betta' than ta' let im' get to me, but hell, I grew up wi' that asshole. We raised hell all ova' this county when we was kids. Red's problem was, he jus' could'nt quit; jus' got sorrier' and sorrier'. There ain't no tellin' how much money I loaned at' prick and neva' got back a dime. Bunch of us went ta' tha' show one saddey' night ta' see Mr. Burt Lancaster's new movie, 'Elmer Gantry'. Well-sir, Red woke up tha' next moanin' with a hard-on, cravin' fried chicken, and swore he'd been called ta' preach. Coincidence? You tell me! Why ya' think e' sounds like Mr. Lancaster? He got tha' whole idea from a pitcher' show. If he's a Preacher, my ass is a Chinese typewriter. Ya' see, once e' announced his 'callin', he figgered' all debts was cancelled, cause he had become a servant of the 'Lawd'. Hell, it wad'n jus'me. He owed everbody' in is' county, and e' got away with it. Tha' women saw to it. Ever' time he goes ministerin' at somebody's house, he' comes out pickin' is' teeth, and zippin' up is' pants! I don't give a tinker's damn what e' says bout' me, r' anybody else, cause all tha' men at' run is' county know tha' truth, and tha' truth, BY GOD, WILL SET YOUR ASS FREE!"

The spirit had a hold of Doil, and I knew he was ready to testify.

"Ya' know this actress is bustin' a gut tryin' to get tha' animal rights people stirred up about ya'."

"Lemme splain' sumpn' to ya'. The very people that insist at' we're descended from monkeys, are tha' ones at' raise tha' most hell bout' me gettin' mine drunk. They say, they look like us, an' act like us, tha' only difference is, tha' monkeys cain't talk. Well-sir, I can add one more ta' that list; they drink like us too, and they ain't gotney' money neither, and I'm gettin' em' drunk for free; FOR FREE! I don't get no damn humans drunk fa' free! So ya' see, tha' way I figger' it, I'm supportin' their damn theory uv' evolution by givin' our furry cousins tha' benefit of human recreational activity, which is more n' I can say fa' most o' them shit-ball dodgin' crybabys. They wont' me ta' send my monkeys back ta' tha' jungle, but my question is; where is a monkey gonna' get a cocktail in tha' jungle?—— You tell me that shit."

Around one o'clock, we expected the phone to start ringing off the hook with reports of the preacher's new crusade against Doil's evil empire, and his plans for the 'dominicker-demon' possessed child of Elsie Freeman, both being held, against their will, at the Pettyjohn compound. One fifteen, and then one thirty came and went, without a single call. Perplexed at this turn of events, Doil called Betty-Fay at home.

"Whad' tha' Preacher preach on taday'?"

We sat reverently, listening to the one-sided conversation.

"Thas' all? Did'n' say nothin' bout' Elsie or tha' kid? Yeah, hallelujah ta' you too," he said, as he hung up the phone.

We waited patiently for the report.

"Nothin'; never mentioned em'. Didn' ebn' raise any hell bout' me. Preached on tha' evils uv' rock&roll an' dancin'. Sumbitch is up ta' sumpn'. Runt, we gotta get them papers to tha' judge quick!"

We all nodded our concern, and agreement, and continued with the service.

27

The drive from Biloxie to northeast Alabama was long and tiring, even in a Cadillac. Arv and Wyvanelle had left after the Sunday lunch crowd had been fed, and arrangements could be made for her to be gone for a few days. It was well after dark when they passed through Birmingham.

"You wanna' stop n' go on inna' moanin'?" asked a bleary-eyed' Arv, hoping she'd say yes.

"No, go on. There's a fairly nice place just this side o' the county line that's got a restaurant an' a lounge. It'll be a good base of operations."

They rode on in silence till they turned in at the 'Shady Lawn'.

"You hungry?" she aked, as they pulled up in front of the office.

"Too tired ta' eat; you go ahead. I'mon' check us in an'fix mysef' a cocktail."

"I gotta' have somethin'. I'll be on inna' while", and she headed for the restaurant.

Sunday nights were always busy, since the only place to get a cocktail on Sunday was a restaurant, even in the 'wet' counties. The tables were all full, so she took a seat at the bar next to a sultry brunette dressed in very expensive clothes.

"This seat taken?" she asked, although she had already taken it.

"It is now", the exotic creature purred as she scanned Wyvanelle's ample bosom with a delighted smile. Intrigued by this vamp, Wyvanelle continued the small talk.

"You look familiar to me. Do I know you?"

"I've been in a few movies."

A playful smile of recognition crossed Wyvanelle's handsome features.

"I thought so. I have seen you; all of you." and she extended her hand.

"Wyvanelle."

The brunette tossed her hair out of her face and gently took her extended hand, not in a handshake, but a sensual caress.

"I see you're not wearing a ring. Do you have a last name——————-Wyvanelle?"

"It's not important."

"I could'nt agree more. My name is Seven. Tell me,——————-Wyvanelle with no last name, did you like what you saw?"

"I suppose so," she said, as she pulled her hand away, a little un-comfortable with Seven's boldness.

"I'm sorry, my profession has made me very direct. I did'nt mean to startle you. Let me buy you a drink, and we'll start over."

"That ud' be nice." She was flattered, and oddly attracted to this bohemian wench.

"What would you like?" she asked, staring directly into her eyes.

Wyvanelle was a street-wise gal, and she sensed that this woman was lonely and vulnerable, and quite obviously well-connected, so she played along with the flirtatrion. She stared directly back into Seven's smoldering eyes for a few moments before answering.

"Martini?"

Seven broke into a broad smile, her perfectly capped teeth glowing like a fluorescent bulb against her dark features.

"Two martinis", she barked at the bartender, and she gave Wyvanelle a devilish look as she added,

"Very dry."

"So what r' you doin' in Alabama; slumming?"

"I'm filming a documentary about animal abuse. It's one of my passions."

"One of your passions?"

"Maybe not the biggest one."

"Really? And you found a lot of abusers here?"

"I'm going to do the entire piece about a barbarian that lives a few miles from here. I intend to destroy the heartless son of a bitch."

"He sounds like quite a scoundrel. Who ise'?"

"Doil Pettyjohn. Do you know of him?"

"I've heard the name", she answered, as her pulse quickened, and amazing possibilities presented themselves, in the form of this very handsome, and very needy woman."I'm starved! Are you hungry?"

"Famished."

"Les' take a table. I wanna' hear all about this barbarian", she said, as she held two fingers in the air, and waved them in a circle, indicating to the barkeep to send down two more of the same, and keep em' coming.

After a few cocktails and some chicken fried steak, they both bared their souls. The shared history of abuse at the hands of evil men, the broken hearts, the sexual frustrations; though from very different backgrounds, they were cut from the same cloth.

Wyvanelle was nothing if not cunning, and though smitten with this erotic mink, she was also not above exploiting the woman's obvious vulnerability to further her own agenda. She told Seven the whole story about her reason for being there; the Preacher, Arvin Kilgore, Elsie Freeman, the kid who clucked like a chicken, and her burning hatred of Doil Pettyjohn.

The dark one was consumed. They made plans to skewer them all; Doil, Booger Red, and Arv; save the child and his mother from these vile and abusive snakes, and realize a handsome profit, along with world-wide critical acclaim, via a documentary film on the rescue and rehabilitation, and in the process, create an advertising icon for Wyvanelle's Kentucky Fried Chicken franchises. For the moment, they'd have to keep their smoldering passions at bay. They still needed the men to gain access to Elsie and the kid. They made arrangements for their first clandestine rendevous, and left the restaurant, the dark one going to her room, and Wyvanelle going to Arv's, to cry themselves to sleep, and dream of the retribution that they planned to visit on the 'male' of the species.

28

Doil was awakened Monday morning by a call from one of his spys, with the news that Arv Kilgore was seen checking into the motel alone, late Sunday evening. He sat straight up in bed.

"You sure it was him?"

The voice on the other end assured him that it was indeed, Arvin Kilgore. He had looked at the register to be sure, because the fella was driving a new 'Coupe de'Ville' with Mississippi plates.

"Probley' won it inna' chicken fight", Doil concluded. "Boy's a hell uva' chicken fighter!" The voice on the other end concurred.

This was a contingency that Doil had'nt counted on, but he was non-plussed, and refused to let it interfere with his daily ritual. A ritual that he had practiced every morning since he was twelve.

He heaped the percolator full of 'Luzianne' coffee and chicory, placed the tone arm of the 'Magnavox' between tracks four and five of a well-worn vinyl copy of 'Ethel Merman on Broadway', and took his place at center stage, in the kitchen. He stood, heel to instep, straight as a fence post, chin up, left arm hanging straight, palm forward, right arm at a '45', palm up, waiting for the curtain. The record made a few perfectly counted scratches, he stomped his foot once, and he and Ethel broke into a blistering version of 'There's No Bidness' like Show Bidness', flawlessly choreographed, and brilliantly delivered.

It was his theme song. It transformed him. Before, he was just a corpulent, monkey ranch huckster; afterward, he was an entertainment wildcat, ready to pounce on the world; 'Swifty' Lazar in dungarees. His mind clear, his course obvious, he got dressed, and headed off to find Pee-Wee.

Pee Wee was an unusual little fellow. He claimed to be a direct descendant of Col.Tom Thumb and his wife Lavinia, who were at one time, arguably, the most famous little people on the planet, thanks to P.T. Barnum, who, oddly enough, was an ancestor of Doil Pettyjohn, or so he said. Pee Wee was not a dwarf in the historic mold, but a perfectly proportioned, tiny little man, who, though in his early twenties, was less than three feet tall, just like his famous forebearers. From a distance, he looked just like a little kid; the perfect decoy.

Doil had known him since he was very young, and had planned to make him as famous as the Colonel, but as he grew older, he became quite un-manageable. Being that small put quite a chip on his shoulder, and he had turned into a tiny hellion. Doil had tried to develop shows around him at the ranch, with Pee Wee performing tricks while riding a dog, but he was constantly sneaking into the back room to drink, which made him verbally abusive to the patrons, and triggered his highly-charged sexual energy, prompting him to 'doodle-dash' the crowd from dog-back on several occasions.

His behavior was not at all condusive to the 'family' atmosphere that Doil fostered at the monkey ranch, and he eventually had to run him off. Since then, he had become quite the public nuisance; looking up women's dresses, weenie-waggin', and picking fights with grade-schoolers. Doil's keen instincts told him to look first at the county lock-up, and that's where he found him.

"Whas' the story on Pee Wee Sheriff?"

"Well, les' see.——-Got drunk fridey' night'n decided he'd gota' tha' show. Slipped in through tha' exit tween' Tha' Bowery Boys, and Tha' Three Stooges. Fount'a box o' popcorn with a little left in it, poked a hole in tha' bottom, and stuck his pecker up in it. A plump lil' mill village gal set down next to im', n'e' ast' was she hungry?"

"Well-sir, she runner' hand down in tha' corn box, n' grabbed her up a big handful o' Pee Wee, hollered SNAKE! and rared' back inner' seat."

"My sister, whod' been in tha' field all day, was settin' behinder' with her shoes off, restiner' pore, tired feet on tha' seat cushion in front of er', an' tha' seat back broke both er' big toes. Everbody in tha' place started fightin' ta' get ta' tha' exit, thinkin' a 'mister no-shoulders' was loose. Two r' three got stepped on, n' they broke tha' door off its hinges tryin' ta' get out."

Cecil leaned way back in his chair, and made a little sucking sound through his teeth.

"Tha' list keeps gettin' longer. Jus' pick one." He said very sarcastically.

"What'll it cost me ta' get im' out?" asked Doil, as he pulled a roll of twenties from his pocket and began to peel them off, one at a time, and drop them on the desk.

"You jus' keep peelin', I'll tell ya' when ta' quit."

When the pile reached two hundred, Cecil said,

"At' oughtta' do it. An' a half-a-gallon o' likker' ta' ease my sister's sufferin'."

"Bless er' heart. Go get tha' lil' prick".

Cecil took the keys from his desk and disappeared, returning a few minutes later with the diminutive troublemaker. He looked like a first grader in the principal's office.

"Well well", said the defiant little criminal,"Tha' man who ruined my life."

"Save it junior", said Doil. "Here's tha' deal; I need ya' ta' do some work fa' me for a couple a' weeks. In return, I'm gonna' pay you outta' this current mess, but you gotta' do what I say, when I say it, an' keep ya' smart mouth shut. Otherwise, you can stay in here fa' a few months. How bout' it Cecil?"

"Bout' twelve months I'd say."

"You're shittin' me! Fa' givin' at' gal tha' thrill uva' lifetime?"

"Well what about it? Can ya' live by my rules, r' not?"

"Daddy!" exclaimed Pee Wee, as he threw his arms around Doil's leg.

29

Having been caught up in the religious fervor at the ranch on Sunday, Waddell and myself were obliged to sleep off the spirituous exitement in Doil's office. We were brought back to life by Doil's booming voice, and an all too familiar laugh.

"Awright' boys, showtime!" said Doil, as he flicked on the light.

Pee Wee, whose hangover was long gone, was laughing hysterically, and intruding on ours. Waddell was on the couch just inside the door, covered with an army blanket, and he managed to open one crusty, bloodshot eye, and focus it directly on Pee Wee.

"You're a sad lookin' bastard, Waddell", said Pee Wee, but before the last syllable had faded, the recumbent plowboy's huge hand shot out, and grabbed Pee Wee by the scruff of the neck, while the other raised the thick wool blanket and shoved him, screaming, under the cover. A muffled,

"Noooooooooooooo" emanated from underneath the olive drab, followed by the un-mistakable honk of pickled egg and beer fueled flatulence. There were muffled screams and curses, and a tremendous amount of thrashing about, before the blanket fell still. Waddell gently raised it, pulled the limp little lump from underneath, and un-ceremoniously dropped him over the side of the couch. Pee Wee exhaled hard as he hit the floor, unable to hold his breath any longer.

"You son of a bitch!" he yelled, and as Waddell reached for him again, he ran behind Doil's legs, and grabbed on to his trousers.

"You two get up an' get dressed. Yall' are on baby sittin' detail this moanin'."

"We aint' babysittin' is' lil' prick", Waddell managed to say, in a slow, muttering monotone.

"Not Pee Wee, lil' Conway; I'm on'go get im'. It'll be tha' perfeck' job for them at' suffer witha' hangover."

"Reckon?" was all I could manage to say.

Doil and the still reeking hellion, went out the front, and climbed into the car. He put the key in the switch, but did'nt crank up. Instead, He leaned back, and pulled a pack of 'White Owl Tips' from over the visor.

"Cegar'?"

"Don't mind if I do" answered Pee Wee, and he took one of the skinny cigarillos and un-wrapped it. Doil produced a clear plastic 'zippo' with a fly fishing lure floating in the fluid, and rolled his big thumb on the wheel. It lit the first try, and he held it over for Pee Wee.

"This aint' gonna' stunt yer' growth is it?"

Pee Wee just kept puffing, with the cigar still stuck in the flame, squinting like a suckling pig.

"Listen Pee Wee, here's tha' deal," and he laid out the whole scenario for him, from the school board, to the plan to adopt little Conway and Elsie.

Pee Wee listened intently, puffing on the 'White Owl', and eyeing Doil with suspicion.

"And you think I'M gonna' pass fa' this kid?"

"Thas' tha' idea."

"It'll never work."

"It can, by God, and it will!" barked Doil, as he looked dead into Pee Wee's eyes.

"You gon' make it work. I know ya' got tha' talent, an' when we make tha' movie, I'm gon' make damn sure there's a big part in it fa' you!"

Ol' Doil was crafty. He knew what people wanted to hear, what made em' tick, and how to get next to em'. Pee Wee's whole demeanor changed. He went from disruptive rascal, to eager pupil in the blink of an eye. That was the power of Pettyjohn; the irresistible lure of show bidness'. He pulled it down in drive, and they headed to the house.

Betty-Fay and Elsie were finishing up the breakfast dishes, and little Conway was sitting at the kitchen table, thumbing through an illustrated book of Bible stories, when Doil and Pee Wee came in. Conway ignored Doil, but when he saw Pee Wee, he jumped up and ran straight to him. They stood, eye to eye, silently examining each other, neither of them quite knowing what to make of the other. They were amazingly close to the same size.

"Has tha' Devil still got a hold on you Pee Wee?" snarled Betty-fay, in her most condescending tone.

"Right by tha' balls" he answered off-handedly, never taking his gaze off the kid, until the dish towel popped him up side the head.

"Shit!" he cried, as he rubbed his stinging cheek. Conway extended his hand and rubbed the spot, examining it carefully, and thoughtfully.

"Awright", said Doil, "les' everbody' calm down. Elsie, sit down here hon'."

He pulled out a chair for her at the table.

"I know what you're up to Doil Pettyjohn, and I aint' havin' no part in it", growled Betty-Fay, as she stalked out of the kitchen.

"Listen honey, Arv's in town."

"I don't give a shit."

"I know, but he could show up here at any time, and he'll try ta' take tha' boy, and we aint' gon' letat' happen."

Elsie caught on quick.

"He aint' ever seen tha' boy," she said.

"An' when e' does he's gon' be twenty sumpn' an' needin' a shave, if ya' know what I'm sayin'."

"I got a purty good idea."

"You two need ta' swap outfits", Doil said to the boys.

Pee Wee grinned at Conway, and cocked his head toward the bedroom door. Conway had taken an instant liking to Pee Wee. He sensed a kinship shared by those who are outside of what people consider the 'norm'. He smiled back, and followed Pee Wee to the bedroom, clucking quietly, almost chuckling. He had found a friend in Pee Wee.

"Imon' take tha' boy down to tha' monkey ranch. Waddell an' ol' Hickey are gon' watch him till we see what Arv's up to."

"You tell Waddell I said ta' be careful wi' my baby."

Doil gave her a knowing smile.

"I'll do that Hon', I'll be sure and do it."

Shortly, Conway and Pee Wee emerged wearing each others' clothes.

"Call me Popeye, an' I'll punch you square inna' balls".

"Come on boy, les' you n' me go see tha' monkeys."

Conway took Doil's out-stretched finger, and followed him out, looking back over his shoulder at Elsie and Pee Wee, who were nodding their approval.

By the time Doil returned with little Conway, Waddell and I had managed to get down a couple of cups of Irish coffee, and some 'Goody Powders' in an attempt to re-join the living.

"Showtime boys", boomed Doil, as he blew into the office with the kid close behind.

"You gotta' be sa' damn loud?"

"S'matter', ya' head hurt? I knowed youse' gon' have trouble wi' that head the first time I seen it," observed Doil, as he burst into a crow cackle.

"Crackin' ya'sef' up aint' ya' gobby? Whater' we sposed' ta' do wi' shawt' stuff here?"

Doil was already headed out the door, and he called back over his shoulder,

"Entertain im'!"

"Maybe he'd enjoy Kaptain Kangaroo, I know I would." I said, very sincerely.

"Not taday' Mr. Greenjeans; taday' we start is' boy's ed-yew-cayshun'!"

From off in the distance we heard Doil yell,

"Waddell, Elsie said ta' tell ya' ta' take good care o' her baby", in a high-pitched sing-song, like a kid taunting him on the playground, and the sound of laughter as he exited the building.

Waddell fished around in his pocket, and came out with an un-opened bag of candy corn.

"Hickey, get at' pack o' bicycles outta' tha'desk. We gon' teach is' boy howta' play some cards."

Conway looked up at Waddell with curiosity.

"Ats' right boy; school is in session."

30

When Doil tried to pull into his driveway, he found it blocked by a shiny new Coupe de' Ville, parked quite a ways from the house. Perfect timing, he thought to himself, as he detoured through the dew-soaked grass, and stopped near the front porch.

"Show time" he said, as he slammed the car in park, swung open the door, and rolled himself out. Arv could hear his heavy footfalls from the first porch steps, and as the screen door creaked open, slammed, bounced open partially, and lightly closed again, big beads of sweat popped out on Arv's freshly shaved upper lip. He was sitting at the kitchen table, like a guilty suspect under the glare of a nekkid' light bulb. Betty-Fay had poured him a cup of 'Luzianne', which he had'nt touched, and she was sitting on the opposite side of the table, eyeing him with contempt, when Doil walked into the room.

"Hello Arv" he bellowed, as he marched straight up to him, hand out-stretched, his commanding bulk completely filling every angle of Arv's vision. His fine-tuned show-bidness' instincts had taught him that the entrance, and the opening scene are paramount in capturing the audience's rapt attention, and he wanted no doubt in Arv's mind as to who the star of this production would be.

"Where ya' been keepin' ya'sef'? Missippi'? I seen tha' plates on ya' car. Bidness' mus' be good! Lotta' chicken fighters in Missippi' are they?"

Doil's rapid-fire delivery did'nt allow any room for Arv to speak. He could only nod his head a beat behind, in affirmation, which was the way Doil wanted it, and deep down, the way Arv wanted it too.

"What brings ya' back ta' these parts, what with ya' doin' sa' well an' all in Missippi'? Didya' come back ta' check on Elsie?————Ya' sorry little bastard?"

Arv was sweating profusely now, and though Doil had left a hole for him to respond to the insult, he was completely intimidated, and did'nt utter a word. Nodding nervously, he fixed his eyes on the rapidly cooling coffee.

"Ya' conscience started botherin' ya' after all ese' years, an' ya' decided ta' come slinkin' back here an' make it right with er'. Issat' it?"

Still unable to speak, Arv only nodded.

Doil stared at him for a long few moments, making him as un-comfortable as was humanly possible, hands-free, then turned to Betty-Fay, who had remained un-characteristically silent through all of this, and very calmly said,

"Go get Elsie."

Doil resumed his icy silence as Betty-fay left the kitchen, and Arv, feeling the full weight of it, sat staring blankly at the coffee cup, tapping the handle very lightly with his index finger. After what seemed to Arv an eternity, Elsie slowly made her way into the kitchen. Had he encountered her on the street, he would not have recognized her, dressed as she was in Betty-Fay's drab, holiness attire, her hair done up according to spiritual law.

"Whatha' hell da' you wont'?"

Arv started to stand, but Doil placed his big hand on his shoulder, and pushed him back down in the hard, wooden chair. He finally found the nerve to timidly speak.

"I got ta' worryin' about' ya'."

"No shit?"

"I kept sendin' money, but tha'post office jus' kept sendin' it back, like you didn' live here no more. I was gettin' scared sumpn' mighta' happem' to ya'."

"Imagine at'. After five r' six years, an' is' pile o' money comin' back, ya' said ta' ya'sef', I best go check on Elsie. She MAY be in some kinda' trouble."

"At's right! At's tha' God's truth."

Big, horse tears began to well up in her eyes, and as tough as she was, her lip began to tremble. Betrayal is a life-breaker.

"I'se' Pregnant when you run off, you son-uva'-bitch!"

The salty tears began to stream down her face.

"I had at' baby all by myself!"

"A baby? You mean ta' tell me you had a baby? Why did'n ya' tell me you's gon' have a youngun'?"

"I did'n know where you was!" she screamed.

"Well, if ida' knowed' that:" The implication being, that the whole tragic 'misunderstanding' was her fault.

In a fit of desparate rage, she grabbed the cup of coffee, and sloshed it in his face, hoping to scald out his lying eyes, but it had completely cooled, and all she accomplished was to get him wet.

He instinctively made a move to get up and get at her, but Doil's hand closed around the base of his skull, and he leaned down and whispered,

"You raise ya' hand ta' her, an' I'll wring ya' goddam'-neck!"

Arv leaned back in the chair, and wiped his face on the sleeve of his shirt.

"Was it a boy r' a girl?"

"Whatta' you care?"

"Cause I gotta' right ta' know."

"What makes ya' think you his daddy?"

"So I gotta' boy, huh?"

"You aint' got shit!"

"I wanna see im'. I gotta' right. He's my blood. If you don't let me, I'll go get tha' law, by God!"

"Don't forget where you're at, Arv."

Doil interjected, and even Arv, who was a 'category five', idiot understood that implication. He was in 'Pettyjohn territory' now. For all intents and purposes, Doil was the law. He paid for the privilege. Elsie gave Doil a questioning look.

"You bring tha' boy to the door there Elsie, and let him decide whether r' not ta'come over an' see im'. You jus' keep ya' seat, Arv. It's tha' boy's choice ta' make."

Elsie disappeared, only to return shortly holding Pee Wee by the hand. He was dressed in the sailor suit, the only difference being that she had folded down the brim of the white sailor's cap to hide Pee Wee's more manly features. She squatted in front of the tiny seaman, and held his exposed cheeks in her hands.

"Honey, that worthless bastard sittin' at tha' table claims' ta' be ya' daddy."

She pinched his ear-lobe gently, the signal worked out before-hand, for Pee Wee to cluck. He made an attempt to sound like a chicken, and although it was a sincere effort, to Doil, it sounded more like a burp. Elsie continued:

"If you wanna' go ova'there an' meet im', I aint' gonna' stop ya'."

She stood and faced Arv. Pee Wee timidly turned to face Arv also, but his eyes were covered by the cap, so all Arv could see was his chin, and his bottom lip. He leaned his head thoughtfully into Elsie's thigh, and with one hand, he grabbed a handful of the colorless dress, while the other, which was hidden from view, he slipped under the dress from behind, and was slowly sliding it up the inside of her thigh, headed straight for home plate.

Elsie stiffened, her eyes bulging, and her breathing becoming shallow, although she did'nt dare let on, for fear of blowing the ruse. It was blatantly obvious to her that the little pervert was going to take full advantage of the situation.

"S'matter wi' you boy? Caint' you tawk'? Comeon' ova' here an' lemme' look atcha'. I'm ya' daddy!"

Pee Wee let his hand slide back down the soft, inside of her thigh a few inches. She slid her hand across the back of his neck, under the hat brim, and buried her thumbnail in the fat part of his ear-lobe, mashing till tears came to his eyes, and he pulled away with a muffled

"Cluck", and slid his hand from under her dress.

"Boy, I said commere'!"

Pee Wee was looking up toward Elsie with a fiendish grin, visible only to her from under the hat brim, and without so much as a peep, he turned toward Arv, and extended his little arm, un-rolled his tiny 'bird' finger, and held it erect and motionless, in a contemptuous salute, before disappearing through the open door.

"At's real damn nice. You doin' a helluva' job raisin' at' youngun' Elsie! Little sumbitch' shoot me a bird! You orta' whoop' is' ass, r' lemme' in nere' an' I will!"

Elsie did'nt say a word. She un-sheathed her own middle finger, and pumped it, with great conviction, right in Arv's face, before she too, turned and disappeared.

"Yeah, by God, go. At' proves right tere' at' you aint' fitten' ta' raise at' kid."

Arv felt Doil's fingers tighten around the back of his neck, pulling him up out of the chair.

"I bleve' we're done here," said Doil calmly, as he walked him toward the door.

"I'mon' go get me a lawyer, Doil. I'mon' get at' boy, an' I got tha' damn money ta' do it!"

Arv felt Doil's grip tighten around his neck as he pulled him close and whispered,

"You better get you a good un'," and he shoved him out through the screen door, and sent him stumbling down the steps.

"I'll be back, by God," he yelled, as he caught himself on the hood of Doil's car, "An' I'm bringin' tha' damn law wimmee'!"

Doil opened the screen, and in an act of solidarity with Elsie and Pee Wee, stuck out his fist, raised his chubby middle finger, and pumped it once, in a perfectly executed flip-off.

"Que sera shit-head, que sera."

31

Waddell picked up his cards, gave them a disgusted look, and dropped them on the desk. He eyed Conway suspiciously, as he began to play a cadence on the wooden desktop with his fingertips.

"You sure you aint' ever played cards before boy?"

The kid was barely visible behind the mound of candy corn, the pile of change and dollar bills, and Waddell's wind-proof zippo lighter. He clucked softly, which to us, sounded for all the world like a chuckle, as he drug Waddell's two-bladed 'Case' pocket-knife into the into the growing pile. I had long since been wiped out, and somewhere in that mound, was my class ring, and the 'coon dick' toothpick that my granddaddy had given me.

"I bleve' we been slip-shucked!", Waddell observed.

"You tha' one wanted ta' teach him ta' gamble."

Just as Waddell and I were about to vent our frustration on each other, Doil blew into the office.

"Hot damn son! We might oughtta' take you ta' Vegas! Lookit' whatta' pile o' loot!"

He reached for the double-bladed 'case', but the moment his fingers touched the knife, Conway jumped straight up, and let out an ear-splitting

"Brrrrrrraaaawwwkkkkkkk"

that caught the impresario completely off guard, and startled him so, that he jumped back, and planted his foot in a Volkswagen hubcap that we were using for an ashtray. It shot out from under him, and he fell backwards over the arm of the couch, releasing a painful moan as the breath left his lungs.

Waddell had just taken the first pull off a fresh Pabst Blue Ribbon, and the last thing that I saw, as I fell out of my chair, overcome by the enormity of the situation, were two foamy white columns shooting out of Waddell's nostrils like jet streams. Laughter had rendered his 'swaller pipe' in-operable, and he too, fell to the floor. Doil finally struggled to his feet, gasping for air, and holding his kidneys.

"Shit boy, you gotta' quitat'. You gon' kill somebody!"

Conway stiffened to repeat the performance, when Waddell came sputtering off the floor, beer still dripping from his nose.

"We give boy, calf rope! Doil; leave is' damn knife alone!"

Conway snatched up the knife and sat back down, examining it carefully, before slipping it into the pocket of Pee Wee's jeans.

"Arv just left tha' house," said Doil, as he rubbed his aching back against the door facing, as large men are want to do.

"De' buy it?"

"Course e' bought it. He's dumb as a chicken. No offence kid. Says he's gon' come back wi' tha' law, but eb'n he knows bettern'at'. He'll try ta' grab tha' kid n'make it back ta' Missippi', but e' caint' do it alone. He aint'at smart. Hickey, you slip down at tha' motel and see has he gotney' body with im'. I heard some boys in tha' store talkin' bout' a woman wi' big knockers an' at' movie star bein' real chummy n'all at tha' café Sundy' night.

Sounds like tha' dumass' mighta' hooked up wi' Wyvanelle for real."

"Reckon?" was all I could say.

Waddell nodded toward the kid.

"You might oughta'take im' wi'ya', since e' started his schoolin' taday'. A boy don't get ta' see a pair like at' too offen'. Come ta' think on it, ya' might orta' take me too!"

He licked the tip of his little finger, and smoothed out his eyebrows.

"You n'at' boy can check out women's knockers later. You take tha' kid out ta' your place and keep im' outta' sight till we find out what Arv's up to."

"What about tha' Preacher?"

"Screw tha' Preacher! We'll worry bout' him later," and he clapped his hands together, and began to shimmy, as he sang that song about the ant, and the rubber tree plant. It was quite entertaining.

"Comon' boy, les' me n' you go find sumpn' ta' get into."

He took off his Caterpillar cap, and held it under the rim of the desk, while Conway raked his winnings into it, candy corn and all.

"Me n' you might have ta' go to tha' show with all is' money."

"Whatever ya' do, be careful," warned Doil as they headed out the door.

"At's' my middle name Doil. Waddell C. Strickland; an' tha' C is for Careful, or Cod, I caint' ever remember which. Right boy?"

As they drifted down the hall, we heard a half cluck, half chuckle, as the door slammed behind them.

32

When Arv returned to the motel, he found a note from Wyvanelle instructing him to come to the private dining room in the café, where she had arranged a meeting with the Preacher. Arv was un-hinged by his treatment at the Pettyjohn place, and had to brace himself with several shots of liquor before submitting to another confrontation. The whiskey was well on it's way to swallowing his brain, as he parted the curtains to the dining room and stepped inside.

He was greeted by an un-pleasant silence, the air hanging heavy with a combination of contempt and lust. Wyvanelle sat on one side of the small dining table, staring over a pair of rhinestone crusted reading glasses at Booger Red, who was sitting directly across from her. To her left, facing Arv, was the dark featured actress, staring at Wyvanelle; big lipped, pouty, smoldering like a butted-out cigar.

The Minister sat ramrod straight, smiling stoically, imagining himself as a hunk of baloney between slices of creamy white bread, and dark pumpernickel. Arv plopped down in the empty chair. Wyvanelle shot him a disgusted smirk, as she introduced him to Seven. The actress acknowledged him with a disinterested nod, and immediately shifted her gaze back to Wyvanelle.

Arv slumped in his chair, unable to speak, staring in utter amazement at Seven's enormous lips. On the table in front of Wyvanelle, was a legal pad, and she was turning a pen over and over in her fingers, putting first the tip to the paper and sliding her hand down to the pad, and then flipping it over and doing the same with the cap. It was clear to all that she was large, and in charge, and impatient to get started. The Preacher was the first to break the icy silence.

"Shall we join hands, and start with a word of prayer Wyvanelle?"

"This is a business meetin', not a revival. Keep ya' hands to yaself'."

"Whashe'doin' here?" Arv managed to say, more as a salacious exclamation, than a question.

"I'd like to know that myself," intoned Red.

"Ms. Bridges is here at my request. She's doin' a documentary film about Doil Pettyjohn, an' I think we can all benefit from her involvement."

"Would ya' care to tellus' how?"

"No, figger' it out fa' yaself', she stays!"

That icy declaration pretty much ended the question of Seven's involvement.

"The question is now, how to proceed."

"Ats' my boy n' Imon' go get im'!"

"Wonderful, but in tha' meantime, tha' Reverend here has proposed a bizness' arrangement, and that's why were havin' this meeting, so I suggest that we let im' lay it out, uh, I mean explain it to us."

Now Wyvanelle had no intention of turning this kid over to the man that had used, abused, and run her off, any more than she intended to let Arv take control of him, but cards were being dealt, and she had to play her hand. The ugly truth was, that everyone at this table was out to screw one, or all of the others, literally and figuratively, and not one of them actually gave two shits about the kid, or his mother. Show bidness' in it's truest form.

Reverend Dalrymple repeated his original offer, of the twenty-five percent share of the expanded ministry, possibly to include television, and delivery of the funds to a foundation in Conway's name, administered by Arv, and Wyvanelle, under a tax free religious umbrella. Wyvanelle took very specific notes, questioning the preacher on every point, causing tiny beads of sweat to appear on his massive forehead, which he wiped repeatedly with a linen hanky, embroidered with his initials and the outline of a fish.

Wyvanelle put forth the possibility of changing the focus of the film to the salvation of the extraordinary kid, and at the same time, exposing Doil as the vile, animal abusing, whiskey dealing, kidnapper that he was. A point on which they all agreed.

Seven became very animated at this point, and led the discussion in points and percentages, distribution rights, foreign liscense, and so forth. Wyvanelle penned every point. It was a discussion more akin to a stock acquisition, than the welfare of a child.

Arv contributed by slipping off his boot, and trying to get his foot on Seven's knee, which, due to the length of the table, and the shortness of his legs, he was never able to do. At one point he had slid so far down in his chair, that only his head was visible over the table, but the other three were so en-grossed in enterprise, that they did'nt notice. The three active participants agreed to immediately file, in Arv's name, for a restraining order against Doil, and petition the court to have the kid put in Arv and Wyvanelle's custody, pending a competency hearing to determine Elsie's mental condition, and her fitness as a mother. At that point, they all looked at Arv, visible from the nose up, and in unison said,

"Well?"

Arv slowly pulled himself up in his chair.

"Whatever suits yall', tickles me ta' death."

I witnessed this whole ugly scene, due to the fact that I had beaten a trail to the motel, observed Arv stumbling from his room, and followed him to the café. A well-placed fiver, in the hand of the waitress who was delivering groceries to the 'private dining' section, had secured my place in the adjacent stall, and due to the fact that curtains hanging from a galvanized pipe were what made the 'private dining' room private, with the aid of a butter knife, it was no problem to part a tiny space in the back corner of the curtain, and enjoy the show.

The meeting ended abruptly, with none of the cordiality usually afforded after such gatherings, and the preacher exited quickly, followed by Arv, hollering

"Where's tha' pisser' inis'place?"

Only seconds after Arv walked away, Seven reached across the corner of the table, grabbed the back of Wyvanelle's perfectly coiffed, bleach blonde hair-do, and pulled her halfway across the table, where she met her with a huge, juicy, open mouthed kiss. It was at that moment, that I dropped the butter knife, ending the peep show, and very nearly causing my capture as a spy. After I made my escape, I high-tailed it back to the ranch, where I reported, in detail, all that I had seen and heard. Doil was transfixed, especially at the last part, which I re-counted as being the high point of my life, up to this point. I repeated the last few moments again, for clarity's sake, his as well as mine, and we sat in silence for a few minutes, while Doil processed this information.

"Right on tha' mouth?"

"Right on it."

"Damn!"

I ended the fantasy-fest with a softly spoken,

"Now what?"

"Runt called. Tha' judge is gon' see us on saddy' moanin' in his office. Won't be a bunch o' nosy bastards runnin' around. Right on the mouth, ya' say? ——— Damn!"

33

"Hold it up to ya' shoulder like is'."

Waddell was on his knees behind the kid, with his arms around him, holding a bolt action '22' calibre rifle.

"Now sight downa' barrel, n' getat' Clo-rox bottle lined up."

Waddell placed the kid's finger very gently on the trigger, and helped him steady the gun.

"Now squeezeit'; don't pull, jus' squeezeit'."

There was a loud crack, and the sound of shattering glass, as the bottle sent a spray of tiny brown crystals showering in every direction. Conway slipped from under the en-circling arms and ran to survey the kill. When he turned back to Waddell, he was beaming.

"You got it boy! You a damn good shot! Good as ol' Sargeant York!"

The kid ran back to Waddell, who was still squatted at eye level, and threw his arms around his neck. Un-accustomed to such open affection, he awkwardly patted the kid on the back with his big, rough hand.

"Les' don't get all squirrelly," he said, as he slowly rose to his feet, and held out his hand to Conway.

"Comeon' boy, les' me n' you see can we find anotha' clo-rox bottle r' two unda' tha' back porch."

He reached up and took Waddell by the little finger, and they walked slowly back toward the house, occasionally stopping for Conway to dig in the dirt with his toe.

34

Pee Wee sat on the back porch at Doil's, in a cane bottom chair, between two five gallon buckets, shelling peas into a beat-up aluminum dish pan.

"This is bullshit", he mumbled, not realizing Betty-Fay had slipped up behind him to make sure he was working. She immediately popped him on the back of the neck with a fly swatter.

"Shit", he cried, as he jumped up, dropping the dishpan, and sending shelled peas rolling in every direction on the rough wooden porch, most of them disappearing thru the cracks in the planks.

"Why you keep hittin' me Betty-Fay?" he asked pitifully, as he rubbed his stinging neck.

"Coz' you're a blasphemin' lil' pervert, and by God while you're in my house, you gonna' act like somebody."

Elsie had heard the ruckus, and came to investigate.

"You go on an' do what ya' got ta' do, an' I'll keep an eye on im'," she said, as she stooped to pick up the overturned pan.

"Pull ya' up a chair an' I'll help ya' shell ese' peas, Pee Wee."

"Gotanotha' dishpan?" she asked Betty-Fay.

"By tha' sink" she answered, "But you aint' gotta' hep' him."

"I need ta' do sumpn' ta' earn my keep, and besides, you wouldn't hafta' be puttin' up wi' slick here, if it wadn' fa' me an' my boy, an' I wont' ya' ta' know I preciate' it."

Betty Fay gave her a faint smile, and nodded as she walked back into the kitchen.

"I preciate' it too", Pee Wee called out sarcastically, but got no response from Betty-Fay.

"Why you gotta' be such a hard ass?"

"So people wont' run ova' me." He shot back.

"Who ya' think's tryin' ta' run over ya'?"

"Everbody'; they don't nobody respect a little man."

"They don't nobody respect a 'shithead'."

"I aint' a 'shithead'!"

"Yeah, you are. A smart mouth, disrespectful, ungrateful, 'shithead'."

"What tha' hell have I got ta' be grateful about. I'm twenty-one years old an' I'm three feet tall!"

"You got people at' care about ya'."

"Like who?"

"Doil, fa' one. I heard him talkin' ta' Betty-Fay, tellin' er' not ta' be sa' hard on ya', cause she don't know what it's like ta' walk in yer' little shoes."

"She hates my guts."

"She don't hate ya', she hates tha' way ya' act."

"And how do I act?"

"Like a 'SHITHEAD'! Now get ta' shellin' em' peas or we'll be out here all day."

Nobody had ever talked to Pee Wee like that, and for a while, at least, he conducted himself in a civilized manner, and he and Elsie actually carried on a normal conversation, while they worked their way through those five gallon buckets. Somewhere along the way, they found common ground in her homliness, and his stature. She still did'nt trust him, but she sort of understood him. Betty-Fay heard them talking, and slipped back to the kitchen door to eavesdrop, fly swat still in hand, just in case.

There was a monumental struggle going on inside Betty-Fay. Through that drab, seemingly impenetrable veneer, a little bit of mothering instinct was creeping out, even with regards to Pee Wee, but her religion, as religion often does, had tempered her compassion with self righteous, judgemental, bullshit to the point that she, and much of the flock, had come to see things, not thru their own eyes, but thru the eyes of the Preacher, which was like accepting, and embracing, the description of a rainbow from a blind man.

The struggle didn't last long. Even though deep in her heart, she could find nothing remotely evil, or sinister, about Elsie or little Conway, and something in her made her want to hold and protect them, Booger Red's self-serving, show bidness' theology had a powerful hold on her, and she tiptoed quietly into the parlor, and called the church office.

35

Arv had gone off in search of 'puscle-gutted' Cecil Dowd to try and out-bribe Doil. Wyvanelle made her way to Seven's room, and demurely tapped on the door. To her surprise, as the door opened, she was greeted by the camera-man, whom she had'nt formally met.

"Come on in, she's on the phone, I'm Steve," and he extended his hand.

"My pleasure, I'm-"

"Wyvanelle, I know. I've heard all about you."

She took a seat at a card table that was covered by piles of script notes and film cans. Steve sat on the bed and pointed to the tri-colored poster, that was thumb tacked to a cork board that leaned against the wall. Wyvanelle studied it carefully, and a devilish smile appeared on her face, as she felt a plan falling into place like the tumblers in a safe. Seven was carrying on an animated conversation, barking and pacing, while stabbing the air with her finger. Wyvanelle glanced from the poster to Seven, and back to the poster. Steve made a Herculean effort not to stare, but he'd been away from home for quite a while, and his gaze kept falling back on Wyvanelle's glorious bosom.

"Damn!" he thought to himself, "damn!"

Seven dropped the phone onto the receiver and spun around to face the buxom blonde.

"He's going to debut the kid at this barbarian orgy!" she announced, pointing to the brightly colored poster.

"How do ya' know that?"

"I went by the office to complain about the air conditioning, and happened to over-hear an idiot inviting the clerk to the game, saying that Doil Pettyjohn had discovered a 'missing link' that's half human and half chicken, and he plans to show him in public for the first time at the game."

She pecked at the poster with a long, red fingernail for emphasis.

"And while I was there, the clerk took a message for Mr. Kilgore, that he was to appear at the judge's chambers at the court-house on Saturday morning, for a preliminary custody hearing. The clerk read it back. We can't take the chance that this be heard in front of a Pettyjohn puppet."

"Are you sure this guy was'nt puttin' on an act for your benefit?"

"Absolutely not! He had his back to me the whole time, did'nt even turn around when I came in. Besides, this rube did'nt look intelligent enough to act. We can grab the kid at the game. From what I hear, once it starts, it's total chaos. We'll be long gone by the time anyone figures out what's happened."

"It could work, I suppose."

"It could work? IT WILL work! With a body like yours, none of those men will be watching that kid."

Steve just sat there smiling.

"That's for damn sure," he thought.

The dumb looking rube that she was referring to was me. Doil had sent me flying back to the motel to plant the seeds of larceny in their tiny little minds. The part about the 'missing link' was my idea, and for a rube, I thought it highly creative.

36

There's something about Friday nights that make them the perfect time for sporting events. It could be, that after five days of chopping cotton, or running a loom at the spinning mill, witnessing a little gratuitous violence might be the only thing that keeps you from taking a plow line to family and friends, or worse. It takes a body back to the time when there was no greater thrill than losing a tooth or two on a Friday night, when you still had a few to spare. Plus, you had Saturday and Sunday to recover, because short of death, you had to be back in the field, or in the mill on Monday morning. No one understood this better than Doil Pettyjohn, and except for maybe Hitler, nobody could turn out a spectacle like Doil. From all indications, Friday night was gonna' be a 'humdinger'.

He had offered to give the ragged little kids that hung around the ranch after school, a nickel a-piece for good, dent-free, empty paint cans, and they had scoured the dump and the ditchbanks, and scrounged up thirty-two of them. Punch a hole in the bottom for the cord, and mount a ninety-eight cent ceramic fixture, and you have theatre quality lighting (practically). The ten cent bounty on 'flood' lamps caused a county-wide, out-door blackout, but Doil soon had a light rig, suitable for filming.

A couple of the more enterprising members of Doil's fan club slipped down the mountain to the Etowah Blue Devil's stadium, shinnied up the poles, and made off with a pair of university horns, and a Bogen public address amplifier, insuring faithful, as well as portable, sound reproduction. Friday night was shaping up to be on par with the Nuremburg rally.

That afternoon, there was a production meeting in Doil's office. We were all there; me, Waddell and little Conway, 'puscle-gutted' Cecil Dowd, and Doil's donkey basketball road crew. After Doil gave the crew their specific assignments and dismissed them, we broke out the fruit jars, and got down to real business. It was decided that Pee Wee would remain in the back seat of Doil's car, parked behind the gym, in the shadows, and the sheriff, as head of security, would post an eager, yet open-minded deputy there to guard him.

The way Doil figured it, they would make their move shortly after tip-off, when everyone's attention would be on the exploding drama in the gym. Waddell was to pick up Elsie, and take she and the kid out to his place, owing to the likely probability that Betty-Fay had spilled her guts to the Reverend. I was to take the plowboy's place at the ball game, with the specific orders to make sure the donkeys are ready, the coach is happy, and the likker's flowing.

"Runt's got us a hearin' with tha' judge at ten o'clock saddey' moanin'. I expect yall' ta' deliver Elsie an' tha' baby, rested n' refreshed, an' be prepared ta' tell tha' judge what a sterlin' induvidual I am, whether ya' believe it r' not."

At this point, he jumped up, opened the door, and as we filed out, he shook hands with each of us, and sang an impromptu version of 'The Impossible Dream'. His motivational skills were without equal, and, he had a pretty fair singing voice.

37

When Doil turned in and steered toward the house, he met Pee Wee halfway down the driveway, headed for the open road, and slid to a stop.

"Where ya' headed?"

"Back ta' jail. I caint' take no more o' this."

"Now wait a minute junior, we had a deal"

"I don't remember nothin' in at' deal bout' shellin' peas, an' bein' beat with a damn fly-flap!"

Doil reached over and opened the passenger door.

"Hop in son, yo' pea-shellin' days r' ova', and ya' movie-actin' days are about to commence".

Pee Wee could'nt resist Doil; nobody could. He could sell an ice-box to an Eskimo. He dutifully climbed in.

Doil shoved it up in park, and turned off the switch. He told the little man about my witnessing the meeting at the café, and the conspiracy that was a-foot to gain custody of little Conway. Pee Wee became visibly exited upon hearing vivid descriptions of Arv's female accomplices.

"Now listen, you gotta' take is' thing as far as she'll go. At' actress woman is plannin' on fimmin' tha' whole shootin' match, an' nat' means YOU gon' be tha' star uv' tha' show. Think about it boy; kidnapped by two beautiful women. It's ever' man's dream by God, and YOU gonna' haver'on film.You'll be tha' heero' uv' ever' man in

Alabama. Little boys'll sing songs about you. Hell, they liable to write a new chapter in the Bible bout' it."

Pee Wee fell silent for a moment, as the newsreels in his head ran scenes of himself and Marilyn Monroe exiting a motel, and waving to reporters. He was jarred awake from his fantasy by a blaring truck horn, and both he and Doil turned in the seat, to see Waddell's truck as it slid around them, with little Conway at the wheel, sitting in Waddell's lap, both of them laughing hysterically.

"Looks like Waddell's found him a buddy."

"Looks like they both have", said Doil, as he threw his arm over the seat and backed down the driveway.

Waddell and the kid cut a few 'dados' in the sage patch that bordered the driveway, before sliding to a stop near the front porch.

"Boy, you sure you neva' drove before? I ain't seen drivin' like at' since 'Fireball' Roberts got killed."

Conway was beaming.

"Wanna' take er' around again?"

The kid's expression was all the answer he needed. He pulled it down in low, and they took off through the yard, sliding sideways between the clothesline and the pump house.

Betty-Fay heard the commotion, and came running out of the house, broom in hand, screaming at the top of her lungs, and smacking the truck with the broom on every pass it made. Elsie was on the screened-in porch, and she began to clap and cheer every time they came around the house, and Conway would wave, and grin like a possum when she did. Soon, even Betty-Fay started to smile, and she waved the broom like a victory flag on every lap. Seeing a kid have that much fun makes a few ruts in the yard seem awfully trivial. By the time they slid to a stop, all four of them were doubled over with laughter. In an odd sort of way, it almost felt like a real family.

Betty-Fay was leaning on the broom handle, her usually sour expression was gone; her face having been flushed with laughter, the scowl replaced by a serene smile.

"Doil told me ta' pick Elsie up, and take her an' tha' boy out ta' my place till in tha' mornin'," said Waddell sheepishly.

"Well go on nen'. I'm proud ta' be shed of em!" she said, but she did'nt mean it. She walked over to the truck, leaned in, and kissed Conway on the cheek.

"You be a good boy", she said quietly, as she turned, and slowly climbed the stairs to the porch, where Elsie stood quietly staring through the screen wire.

"He's waitin' fa' you."

"I ain't got tha' words ta' thank ya'."

" I don't need no thanks honey. Seein' at' youngun' smile is thanks enough fa' me."

She stepped forward and hugged Elsie hard. They both teared up, and held each other for a long time, then Elsie made her way down the steps, and climbed in the truck, and they drove away. Betty-Fay watched as Conway steered the truck around the corner of the house. She suddenly felt more alone than she'd ever felt in her life, and she stood on the porch and cried for a long time, but she did'nt know exactly why.

"Bye baby," she whispered, "Bye baby".

38

At the motel, Wyvanelle and Seven were finalizing their plan for the dismantling of one empire, and the assemblage of another. Steve wanted no part in the plot, but he was torn between his sense of moral outrage, and his burning desire to be taken seriously as a photo-journalist. That, and the fact that he too, was smitten with Wyvanelle. The picture of her magnificent bosom, that was etched on his brain like a jail-house tattoo, sealed his fate as a co-conspirator. He provided them with walkie-talkies that he carried with his equipment, and instructed them in their use.

It was decided that he and Seven would arrive the gym early, and go about filming the pre-game rituals, rumored to be quite ghastly, and attempt to locate the kid, or at least determine at what point in the evening that Doil planned to show him.

Arv would park as far away as the range of the walkie-talkies would permit, and wait for the signal to move in for the pick-up. Wyvanelle would be responsible for distracting the guard. It was decided that if Elsie were with him, they would grab them both, and engineer her commitment later. All the plans were falling into place, guided by the unseen hand of Doil Pettyjohn. The only wild card in the deck, was Booger Red. Doil considered him a snake, and thus un-predictable.

"Ya' never know when r' where they'll strike," he would say,

"Tha' onliest' way not ta' get bit, is avoid em!" and that's what we planned to do.

To get to Waddell's place, you had to turn off the blacktop, and travel for a couple of miles down a dirt road that forked in a wash. The left fork took you to the Strickland place. The right one, took you to Datherd Dimond's.

Datherd Dimond was a pulp-wooder, as had been his daddy, and his gran-daddy, and a meaner son-of-a-bitch has never walked this earth. Datherd had four daughters ranging in age from fourteen or so, to twenty, and all were pin-up quality. Ol' Datherd hovered over those 'hormone-geysers' like a meth-driven prison guard, and many an insurance debitor, and Fuller Brush salesman had felt the sting of rock salt from Datherd's bird gun for daring to peep into the window at these virginal flowers. It was rumoured that vinyl siding peddlers, and a few would-be suitors, had disappeared altogether, but none of this could be verified. The one thing that we knew for certain, was that if you planned to call on the Dimond place, you'd better be ready to take on Datherd, and few that we knew were that tough, or that ignorant.

Doil reasoned, and rightly so, that the Preacher had never been to Waddell's, or to the Dimond home place, since he tended to deliver his message to those with stature and influence, not moonshiners, and certainly not pulp-wooders. At the fork in the road, were two hand-lettered signs, with arrows pointing the direction to each man's respective place. Doil had Waddell switch em', just in case the Preacher should suddenly become concerned about the heathen element in the community, and plan a visitation.

39

The coach was an amiable sort, and after a few fellowship charging swallows of sweet mash, he was diapering donkeys with Hooleo & Hooleo, the twin migrant workers that Doil had dubbed his 'road crew'. He even helped them climb into the rafters, and suspend the 'paint can' lighting rig with bailin' twine, which was dangerous, but I suppose no more so, than attempting to ride a pissed-off donkey on a hardwood floor.

The first few volunteer players drifted in to claim the choicest mounts, and to linger around the player's buffet, which consisted of Vienna sausages dumped in a bowl of barbecue sauce, a big hunk of 'commodity' cheese, and several boxes of saltine crackers. The more cheese and crackers they ate, the less likely that they pass out before game-time, so I made sure that there was plenty of both.

Doil drove up, with Pee Wee in the back seat, the sailor hat pulled low on his head, and motioned for me to come to the car.

"Any sign ob'em' yet?"

"Aint' seen nothin'."

I leaned down to have a look at Pee Wee. He cocked his head to reveal one eye, and flipped me a bird.

"Ya' really think this is gonna' work?"

"Does a fat baby fart? Thow' a couplea' saw hosses' cross' the drive, sos' we can keep people from parkin' in here. We don' wanna' make is' too hard fa' Arv. He's a simple soul."

"But a hell uva' chicken fighter."

"Thateis', thateis' answered Doil, as he attempted to

turn in the seat.

"Are ya' ready Valentino?"

Pee Wee neither raised his head, nor uttered a sound. Once again, he raised his tiny middle finger, ever so slowly, and held it motionless, pointed skyward, as Doil rolled out of the car.

"Method actor," Doil whispered, as we walked away.

40

Betty-Fay was in a foul mood, like she'd been up all night ironing, with a briar in her foot. She was confused, angry, and lonely. Conway and Elsie had only been gone for a little while, and she already missed them. She wanted to believe that the preacher was some religious superman who had a pipeline to the almighty, but somewhere deep in her heart, she knew that he was no more than an opportunistic parasite. He just happened to look like the movie Moses, who, to a whole generation of Americans, was the personification of God and religion, virtue and manliness. The real Moses probably looked like Wally Cox. She was struggling with the absurd notion that anyone so young and innocent as Conway, could be consumed with evil, and that Elsie, though admittedly a little whacky, was nothing more than a lonely, frightened, and somewhat angry woman, just like her. She needed to talk. She needed guidance, and the only one she felt she could turn to, was the Preacher. She fell right into his baby soft hands.

41

Conway sat in Waddell's lap and steered the truck, with a little help, all the way to the house. As they rolled to a stop, Waddell said,

"We aint' got nothin' ta' cook fa' supper. Reckon we oughta' go down ta' tha' pond and see can we catch a mess o' bream?"

The look on the kid's face was all the answer he needed. He flashed Elsie that famous grin.

"You bait a hook?"

"Hell yeah I can bait a hook."

"There's some cane-poles leaned up by tha' porch. You come wi' me boy, an' hep' me catch a tube o' them crickets."

Elsie watched, as Conway took Waddell by the finger, and they walked toward the barn, stopping to let the kid kick at something on the ground, like kids, and chickens will do. She was overcome with guilt, but when she saw Waddell squat beside him and rub his 'comb-like' shock of hair with his big hand, the guilt turned to hope, and she started to smile, and climbed out of the truck to gather up the fishing poles.

It was getting on about dusky dark, and they were catching fish as fast as they could bait the hooks. When they had caught enough for a mess, they slowly walked back to the house, and Waddell taught the kid the fine art of cleaning fish. Elsie fried em' up, with a big plate full of hush puppies. After they had eaten everything but the plates, Waddell taught Conway his technique for projection belching, much to Elsie's delight. It was the most satisfying meal that any of them had ever had.

42

The tip–off that night was a glorious event. Doil's paint can light rig lit him up like a fat Christmas tree, the gleaming whistle in his mouth sending out reflected rays of light like the Star of Bethlehem. The gym was packed, the players were drunk, the donkeys were mad, and the film was rolling! It was a showman's dream. The laughter, the screams, and the braying grew louder and louder, until it became a deafening roar. It was a scene that stretched as far back as the Roman Collosseum. Warriors hungry for glory; crowds hungry for violence, and Doil Pettyjohn as a modern-day Caligula.

Outside this roaring temple, Pee Wee sat in the back of Doil's car, patiently waiting for his cue, dreaming of fame, fortune, and sexual conquest, discreetly sipping on a fruit jar full of mash that he had managed to pilfer at some point in his journey. One of Cecil's deputys, a young man with no experience in law enforcement, and even less with women, guarded the car.

Wyvanelle materialized out of the shadows like an apparition, walking slowly and deliberately, toward the awe-struck deputy, her platinum hair hanging wantonly over one eye. She was wearing a slinky, shimmering silver dress that was so tight that it looked as though she'd been dipped in it; the peaks and valleys in that magnificent body casting dark shadows across her meaty midriff. Her open-toed, six- inch spike-heeled pumps revealed a fresh coat of corvette-red nail polish. Her Lee 'press-ons' glistened with the same. The dress was cut low, and was strained to bursting by the breath-taking bosom gathered under her chin, that undulated gently with every step she took. In one hand she carried a glass of champagne that she sipped sensuously as she glided toward him, and in the other she carried the bottle, holding it loosely by the neck, like she was dragging the whole state of Alabama by its erect manhood. She was, in a word, magnificent.

Nothing could have prepared this young deputy for an assault such as this. As Wyvanelle drew nearer, the smell of her 'Jungle Gardenia' intoxicated him, his breathing grew shallow, and he became light-headed. She oozed straight up to him, her pillow-soft breasts covering his badge and name tag. She did'nt utter a word, but silently brought the glass to her glistening red lips, and took a slow, sensous swallow, before moving the flute to his mouth, and tilting the remainder down his throat. He stared helplessly, trying not to choke, as she raised the bottle and filled the flute again. He had no way of knowing that the champagne in the bottle was drugged, and it would'nt have mattered anyway, because even if he had been told it was strychnine, which it was'nt, he would have gladly taken anything she offered, so helpless was he under her spell. He was fast approaching a sexual fantasy nirvana, when the hyper-ventilation and the drugged wine rendered him un-conscious.

In the back seat of the darkened car, Pee Wee, now quite drunk himself, had watched this entire scene unfold, and from the moment that Wyvanelle had appeared out of the shadows he had fought back his animal urges, trying bravely to remember what Doil had instructed, not wanting to blow what might be his only chance at stardom. It is a fact however, that men, whether they be large or small in stature, when confronted with a situation involving a gorgeous woman with huge breasts, in a skin tight dress with spike heels and red toe-polish, will lose all sense of reason, start sprouting hair, and slobber like a 'were-wolf'. He watched as the deputy sank out of sight, and he lowered his head, the down-turned sailor cap hiding a fiendish grin, and waited for his chance to pounce. He did'nt have to wait long.

Seven and Steve had filmed their way out the back door of the gym, and she and Wyvanelle had drug the lifeless deputy out of camera range, and were preparing to capture on film, the first glimpse the world would see of the feral 'chicken child'.

Now it's interesting to note, that Pee-Wee was of miniature scale in every area but one. It was said that his Momma used to tell people that Pee-Wee would have been six feet tall, had he not gone all to pecker. As he sat motionless in the back seat, with his head down, he noticed that the biggest part of him was practically touching his hat brim. To his credit, he had enough presence of mind to realize that this could pose a major stumbling block in the deception, and he quickly reached into the floorboard and fished out Doil's dirty denim jacket, and put it on. It covered him like a circus tent from his neck, to his tiny little feet. Luckily Doil, like all the males in this part of the country, had cut the sleeves out of every shirt, and jacket that he owned, so Pee Wee was un-encumbered, and appeared to be wearing a denim mu mu, thus hiding the appurtenance that stuck out below his belly. He stood on the back seat, in the corner, farthest from the spot where all the activity was taking place.

Seven and Wyvanelle positioned themselves on either side of the back door, and Steve framed it with a tight shot to capture that first magic moment, when the child emerged to step into celluloid history.

Unbeknownst to the conspirators, Doil and myself had watched them slip out the back door, and we had taken up a position in the gym's bathroom window, overlooking the scene un-folding in the dusty lot. He had procured a 'Brownie 8' movie camera, and with the aid of a few well placed paint can flood lights, I was filming the crime as it transpired, for viewing at the adoption hearing, and in re-run during Sunday services at the ranch. So far, everything was going according to plan.

43

The Cadillac snaked it's way up the darkened drive, and stopped fifty feet or so from the front porch. Betty-Fay had watched through the blinds, and stood motionless, holding down a single blind with two fingers, as the behemoth rolled to a stop, and sat idling, the lights illuminating the front porch.

Betty-Fay had reached the crossroads, although in her narrow-minded view, she may not have realized it. Like so many women approaching middle age, she felt neglected and un-fulfilled, and she was looking outside herself for those things that she had been raised to believe that she needed.

That fifty foot walk in the glare of the headlights to the waiting car, could be the equivalent of dragging an eraser over the penciled-in pages of her life; fifty feet of ground that could separate her forever from the person she once was. The longing that had been stirred up with the departure of Elsie and the baby, and her un-wavering belief in the Preacher, and his home-grown, hedonistic religious principles, made her willing to attempt to rescue those who don't seek rescue. She had no inkling that the one she was trying to rescue was herself. She slipped her fingers out of the blinds and walked to the front door, picking up the crudely drawn map that lay beside the phone as she walked by.

44

Pee Wee emerged from the dark shadows, and stood unsteadily, crouching slightly, in the open door. Doil's sleeve-less jacket, and the downturned sailor cap, gave him the appearance of a Christmas tree ornament. He attempted a few feeble 'clucks', but his attempt at mimicry was at best, pitiful. Wyvanelle stepped into frame, and extended her hand.

"You wanna' get out honey?"

Pee Wee, cramped in the in the space between the seat cushion and the roof, and holding on to the back of the front seat to steady himself, cocked his head ever so slightly, just enough to peek out under the hat brim and get a close-up view of that show-stopping bosom. Then suddenly, without any sort of warning, he dove face-first into the shimmering chasm under her chin, twisting his hips to the side to conceal the fact that he was blessed beyond circus hope for a lttle kid, and burrowed into her spectacular 'playground' like a mole. Wyvanelle staggered slightly, and was totally shocked, but she was a sturdy woman, and caught him with no more effort than one would catch a fly ball.

"My God, this kid's starved for affection!"

Now at this point, I thought the whole scheme was blown, because Doil slid to the floor, banged his knees, and fell over with a huge crash, against the bathroom stall. I struggled to keep the camera aimed, but it was no use, and I left it on the window sill, and joined Doil on the floor, biting my lip to keep from cackling out loud. Pee Wee continued to burrow, attempting to stay in character with the occasional cluck, but now, with his face buried between her breasts, it sounded more like a hog rootin' in damp dirt. Over Doil's choked laughter, from somewhere in the shadows, I heard Arv yell,

"Les' get tha' hell out from here!", and they all disappeared into the darkness.

45

Waddell sat straight up in his chair, the newspaper still in his lap.

"Hoddam', I nearly forgot! Elsie, putya' shoes on. We got somewhere ta' go!"

"Doil said fa' us ta' stay out here."

"You did'n' see Pettyjohn wrote on my mailbox when we turned in didya'?

Come on boy, n'gettina' truck. We got ducks ta' pick up!"

"What in tha' hell r' you talkin' about?" muttered Elsie as they climbed in.

"Issa' surprise! You like surprises doncha' boy?"

Conway gave him a questioning look, and the cluck equivalent of 'I guess'.

As they barreled past the fork, no one noticed the ominous Cadillac sedan, parked a few yards down the narrow lane that led to Datherd Dimond's place, momentarily to be blanketed with a thick layer of dust. Just minutes before, there had been a prayer meeting of sorts in the Cadillac, as the Preacher gave last minute holy orders to a smitten Betty-Fay, while he held her clammy hand.

"Yea' though I walk, ya' know how this goes, doncha' sister?"

He gently lifted her hand and kissed it. She became all moist and giddy.

"Halleujah", she whispered, "halleujah!"

They could see the sky lit up for a couple of miles, before Waddell slid the truck into the dirt parking lot at the fairgrounds. Conway was standing in the floorboard with his chin on the dash, staring in wonder at the garishly lit rides on the midway.

"See at' bigun' inna' middle? At's tha' ferrist' wheel, and me an' you an' ya' mamma' gon' ride tha' hell out uv' it!"

Conway was bouncing like a golf ball on a concrete slab. Elsie smiled sweetly at Waddell, flashing her big, chinaberry colored teeth.

"You're a purty good ol' shit, Waddell."

"Don't tell nobody. It'll rurn' my image."

The boy's eyes were open so wide, that the entire midway was illuminated in them.

"Damn, atud' make a purty' pitcher."

Waddell and Elsie each held out a hand. Conway grabbed a finger on both, and they headed down the midway.

"Looky here."

They stopped in front of a tent with a hundred or so wooden 'stobs' sticking up inside. Each 'stob' held a worthless, yet strangely compelling prize, fastened with a big rubber band. There were fat, plastic babies smoking cigarettes, and nekkid' women key chains, and the occasional gaudy, plated wristwatch banded to a 'stob' that, even from a few feet away, appeared to be greater in girth than the ones the kazoos and pennywhistles were on.

Standing next to this glittering array, was a shiftless looking greaseball in a filthy red apron, with teeth like a yard rake. He was holding a handful of dirty wooden rings, and as he jabbered incessantly to everyone in earshot, he would toss a ring that would land perfectly around one of the more appealing of the worthless novelties.

"How much?"

"Three trys fa' fitty' cents."

"Whatya' think boy? Wonna' giver'a try?"

Conway shook with anticipation. Waddell handed the carny' two quarters, and he, in turn, handed three of the filthy rings to the kid. As he extended his hand, Elsie noticed that he had f.u.c.k. tattooed, one letter per finger, on the back of his hairy knuckles, obviously not the work of a professional. She gave him a disgusted look.

"Awright boy, pick out tha' one you want n' aim for it."

Conway took careful aim and tossed the ring, just the way the carny had done it. It bounced once, and disappeared into the maze of upright stobs. Disappointed but determined, he tossed the remaining two, and they bounced, clicking, to the ground. Conway was crestfallen. All the joy seemed to run from his face. Waddell handed the carney' two more quarters.

"You bouta'get tha' hang uv' it".

Conway took careful aim, and missed again. A look of steely determination crossed his face as he took a ring in his other hand, and with the grace of a ballerina, tossed it in a high arc. It came down in slow motion, almost like a feather floating in the air, and slowly spun around the wooden stob the way a basketball sometimes circles the rim, tempting fate and the laws of probability, and dropped, precariously hanging on the edge of the stob, but hanging none-the-less. Elsie screamed.

Waddell hollered,

"Hell yeah!", and they all bounced in place, as though riding imaginary pogo sticks. The dirty-knuckled 'carney' reached under the tent skirt, and handed little Conway a fresh rubber chicken. He stared at it, then hugged it, and stared at it some more.

"Don't take much ta' tickle im' does it?" Waddell said, as he put his big hand on the kid's head, and they wandered on down the midway.

46

The Preacher and Betty-Fay made their way down the dusty dirt road, he holding a flashlight, and she a feed sack full of bones, picked up from behind a deer processs-ing shack, that belonged to a cousin of the Reverend.

"How do ya' know he's got dogs?"

"This is the country. Everybody's got dogs."

He had no more than whispered it, when a chorus started howling in the distance. They stopped and stood quietly in the road as the barking and howling got louder and closer.

"Hand me tha' sack."

He quietly handed the flashlight to her, and proceeded to scatter the bones across the road. When he had emptied the sack, he threw it into the ditch, and taking the flash-light in one hand and she in the other, led her into the edge of the woods, behind a huge sweet gum. Within sec-onds, the yelping herd charged into the bone-yard and fell silent.

The Preacher and his smitten disciple stood silently, and remained completely still, until the only sounds they could hear were the grunts and crunches of the ecstatically happy pack. He was still holding her hand, and she was smoldering like a burnt match. A little ray of moonlight had made it's way through the sweet gum canopy, and was illuminating Booger Red's massive, white hair-do, the reflected luminance giving her pale skin a ghastly pallor, like the 'Bride of Frankenstein'.

She started to lean toward him, her lips throbbing like a stumped toe, when he abruptly stepped from behind the tree, causing her to plant a dripping wet kiss, on a big patch of green moss, as he very nearly jerked her arm out of its socket.

"Come on! We gotta' get this done before tha' new wears offa' these bones."

47

The plan was simple enough. They would drive casually back to the motel, and go to their respective rooms, and since they assumed that no one had made the connection between Wyvanelle and Seven, it had been decided that the kid would stay in Seven's room. In the morning, she Steve and the kid, would start toward Birmingham, for an eventual rendevous with Arv and Wyvanelle, who would hang around long enough to fend off Doil and his cronies.

Pee-Wee was burrowed like a mole in Wyvanelle's powdered bosom, and she, having no children of her own, assumed that all of this nuzzling and rubbing was perfectly natural, although she had to constantly remind herself that this was a little boy, and suppress her feelings of arousal, as Pee-Wee rubbed a very erect nipple between his thumb and forefinger, like a child would rub his 'gowny'. By the time they reached the motel, beads of sweat had popped out on her lip, and her breathing had become labored.

The actress and her cameraman had followed at a respectable distance, and parked on the opposite side of the parking lot. As she approached the car, Pee-Wee raised his head ever so slightly, and peered out of one eye at the exotic creature with the huge, pouty lips, slinking her way toward him. As she opened the door, he gave Wyvanelle a parting tweak, and standing up, head down, arms outstretched, he dove towards the actress, expecting to be caught in mid-air, as Wyvanelle had done.

Seven however, was by nature, not one to tolerate uninvited contact, and startled, she jumped back. Pee-Wee executed a perfect belly flop onto the parking lot, emitting a man sized grunt as he hit the ground, and very nearly driving his manhood into the earth like a tent peg. He managed a few feeble clucks before Wyvanelle reached down, and snatched him up by the collar of his denim 'mu-mu'. He came up so fast that he had to grab the brim of the sailor cap with both hands to keep it from flying off, and blowing his cover.

"Why tha' hell did'n you catch im'?" snarled Wyvanelle.

"I don't do circus tricks."

"He coulda' been hurt!"

"He looks fine to me!"

Pee-Wee forgot all about the discomfort in his groin, when he realized that these two she-devils might actually tear into each other. He glanced over his shoulder at Arv, who out of pure male instinct, gave Pee-Wee the thumbs-up, and bit his lip, feeling the same rush of exitement that he always experienced in the seconds before a well-advertised chicken fight.

Seven grabbed Pee-Wee by the hand.

"Come on kid."

She stalked away, half dragging the slightly wounded, and extremely dis-appointed abductee toward her room. Arv muttered

"Sheit!" under his breath, as he climbed out of the car. Wyvanelle remained seated for a short while. Arousal, anger, and the thrill of criminal activity having suddenly taken a toll on her.

Seven stalked into her room, and poured herself a snifter of brandy, leaving Pee-Wee standing in the open door. She took a couple of sips before she realized that she had left him outside.

"Well, come on in and close the door."

She walked to the bathroom and turned on the water in the tub. Pee-Wee stealthily hung the 'Do Not Disturb' sign on the knob, and on tip-toes, latched the safety chain.

"I can't believe that bitch turned on me like that, after what we've shared. And you, you little shit, you just had to jump did'nt you?"

She bitched and drank, drank and bitched, and every time she put the snifter down and walked back into the bathroom to check the water, or take off another article of clothing, Pee-Wee would fill the glass back to it's original level. By the time the tub was full, and she was down to her 'Fredrick's of Hollywood' dominatrix bra and panties, she was getting seriously drunk. Pee-Wee was developing a pretty good buzz himself, from slugs off the brandy bottle. He sat on the bed, ears ringing, almost swooning, as blood intended for his brain was siphoned off to another part of his anatomy. He could hear Doil's voice playing over and over in his head:

"Take is' thing as far as it'll go. Don't blow it! Don't blow it! Don't blow it!"

Seven lit a candle that she kept by the tub, and turned out the light, throwing the whole place into darkness, except for the flickering bit of light that escaped from the open bathroom door. Pee-Wee could see her silhouetted in the dresser mirror, as she dropped the naughahyde bra and panties on the floor, and sinuously slipped into the tub. He sat motionless, waiting for the steamy water to melt the brandy into her brain like butter in a hot skillet. When he heard an audible sigh come from the bathroom, he tip-toed in, and stood next to the tub at her perfectly proportioned feet, absent-mindedly stirring the water with his finger, as his eyes scanned her from the corvette red toe-polish, to her enormous lips, that glistened in the candle-light like two fat eels. Accordingly, he made a feeble attempt to cluck. Her large, dark eyes were half-open, and beginning to glaze over.

"You can get in if you want."

Her speech was beginning to slur.

"You're a little kid, for God's sake. Sit in the water and play with a damn duck, or something."

Pee-Wee quickly peeled out of the denim mu-mu and the sailor suit, but he left the hat pulled way down over his eyes. Seven was leaned back, head resting on the tub, water up to her neck, half watching him as the brandy swallowed her senses. As he climbed over the foot of the tub, she blinked hard, and tried to bring her eyes into focus.

"Oh my God!," she whispered, "oh my God!", but by then, it was too late.

48

Betty-Fay stood at the edge of the woods, fifty yards or so from the house, as the preacher crept up to the porch, and tip-toed to a window with the shade pulled to within an inch or so from the sill. She watched as he dropped to his knees, trying to gain a vantage point from which to try and spot the kid through the crack; the light from which illuminated him in silhouette. To Betty-Fay's eyes, he had dropped to his knees to pray, and the exitement of the moment sent her into a religious 'quiver', and she began to whisper in 'tongues', and march in place to a heavenly cadence, that only she could hear. She was choking back a shout, when out of the darkness, she saw a long, thick shadow emerge and come to rest just behind the preacher's ear, and the un-mistakable click of 'rabbit-ears' being cocked. She tip-toed silently back to the road, and broke into a dead run for the car. The preacher felt the cold steel of the barrells pressing into his skull.

"Don't shoot brother, I'm a man uv' God."

"And you was doin' a little prayin' on my porch was ye'?"

"In a manner of speaking."

"You-us' prayin' em' gals' o' mine us' gonna' openat' winder' you suva'bitch!"

Reality struck the preacher like a shot to the back of the head.

"This ain't the Strickland place,—— is it?"

"You know Goddam' well it ain't the Strickland place, now git yo' ass up!"

He dug the barrels into the back of his skull like a hay fork, and lifted him to his feet.

"You putya' hands on top at' purty' hair-do, and don't move Elvis."

Betty-Fay charged back through the dogs, who were too concerned with the bones to even notice. She had thrown a sensible shoe, was soaked with sweat, and her high holiness hair treatment had blown apart as she ran, huge clumps of which had fallen in every direction, giving her a post-neanderthal appearance. She jumped into the Preacher's car, pushed the matted hair out of her eyes, and took a couple of deep breaths. She suddenly took on the determined, yet serene look of a Mennonite at mule-day. Reaching into the floorboard, she found the keys, cranked the car, turned on the lights, and rolled down the windows. As she began to sing 'Bringing in the Sheaves' at the very top of her lungs, she yanked the caddy' into drive, and buried her foot in the carburetor, sending dirt, rocks, bones, and dogs flying in every direction, as she barreled off to effect the salvation of her would be holy man lover.

Datherd Dimond had begun to push the preacher toward the darkened end of the porch.

"You wantin' ta' talk ta' God, Elvis? You fixin' ta', see im' face to face."

The Preacher, though for no other reason than fear, had re-signed himself to his martyrdom. Too scared to speak, his thoughts should have been on his great reward, but the only thing on his mind, the only face he could see, was Doil Pettyjohn. He hung his hair and waited.

It was very faint at first, but it grew louder very quickly, as if someone were cranking the volume knob on a cheap radio; an eerily off-key voice singing the chorus of 'Bringing in the Sheaves', with a hound dog choir howling in the background. The wind picked up, the singing and the howling grew louder and louder. Datherd pulled the barrells from the preacher's head, and turned, slack-jawed, toward the road. For a split second, everything fell silent. They both held their breath, expecting any second to hear the opening trumpet of judgement day, when the caddy, like a roaring chariot from heaven, burst through the scrub pines and crepe myrtle, taking out a cross-pole full of 'martin gourds' and Datherd's mailbox, and cannon-balled straight at them, sliding sideways when it hit the dew-slick yard.

Betty-Fay's un-furled hair was streaming out the open windows like the banners at Joan of Arc's coming out party. Datherd dove into a box-wood, as the careening car slid to a stop, just before smashing into the porch. The Preacher had lifted his eyes, still holding down his hair-do with his hands.

"Les' go!" she screamed, and Booger Red, not having to be told twice, executed a 'Johnny Weismuller' dive off the porch, landing belly-first in the back seat, as Betty-Fay stomped the accelerator, hooking the car into the corner of the porch, taking out the end column, and sending the tin roof crashing to the ground. As they roared out of the yard, she broke into yet another deafening verse, the end of the first stanza punctuated by a shotgun blast that exploded the rear window.

49

Up to this point, Steve had been a willing participant in this non-sense, but as everyone stomped off to their respective rooms, and he stood there alone in the parking lot, having not received a 'fare thee well', or even a 'kiss my ass', he saw a pattern emerging. The 'double-D' cataracts that blinded him were locked safely away, and the fuzzy vision he had seen of fame, and sex, and awards for photo-journalism, in sharper focus became hand-cuffs, and tabloids, and a long vacation in an Alabama penal facility. He climbed back into the truck, and headed for the monkey ranch.

The road crew was busy un-loading and feeding the ex-hausted donkeys, and a few of the stalwarts, myself included, were in the office, toasting another stellar evening of entertainment with adult beverages, when Steve appeared at the door.

"Come in son, come in an' fix ya-sef' a cocktail. I don't bleve' you met tha' high-sheriff and his posse".

Steve could feel the blood draining from his face, and though his first, and most logical urge was to run, he stepped inside, and prepared to take his medicine. He glanced toward the couch, and there stretched out, with a wet wash-rag on his fore-head, was the deputy Wyvanelle had drugged at the gym. Steve could feel the noose tightening around his neck.

"Tell me he's gonna' be all-right!"

The deputy raised his head, pulled off the wash-rag, and eye-balled Steve.

"Why hell yeah I'm gon' be aw-right'!"

The office erupted with laughter. Steve felt like a city kid at the conclusion of his first snipe hunt.

"You people do realize that I was involved in a kidnapping tonite!" He blurted out, surrendering to the need to un-burden himself.

The laughter grew even louder, to the point that the monkeys were screaming, and the donkeys braying, but Steve's conscience had started to consume him, and he found no humor in the situation. He imagined that this was what hell must be like. Doil finally quit laughing long enough to speak.

"God hon', you killin' me. Hickey, fix the camry-man' here a cocktail. Pull you up a chair son, an' lemme' splain' sumpn' to ya'. You out here among po' folks. Good, hard-workin' folks that break their backs farmin' or mill-workin', day-in and day-out, all o'their all too short lives. A little show-bidness' is all ese' people got ta' puta' little color in a drab, and color-less world. Ya' see son, I scratch out a meager livin', tryin' ta' create diversions ta' hep' ese' folks fa'get how hard their lives are for a minute, an' if they feel tha' need fa' more immediate diversion, I sell em' some likker'. I make ever' effort ta' see that they get tha' most bang fa' their entertainment buck. Now unfortunately, they are others with show-bidness' aspirations operatin' in ese' parts, whose motives are not as pure, or as well-defined. Where tha' price uv' admission greatly exceeds tha' quality uv' tha' show. At' crooked-ass' preacher, for example. Now his interest in tha' child at' YOU say, you was involved in kidnappin', has nothin' ta' do wi' concern fa' tha' baby's welfare, or compassion fa' tha' baby's momma', an' everything ta' do wi' raisin' tha' entertainment value of his production, ta' justify his exorbitant entry fee. Likewise, tha' three that involved you, are all operatin' witha' same, selfish motives."

Doil leaned forward and placed his hand on his heart, his sincereity running like a snotty nose.

"I gotta' responsibility ta' that young'un, an' his momma, an' to tha' good people uv' this community, ta' protect and serve, an' provide high quality, yet affordable entertainment, in ese' un-certain times. Ya' see, deep down, everbody' wonts' ta' be in show bidness'. Aint' nobody satisfied wi' who they are, an' from time ta' time, they feel tha' need ta' act like somebody else. I bleve' it was Elvis at' said "Tha' world isa' stage, and we'se all jus' actors."

"Like tha' deputy here, who acted like he was drugged, an' tha' vetenarian' who acted like he was sellin' a powerful strong tranquilizer ta' Arv Kilgore, who acted like he was buyin' it ta' use on a wounded rooster, an' tha' twenty-one year-old, sex-crazy dwarf, who acted like a little boy who could'nt talk, but made cluckin' noises like a chicken; an' me, who acted like I was runnin' a donkey ball-game, when I was heppin' ol' Hickey here, as he was fimmin' yall' kidnappin' a midget. Do ya' understand what I'm sayin' to ya' son? That,— by God,— is Show Bidness'!"

Humbled and embarrassed in the presence of greatness, Steve squirmed in his seat, and drained his cocktail.

"So I've been?"

"Had."

"And the pill they dropped in the champagne?"

"A fizzie."

"The deputy with the rag on his head?"

"Actin' gives him a head-ache."

"And the little person we kidnapped?"

"Hung like a stud hoss'."

So now it looks like I'm working with you, but I act like I'm working with them."

"Looks like it."

50

Betty-Fay skillfully piloted the steamboat-like caddy between the ditches on the winding dirt road, like a holiness whiskey hauler. When she hit the black-top, she had a full head of steam, that big v-8 suckin' in the wet night air like a shop vac, and burying the speedometer needle. They were just a blur when she met them and blew by, almost sucking the truck into her lane as she shot past.

"What tha' hell was at'?"

He fought the truck back into his lane. Elsie was turned in the seat, and little Conway stood in it backwards, both of them watching the tail-lights disappear into the blackness.

Waddell was watching in the mirror.

"Whatta' ya' think boy? Had ta' be doin' a-hunderd' r' better. Reckon it was a ufo?"

Conway stared into the enveloping darkness for a moment, but he was exhausted. His belly was full of cotton candy, sno-cone, and candy apple, and his eye-lids had grown so heavy that they dropped like a theatre curtain. He leaned into his momma, and slid into her lap, still clutching his rubber chicken, and fell fast asleep. She traced his candy-stained lips with her finger, and smiled at Waddell.

The Preacher was still lying face down on the back seat, covered from head to toe with rhinestone sized chunks of the rear window, whether praying, or cowering like a scared little girl, only he knew. The wind rushing through the open windows of the speeding car created a roar that perfectly accompanied Betty-Fay's a-tonal caterwauling. She was well into her third screaming stanza, when she shrieked past the on-coming truck. It was only a flash of color in the corner of her eye, that took a few moments to register, but when it did, she abruptly stopped her wailing.

"Waddell!"

The Preacher, noting that the un-godly singing had stopped, assumed that it was safe to get up and raised himself. The force of the wind blew the glittering shards from his hair-do, and it whipped violently in every direction.

"Whad' you say?" He yelled over the howling wind.

"Waddelllllllllllllllllllllllllllll!" she screamed, as she planted her one sensible shoe, and her support hose covered foot on the brake pedal. Pulling the sides of the steering wheel like the chains on a playground swing, she pushed it to the floor, as a kid would do, trying to launch her-self into space, feet first.

Aero-dynamically, the Cadillac had much in common with a boxcar. As long as it was going straight, there was at least the illusion of control, but with the brakes locked, it took on all the characteristics of a tilt-a whirl, spinning wildly, clock-wise, then counter-clock-wise, then clock-wise again. It went backwards, the force of the whistling wind through the empty hole where the rear window used to be, parting the Reverend's hair up the back of his head, and filling the windshield with Betty-Fay's years of holiness growth.

The high-way had been an old stage trail in the distant past, and some said a buffalo run, in the eons before the white man and civilized paving practices. It was sunk in the soft earth like a gigantic wagon rut, with tall ditch banks on either side, which contained the screaming, steel capsule as it bounced from side to side like a pinball, knocking down anything in it's path, and taking out an entire section of Doil's 'Burma Shave' style ad campaign. When it finally slid to a stop, a quarter mile or more from where she locked the brakes, they were pointed back in the direction from whence they came. The body of the mangled caddy was resting belly down in the soft dirt of the shoulder, like a hog in a waller', with the engine still running.

The Holy-Man was sitting bolt upright, shell-shocked, his hair folded around his ears from the part in the back, like a halo. His arms were outstretched, and he had a death grip on the 'God-a-mighty' handles that hung from the inside of each brocaded door panel. He seemed unable, or un-willing, to let them go.

Betty-Fay was un-fazed by the hair-raising ride they had just taken, and was revving the engine wildly, with her head poked out the open window, looking toward the rear wheels as they sent a cloud of dust and dirt spewing into the damp night air. The tires had peeled off the rims somewhere back down the road, and the empty wheel on the pulling side, was buzzing as it spun in the dirt, like a bumble-bee in a mason jar. Booger Red, beginning to suffocate from the choking dust, opened a door and climbed out, coughing, and trying to wave the steamy smoke out of his eyes.

"Sister Pettyjohn——-SISTER PETTYJOHN, IT'S NO USE, IT'S STUCK!"

He yelled over the roar of internal combustion, and external circumstance. He still had'nt seen the condition of the car, only a faint outline through the dusty haze. Betty-Fay grudgingly turned off the switch, and climbed out.

"They're gettin' away, they're gettin' away", she repeated over and over, like a broken record.

The Preacher had been momentarily blinded by the dirt in his eyes, and he was standing, his back to her, gingerly wiping them with his monogrammed hanky. The dust settled quickly in the dampness, and his tear ducts finally flooded his lids enough to wash most of the clods from his line of vision. They piled up in the corners, next to his nose, like clumps of brown mascara. As his eyesight slowly returned, he dusted himself, and turned to access the damage. He jumped back, startled, when he got a look at Betty-Fay.

She was standing right behind him, her extremely long, sanctified mane was matted, hanging, arched, twisted, teased, and filthy; her face crusted with dirt, a dark brown outline around every tooth in her head, like she'd just finished eating a mudpie.

"They're gettin' away, they're gettin' away!"

It was at that moment, that he got his first look at his cherished Cadillac.

"Good God!——Good God!———Look what you've done to my car"

"They're gettin' away!"

"Look what you've done to my damn car!"

"They're gettin' away I tell ya'!"

"I don't give a shit! Ya' hear me? I don't give a shit! Look at my goddam' car!"

"But what about tha' baby? What about our baby?"

"You goofy bitch! Do you know how many Sundays I had to work, and how much shit I had to put up with to buy that car? All I ever wanted was at' Cadillac, and you've ruined the son of a bitch!"

"But tha' baby!"

"Forget tha' damn baby, an' be figurin' out how you an' at' whiskey-peddlin' smart ass of a husband you got are gonna' pay for this shit!"

Betty-Fay was shook to the foundation. Everything she thought she believed, her hopes, her dreams, probably her marriage, lay shattered around her like the glass from the smashed headlights. But the thing that hurt the most, the thing that caused her the most shame, was that her husband was right about the Preacher all along. She was so convicted by his professed moral superiority, and the drab cloak of righteousness that she wore, that she had forgotten that life is real, and real people hurt. They have kids with problems, and have problems themselves. They fall down, and they get up again. They curse when they're angry, and tell dirty jokes, and laugh when they're able to laugh, and don't cry nearly enough. A little ray of light opened in her head, and she saw things as they really were for the first time in a long while.

"This is from me and my whisky dealin' husband!"

She took a couple of steps forward, and with that one sensible shoe, she kicked as hard as she could, and sent the preacher's consecrated testicles flying backwards up his 'swaller pipe'. He fell face first into the dirt, gasping for breath. She stood over him for a moment, and raising her arms, cried,

"And tha' truth shall set you free!" and gave him one more swift kick in the ass, before taking off that sensible shoe, tossing it into the car, and starting off toward what she hoped was still her home and husband, bare-foot and free.

51

"You think you could stop drinkin' for maybe five minutes so we can figure out what we're gonna' do?"

"Do bout' what?"

Arv was already down to his boxer shorts, and a Stanley Kowalskie style undershirt. His skinny, hairless legs looked like a pair of toothpicks stuck in a cocktail frank.

"Would you wake up, fa' God's sake! Pettyjohn'll have everbody' in tha' county lookin' fa' that kid."

Wyvanelle was pacing the floor, smoking furiously. She was still wearing that breathtaking dress, and though she had kicked off the spike heels, which made her a little less imposing, she was still a blistering eyeful.

Arv lay on the bed, one skinny ankle crossed with the other, a 'Lucky Strike' dangling from the corner of his mouth, the ash hanging precipitously, about to drop on his bony chest. He eyed her with a bleary-eyed salaciousness, as he sipped on a cocktail, and waited for her to look in his direction. When she finally glanced his way, he patted the bed invitingly, and cocked his head back in a macho, movie gangster, moll demand.

Un-fortunately, the quick movement of his head caused the hot ash to fall, and it landed on his bare white chest, just above the neck of his 'wife-beater'. He jumped, spilling the cocktail all over himself, and started digging with his bony heels, trying to push himself backwards up the headboard, and away from the burning ashes.

Wyvanelle picked up one of the spike heels, and flung it at him. It bounced off his head.

"Oh, sheit'! Whad'yu do at' for?"

"Because I'm surrounded by assholes!"

"But there aint' nobody here but me!"

"Exactly!"

52

"Awright' boys, yall' gather up here. We bouta' compose a luv' letta'. Mista' camryman', can you type?"

"With two fingers."

"At's one moren'me; take a letter."

Doil had an ancient Remington typewriter sitting on his desk, and he got up and held his chair for the reluctant Californian.

"We ebn' got stationery."

Sitting beside the Remington was a stack of official 'Shady Lawn Motor Court' letter paper, complete with matching envelopes, bearing a color picture of the motel and café, that gave them the look of those old-timey post cards from the thirties.

"Dear Red,"

Steve gave Doil a questioning look, amid the chuckling, and out right laughter that filled the office. He ignored his non-verbal query, and the laughter, and continued.

"Dear Red, my heaving bosom aches for you. No man will ever be able to satisfy me after I've had the best! The burning bush is————-burning for YOU!"

The cackling became deafening at this point, and we had to stop the dictation until all, except the camera-man, had laughed till we were gasping.

"Come to me at midnight. Number thirteen. The lights will be off, the door will be unlocked, and I'll be in the bed, naked, smoldering, holding my breath until you take me like the biblically hung animal that you are. Counting the minutes till I EXPLODE!   Wyvanelle."

As we loosened our collars, and wiped the nervous sweat from our brows, Doil reached into the desk and produced a tube of bright, red lipstick and a compact, and proceeded to paint his lips, following his progress in the tiny mirror, like a seasoned professional. A sudden hush fell over the crowd, as he gave himself a final check, rolled his lips in on each other like the wringer on an old time washing machine, and pulled the letter from the Remington. We watched with intense curiosity, as he pressed it to his lips, leaving a huge, perfectly executed, bright red lip-print on the paper.

"Nice touch," I said. "We were startin' ta' get worried."

Doil wiped his lips with his handerkerchief.

"Can I ask ya' sumpn' Hickey?"

"I reckon."

"Da' these shorts make my butt look big?"

The office erupted into laughter once again, and we all, including Doil, availed ourselves of the tension relieving jocularity. Steve, being a relative stranger to those present, and having had recent, all-consuming fantasies concerning Wyvanelle, was struggling with the huge lump in his throat, after Doil's sexually charged recitation.

"S'matta' Steve, got sumpn' stuck in ya' craw'?"

"No, I mean, I just did'nt know,"

"Lissen' son. At' gal aint' no amateur. She been roun' tha' block a few times. I figger' if she wrote a letter, that ud' be tha' kind o' letter she'd write."

"You really think so?"

"Why hell yeah, I know so! I saw tha' tattoos."

"Tattoos on who? What are you talking about?"

"On her, but it's a long story, an' we aint' got much time, so I'm gonna' give ya' tha' opportunity ta' find out fa' ya'self. I need her outta' that motel room fa' thirty minutes, from eleven fawty'-five, till a qwater' after. I don't care whatya' have ta' say, r' whatya' hafta' do, but she needs ta' be gone. You a bright boy, been around show bidness' quite a bit; improvise:

"Wait a minute. How am I suppose to get her to leave?"

"Thas' up ta' you. Jus' make it happen. I will share one little bit o' infamation' wi' ya', sort of an' incentive."

Doil motioned for him to come closer, and he leaned over and whispered in his ear.

"Tha' burnin' bush tattoo is real."

"No kidding?"

"Look at dis' face. Would I kid you?"

"O'kay, I'll try."

"Don't try, do it! Remember, I got fim' on ya'."

"Consider it done."

"Now thas' what I like ta' hear. I'm wavin' bye now," and as Steve left the office, Doil put his hand up next to his ear waved him out of sight, like a circus bear.

53

Oblivious to the carnage in their wake, Waddell and his charges made it back to his place without incident. He carried Conway, who was out for the night, into the house and bedded him down on the couch, and he and Elsie made their way to the back porch, where he had installed a big, wooden swing.

"Whaddaya' think bout' a little nightcap?"

"Soon to as not."

He walked over to the pumphouse, and wiped the cobwebs from a fresh jar of 'mother's milk'. The moon broke through the clouds, bathing the yard in soft moonlight, and revealing a dewey mist, like the fog from dry ice, hovering over the wet grass at ankle height, giving a 'Bela Lugosi' feel to the whole place. As Waddell walked back to the porch, he left a trail in the mist. Suddenly Elsie had a cold chill, and drew up on the corner of the swing with her arms folded tightly about her.

"Whas' wrong wi you?"

"At's' spooky as shit," and she pointed to the dripping, hollow trail that he'd left cut in the mist.

"You aint' gettin' scared, are ya'?"

"Just a little chilly."

He took off his sleeveless, tablecloth print cowboy shirt, and wrapped it around her, in a gesture more romantic than practical, and sat down on the swing, causing it to shimmy and sway. Unscrewing the lid, he offered the jar to her.

"This'll knock tha' chill off."

She took the container and held it to her nose, drawing back quickly as the fumes blistered her olfactory.

"This ud' knock a buzzard off a gut wagon!"

Raising the jar in a silent toast, she took a slug, and handed it back. Wiping her mouth on the collar of the shirt that he had wrapped her in, she caught a hint of his distinctive smell. As he took a long swallow from the communal cup, she held the collar under her nose and inhaled deeply, his intoxicating aroma; a combination of sweat, testosterone, and 'Aqua Velva'. There was a ragged guitar case leaned up in the corner of the porch.

"You pick tha' gittar'?"

"I aint' too good at it."

"Pick me sumpn'.I love me some gittar' pickin'."

He ambled over, opened the case, pulled out the beat-up Harmony flat top, and ran through the tuning, stopping to strum a 'g' chord, then fine tuning again, and checking his tonality with a 'c' and an 'f'. When he was sure he had it close enough for country, he returned to the swing, and took another long drink from the jar, lit a cigarette, and stuck it between strings and the headstock of the guitar. Elsie had pulled her feet up under her, with her arms wrapped around her legs, and her chin resting on her knees.

Waddell turned to her, crossed his legs, and launched into 'Ol' Shep', the single most heart-wrenching song in the history of music, for my money. Waddell's 'ear-tuning' of the guitar was a disaster, and he sang like he had a mouthful of marbles, but by the time he got to the end, tears were rolling down Elsie's face, and she had to blow her nose on the shirttail of his 'western wear'.

"At' damn song breaks my heart," she whispered.

Waddell grew wistful.

"My daddy usta' sing it to me when I wadn' no biggern' lil' Conway in ere'. Made me wanna' cry ever' time I heard it. Now it makes me think about him. He's been gone a long time. Choked onna' neck bone. Makes me miss im'. Boy oughta' have a Daddy. Still sometimes makes me wanna' cry. Hey, here's one ya' might like. Aint' hardly as 'weepy' as at' last un'."

He took a long drag on the cigarette, and stuck it back in the strings on the headstock. It took a long time to compose himself, and then, he looked deep into her eyes.

"Hello Darlin', it's beeen a long tiiiiiiiime,"

She gasped, and put both hands over her open mouth. Waddell sang it like it was the last time anyone would ever hear it, and never took his eyes off Elsie's. By the time he finished, sweat was pouring down his face, and Elsie was practically hyper-ventilating. They stared at each other for a few moments, with wild looks of un-bridled anticipation. He pulled the guitar over his head, and the instant it cleared, they crashed together like two big-horn sheep, each, apparently, trying to swallow the other whole.

They rolled off the swing onto the porch, and after rolling all over the porch, they rolled off into the yard, displacing the hanging mist everywhere they rolled, the heat from their burning bodies sending little clouds of steam into the damp, night air. By the time the first rays of dawn had pierced the darkness, they had rolled all the way to the hall of the barn.

54

Shirley was on her way to the 'Veterans of Foreign Wars' Post 5173, when she spotted the disheveled woman walking slowly up the road, and pulled over to help; not out of any great sense of compassion, just to satisfy her incessant nosiness. The woman continued to walk slowly up the shoulder, as Shirley crept along side her, with the window down.

"Hey, you in trouble? Ya' need some hep'? Where's ya' shoes? Jew' havva' wreck? Wanna' ride? Was you headed ta' tha' V.F.W.?"

Betty-Fay took this barrage as long as she could, but even pentinents have a breaking point. She whirled around to face nosy Shirley.

"Fa' God's sake Shirley, are you writin' a book?"

Shirley slammed on the brakes, causing her to bang her chin on the steering wheel. Up to this point, she had'nt recognized the woman through the matted tangle of hair, that practically covered her whole upper torso.

"Aint' Betty-Fay, issat' you? Aw God-a-mighty, what happened ta' you? You got raped didn' ya'? Did ya' get raped? Who was it? Jew' know im'? Aw God-a-mighty!"

"SHIRLEY! Wouldya' shuddup' aminnit?"

Betty-Fay shook her matted head in dis-belief, opened the door, and climbed in. Shirley was about to bust, biting her tongue in wanton anticipation of the juicy explanation that she could feel was forthcoming. Betty-Fay held up her palm.

"Jus' be quiet, an' lissen'. I was in a little accident. I was not raped. I am not hurt. Will you take me home? If tha' answer is yes, I will tell ya' what happened when we get there."

Shirley exploded.

"God, yes yes, ya' know I will. I'm so sorry. I did'n' know who you was. I just seen is' person walkin', ya' know, an' I thought my God, she's hurt,"

"Drive Shirley,——— just drive."

Steve had'nt been gone thirty seconds, when Doil pointed at me, and then turned his palm toward the ceiling, and wiggled his finger back and forth, like he was scratching a dog's chin. Faithful dog that I am, I came when called. Doil carefully folded the letter and reached into the desk, producing a vial of 'Jungle Gardenia,' which he sprinkled liberally on the folded page.

"At's what I smelled at tha' gym."

"Very observant;'Jungle Gardenia'; sposed' ta' make ya' horny; it's Wyvanelle's favorite. Hot woman put a 'scosh' behind each ear, an' you can smell er' fa'aqwawta' mile r' more."

"I thought it was tha' deodorant cakes in tha' urinals I was smellin'."

"Ya don't get out much, do ya'son? Now pay attention. We aint' got much time, an' you got a pivotal role. Whatcha''Timex' say?"

"Huh?"

"Ya' watch boy, what time ya' got?"

"Oh, ten minutes after nine."

Doil removed his own time piece, and screwed the winding stem slightly.

"Ten minutes after niner', set! Awright Hickey, we symonized'. Now get you a pencil, an'a sheet o' that motel paper. We gotta' write anotha' letter."

I found an Eagle #2 in the desk, and sharpened it with Doil's pocket knife, mine having been lost in the poker lesson, before taking my seat at the stenographer's desk. Doil paced slowly, back and forth, in deep thought, cupping his right elbow with his left hand, while his right hand held his chin, the index finger tapping nervously on the groove that ran from the bottom of his nose to his upper lip.

"Ready?"

"Go ahead on."

"Mister Kilgore, your son is asleep. That bitch Wyvanelle left with my cameraman. They were holding hands! I am sick and tired of being treated like dirt by women, and I'm sure you feel the same way. Why don't we screw each other's brains out, JUST FOR SPITE! THESE THROBBING LIPS NEED RELIEF! If you're not offended by this proposal, leave the door unlocked, and the lights OFF. I'll come to you at midnight.

P.S. I like to wear men's suits, and play rough. Seven"

"You're a damn genius."

"I know, it's quite a burden. Now, here's what ya'do. Round up tha' 'Brownie', and at' light bar with tha' four bubs'. They's a new drop cord in tha' closet. Get it, an' put all at' stuff, an' tha' two letters in tha' car. When ya' leave here, drive straight to tha' parsonage. Hold outcha' hand."

I reluctantly extended my open palm, and he dropped a pair of pierced ear posts into it.

"Take ese' ear bobs', an' think uvem' as thumbtacks. Use one ta' stick through tha' first letter, tha' one at' Steve typed, into tha' door facin' at tha' Preacher's house. He always uses tha' front door, so tha' neighbors can see him comin' an' goin', like he's doin' sumpn' impawtant'. If he aint' home, jus' leave it, an' take off. He'll be home by ten. It's in tha' Preacher's code book. Iffe' is home, tip-toe up, pin it to tha' facin', ring tha' bell, an' haul ass. He'll have ta' come to tha' door. At's inna' book too. Are ya' wimme' so far?"

"I reckon."

"Now here's where tha' timin' gets critical. When ya' leave tha' Preachers, you gotta' get to tha' motel as fast as yo' little ass can go. Find Arv's Cadillac. He neva' leaves it locked. Pull tha' headlight switch out one click, so jus' tha' parkin' lights come on."

He reached into his pocket, and fished out a handful of 'Double-Bubble', started unwrapping, and poking them into my mouth.

"Chew is' up good, an' stick tha' whole 'wad' behind tha' headlight switch. It'll buy ya' a little time. When ya' get out, lock tha' doors, an' go to tha' office. Tell tha' clerk ta' call room thirteen, an' tell im' e' left is' lights on. Arv'll be drunk, an' he'll tell tha' clerk jus' to turn em' off 'hisself'. You tell im' you tried, but tha' doors was locked. Here's tha' tough part. When Arv comes down ta' turn em' off, you gotta' stick tha' second letter on his motel room door with tha' ear bob, slip in tha' room, find a plug, run tha' drop cord aroun' tha' wall, an' into tha' closet. Then YOU get IN tha' closet, close tha' door, plug tha' light bar in, an' get ready. Arv's gotta' be in tha' bed, wi' tha' lights off, by midnight. When you hear bed-springs squeakin', an' tha' first hint of a moan, r' smell shit an' hear glass breakin', come out fimmin' an' don't stop, no matter what."

"What if e' locks tha' door when e' goes out?"

"If he don't lock at' new car, he aint' gon' lock at' shitty' motel room."

"Spose' e' does?"

"He won't!"

"Reckon? Spose' ey' decide to whip my ass?"

"You jus' keep at' camera runnin'. I'll make sure nobody gets their ass whooped'."

"I aint' worried bout' nobody's ass but mine."

Doil took my cheeks in his chubby hands, as they rose and fell, struggling to soften the huge wad of 'blow-gum'.

"This aint' about me, Hickey. Hell, if it was, Ida' quit a long time ago. It's about all uv' us. It's about tha' possibilities, tha'what if's'. It's about you lookin' in tha' mirror when you an ol' man, an' singin' 'I Did It My Waaaaay.' At's whatis' whole thing is about. But jus' fa' tonite, sos' we all will have at' opportunity, we gon' do it my way. Now GET YO' ASS ONNA' ROAD!"

55

The Preacher struggled to his knees, but left his forehead in the dirt, attempting to drain the blood back into his head and feet, and away from his throbbing plums. When he was finally able to stand, he dusted himself off, as best he could, cupped the damaged goods in one hand, and started off down the deserted highway toward home, taking wide strides, as one would take if one were 'galded', which is to say, chafed with extreme prejudice.

He had taken only a few waddling steps, when he heard a rumble in the distance, and turned to see a pair of headlights barreling toward him. He stood on the shoulder, facing the rapidly growing lights, and waved his arms over his head, using the monogrammed hanky with the embroidered fish as a sort of celestial distress flag. As the lights grew near enough to illuminate him, he heard the brakes lock, and the screech of sliding rubber, and he had to dive for the ditch, as a beat-up, rusty truck slid sideways past him and came to a shuddering stop, crossways in the highway.

The Reverend climbed out of the ditch, naively assuming that he had startled a farmer with his sudden, and un-expected flag waving. As he started toward the truck, he heard the now all too familiar click of rabbit-ears, and terror stricken, he dove back into the ditch, just as a load of number eight bird shot cut a gaping hole in the damp air, right through the spot where he was standing, and peppered the ditch bank behind him. The blast had the effect of a morphiene drip, as memory of his booted crotch was forgotten, and as adrenaline flooded his senses, he sprinted like an Olympian underdog up the dew-slick ditch bank, and into the broom sage that bordered the road, just as the second blast sent hundreds of tiny lead missles whistling over his hair-do. He heard the shotgun breach, and Datherd Dimond's angry curses, but they were fading quickly, as he put all the distance he could between himself, and that rabbit-eared gun.

The moonlight illuminated the sage patch, and Dathard could see the preacher's fluorescent hair bounding away, but he was already out of range, and not eager to leave his truck perched sideways in the highway, he climbed back in and headed toward town.

The frantic Minister did'nt stop running until he crashed into a pasture fence, tearing a few gaping holes in his sharkskin suit, and smashing the crystal on his expensive dress watch, with the alligator band. Out of breath, and relatively sure that he had out run Dathard, he followed the fence line to a farmhouse, where he spotted a balloon-tired Schwinn bicycle, leaned up against a tree. The family dogs were starting to yelp and growl, and not anxious to have a repeat of the incident at the Dimond home place, he jumped on the bike and tore out down the road, in the general direction of the parsonage, with the dog pack nipping at his heels.

56

Steve approached room thirteen without a clue as to what he would say when Wyvanelle answered the knock, but hoping against hope that it would be her, and not Arv. He had recited the litany of possibilities all the way from the ranch, but as he drew closer, they all seemed to vanish at once, and he could'nt recall a single one. He stood in front of the door for what seemed like an eternity, struggling to remember anything that might coax her out, but his brain was as empty as a drummer's bank account. It had come down to the moment of truth, and facing the object of his fantasies was infinitely more preferable than seeing himself on the local news, so he swallowed hard, and knocked.

Wyvanelle must have been standing just inside, because he had'nt even taken his hand down before she snatched the door open, and stood face to face with him. It was not humanly possible for him not to take at least a glance at her, from those delicious red toes, to the touseled platinum hair that she pushed out of her eye.

"Well?"

"Are you thirsty?"

It was his intention to say something more charming, but his brain was numb, and that's what rolled out.

"What?"

"Oh, I had a couple of ideas about the film, and I just thought that you might want to maybe get a drink, and I could amaze you with my intellect, and we could talk business, or child rearing, or what my part is in all this."

She glanced back at Arv, who was digging in his bony ass through his baggy boxers, and pouring himself yet another cocktail.

"Yeah, I could use a drink. Gimme' just a second."

She closed the door, and he could hear muffled conversation from within before she re-emerged, wearing a pair of flat shoes that concealed her flaming red toe-nails, much to his disappointment.

"Thanks, it was gettin' a little stuffy in there."

"I know what you mean."

"Do ya?"

She caught him off guard with that, but the inference was clear. At least, that's the way he read it.

"It's just an expression. I did'nt mean—-,"

"Don't worry about it. I know he's a prick."

They walked on in silence, and when they reached the café, he opened the door for her, and she gave him a surprised look. When he pulled out her chair, she gave him a sweet smile.

"It's been a long time since anybody treated me so special."

"A woman like you deserves special treatment."

Steve gave a nod to the bartender, who he had gotten to know during his tenure in Alabama.

"Two martinis."

"Even orderin' for me. Where DID you learn your manners?"

"My family has money. We were expected to mind our P's and Q's."

"Really; you know, I've never heard you mention your family name."

"It's Sanders; my grandfather was a Colonel. But enough about me. I want to hear about you."

Wyvanelle eyed him suspiciously, searching his face for signs of disingenuous intention. She found none.

"I thought you wanted ta' talk about tha' movie business."

"I was lying. I just wanted to have a drink with you."

Wyvanelle kicked off her pumps, and pulled her feet up under her. She had never noticed how handsome Steve was until now, and how comfortable he made her feel. She stirred the cocktail with the olive.

"Whatta' you wanna' know?"

"Everything."

"That could take a while."

"I've got nothing to do, and all night to do it."

He spun his finger over his head to signal his buddy, the bartender, to keep em' coming.

"Start at the beginning."

57

With Steve and myself on the road to stardom, it fell to 'puscle-gutted' Cecil Dowd to receive the last of the stage directions, and become the 'lynch-pin' in the unfolding drama. His acting abilities negligible at best, his role would have to be simple and direct, with minimal dialogue, and no heavy lifting. Doil excused all others, and requested that Cecil sit at the desk, and give him his undivided attention.

"Cecil, you an ' at' play-actin' deputy need ta' ease on down ta' tha' motel, but no sireens', no lights, and no hoo-rah'. Jus' find a park where ya' can keep an eye on room thirteen, an' wait inna' car. Tha' room'll be dark, if ever-body's' followed tha' script. When ya' see bright lights come on, high-tail it in ere', an' say,

"Sherriff's department, investigatin' a kidnappin!"

"You want me ta' arrest anybody?"

"Naw, jus' act real surprised, an' say what tha' hell's goin' on here?"

Ol' Hickey's gonna' be fimmin' tha' whole thing, so stay out of is' way, and whatever ya' do, don't let nobody stop at' fimmin! May be a little pushin' an' shovin'. I don't wont'ne'body gettin' hurt, but I don' wanna' miss a minit' uv' it. Play this right, an' you liable ta' be as famous as BUFORD PUSSER!"

That was all that Cecil needed to hear. To lawmen, and those who ever dreamed of being lawmen, the name Buford Pusser was sacred. Everybody in the south knew the story. Cut from asshole to appetite by philistines, he was left in a ditch to die. A few weeks, and several thousand stitches later, he rose up, cut hisself' a hickory stick, and proceeded to bust the skull of every evil-doer in the county. Those who were still able, ran out, dragging their badly bruised tails, and their gaudily painted whores behind them.

Superman in a sherriff's uniform; a saint with a badge. By merely invoking his name, Doil insured himself a stellar performance from a woefully inadequate actor, once again proving the power of show bidness', the power of Pettyjohn.

"So what'r ya' gonna do Sheriff?"

"My duty, BY GOD!"

Cecil left the office, walking a little taller.

58

When I entered the office, the phone was ringing off the hook. Royce, the desk clerk, was engrossed in an article about artificial worms by Tom Mann in the latest issue of 'Field and Stream', and was somewhere on the river, with a record breaker on the line. He did'nt even look up when I came in.

"Royce,————ROYCE! THE DAMN PHONE'S ABOUT TA' MELT!"

"Shit! Be wiya' inna' minnit' Hickey."

He snatched up the phone.

"Front desk;—— what kinda' noises? Fa' how long?"

Only hearing one side of this conversation, I had to assume that one of the guests was being flustered by some type of auditory disturbance, though I had no clue as to it's nature.

"What makes ya' think at'?"

We would stand in awkward silence as the dis-embodied voice presented it's case, to which I was not privy. The silences were interspersed with incomplete, and though I failed to notice it at the time, grammatically in-correct sentences from Royce.

"She gimme' orders not to. I got an ol' cat at's in heat, an' she carries on moanin' an' whinin' like somebody's stabbin' er' witha' pitchfork, an' she's probley' out bahind',——-hello, hello?'————Ol' bitch hung up on me."

"What was at' all about?"

"Ol' lady rented tha' room next ta' at' actress. Says she been hearin' all kindsa' moanin' an' scratchin' comin' from tha' room next door. Wonted' me ta' call ova' there. I ain't doin' shit! At' puffy-lip' bitch's chewed my ass out sa' many times it looks like a wad o' blow gum."

"Imagine nat'" I said, finding the reference to 'blow-gum' interesting, under the circumstances, and knowing full well what the moaning was all about.

"Jew' need a room Hickey?"

"Naw; Doil sent me."

Once again, the invocation of a magic name opens doors, and creates possibilities.

"Whad' yall' need?"

"Call up ta' room thirteen and tell Kilgore his park lights are on."

"He'll jus' tell me ta' go turn em' off."

"Tell im' ya' tried, but tha' doors was locked, an' tha' lights r'gettin' dimmer. Wait five minutes before ya'call. Ya gotta' gimme'time ta'get in place."

"Whatcha' gon' do?"

"If I told ya'Royce, I'd hafta' kill ya'."

"No shit?"

"Jus' wait five minutes an' call im'."

I ran back to the car, and gathered up the tools of my clandestine assignment. A young woman, who shall remain un-named for security purposes, had left one nylon stocking in the back seat, obviously anticipating my involvment in just such an operation, and I deftly cut two eyeholes, and a mouth slit, and pulled it down on my head till I achieved the proper alignment. Leaving the biggest portion of the leg, and the foot, trailing down my back, I snuck across the parking lot, and took position behind the drink box. I hunkered down, waiting for Arv to emerge from room thirteen. In my hand, I carried letter number two. I was nervous. I knew if I was caught, I'd have to eat it, envelope and all.

Presently, a small bony figure appeared at the door, true to form, in baggy boxer shorts and 'Stanley Kowalskie' wife-beater, staring bleary eyed across the parking lot, and digging in his ass. He started across the lot in a slow shuffling hop, his tender bare feet being pierced and poked by the gravel, oohing' and cursing intermittently as he went.

I waited, my heart floppin' like a flat tire, until he was almost to the car, and I made a mad dash for the room. As luck would have it, he had left the door un-locked, and as I slipped in, I stabbed the door with the ear-bob, securely fastening letter number two in full view. Quickly, I closed the door behind me and searched for a wall socket.

I was exhilarated; 'Napoleon Solo' in a stocking cap. The drop cord plugged, I ran it inconspicuously around the baseboard, and into the closet at the foot of the bed. I wormed my way in behind the hanging cleaner bags that contained Wyvanelle's couture', and settled down to wait, closing the bi-fold doors with my feet. After what seemed an eternity, I heard a muffled,

"Bring it on!"

Then, everything went dark.

59

Betty-Fay rode along in silence, blankly staring at the fence posts as they clicked past like the frames in a silent movie. Shirley's tongue was beating the enamel off the back of her clenched teeth. After what seemed to her an eternity, Betty-Fay turned toward her.

"You gotta' key to tha' store, doncha'?"

For Shirley, the release was as satisfying as a morning movement.

"Oh yeah, I opem' up ever' mornin', an' lock up ever' night. You need sumpn? You need ta'stop? God-a-mighty, what am I sayin'? You'uz just inna'wreck! Need some 'Campho Phenique'? We got tha' big bottles, ya' know, tha' greenuns', an' 'Goody Powders', you probley' need a box o' them, an'a tube o' them 'Doan's Pills', ya' know, fa' ya' back. Some obem' said they work, I don' know, I ain't ever had no back trouble, have you? I mean before now?"

Under normal circumstances, Betty-Fay would have had Shirley's ears pinned back by now, for being so damn nosy, but all the fight seemed to be out of her, replaced by a melancholy vulnerability that was so out of character, as to make her seem like a different person.

"No, I never had back trouble. Don't have it now. Can I ask you a Question?"

"Well of course you can, I'll tell ya' anything you wanna' know, if I know it. You jus' ask away."

"That color you put on your hair; do yall' sell that at tha' store?"

"Oh no, honey, this my real hair color. I don't put nothin'on it. Ize' born blonde." For the first time since the accident, Betty-Fay smiled.

"Well, suppose I wanted ta' make my hair tha' color of yours. Yall' got anything in tha' store that ud' come close?"

"Now we do carry some 'Miss Clairol' products in tha' personal hygiene section, and seems ta' me like, when I was puttin' at' last awder' onna' shef', I seen one at' did look purty' close."

"You happen ta' remember tha' name of it?"

"Let me see. Ya'know, I bleve' tha' name of it's 'Born Blonde', cause I thought, well how odd. Here I am a born blonde, an' I'm puttin' up stock called born blonde. Don'tcha' think at's odd? Anyhow, what r' you askin' for? You ain't thinkin' bout bleachin' ya' hair are ya'? I mean, not tryin' ta' be disrespectful, but aintat' a no-no wi' yall? Besides, much hair as you got, itud' take ever' box in tha' store ta' color it all."

"Not after you cut it."

Shirley ran off the shoulder, and Betty-Fay grabbed the wheel and helped her pull it back in the road.

"Da' you know what you're sayin? Da' you know what you're askin'? Cain't I go ta' Hell fa' that? Aint' at' what dey' burnt at' Joan uv'Arc' woman for? Cuttin'er' hair off?"

"You ever seen a picture of Joey Heatherton? I saw one in a magazine. That's what I wanna' look like. I wont' you ta' cut my hair jus' like hers."

"Aw' God-a-mighty, God-a-mighty, her hair's cut like a man! You musta' hit ya' head innat' wreck an' jus' don't remember. Good God-a-mighty! I'll get fired AN' go ta' hell!"

"I don't think it's considered a sin to cut somebody's hair."

"It is if ya' don't know shit about cuttin' hair!"

"I'll talk ya' through it."

"Don't look ta' me like you know too much about it neither."

Betty-Fay sniggered, surprising herself with such an uncharacteristic outburst, and slowly broke into what would become a heart-healing belly laugh, that was so infectious that nosy Shirley got caught up in it, and as they rolled up in the parking lot at the ranch, they were laughing so hard, that neither one could speak. Shirley stumbled from the car, and motioned Betty-Fay to follow, as they entered the store to gather up the tools of her physical transformation. She held her finger to her lips, and mimed a tip-toe, to warn her that Doil might still be in the office. Betty-Fay quietly slipped out, and followed her in.

60

Datherd prowled the highway and the side roads, sure that sooner or later, the big-haired 'dandy' who had dared to peep on his daughters would have to show his face, and when he did, his ass would belong to him. As he rounded a curve onto a straight, secluded quarter-mile stretch of road, known as a spot frequented by drag racers, he spotted several jacked-up cars, and a group of greasy youth in the darkened parking lot of an abandoned service station, and pulled in close enough to speak.

"Any you boys know a fancy dressin' sumbitch' wiv'a white Evis' hair-do at' drives a Cadillac might live round' here?"

The one nearest walked over to the truck.

"Sounds like Booger Red."

"Red? Naw is' guy's hair's white."

"Itus' red when heus' a kid. Preacher now."

"Preacher my ass. Heus' apeepin' on my girls!"

He leaned in slightly, and spotted the rabbit-eared shotgun in the seat.

"You Datherd Dimond, aint' ya'?"

"Howd' you know?"

"Just a guess. Aint' seen tha' preacher."

"Ya' know where e' lives?"

"Next door ta' tha' church house."

"How ya' get there from here?"

61

The Preacher had been peddling furiously, and his legs, weak from too much fried chicken and inactivity, were failing him. He had to dismount, and push the bike the last couple hundred yards to the parsonage. He leaned the bike against the waist-high porch, sat down, and eased himself backwards, till he was lying down, with his legs dangling over the side. It had been a harrowing night, and he was lucky to be in no worse shape than he was, due no doubt, to his special arrangement with the All-Mighty. As he lay there, his fingers locked behind his head, giving his lungs all the room they needed to re-inflate, he happened to glance back, and up, at the door, and spotted the letter pinned to the door facing.

"What tha' hell?", he thought, and although he was still throbbing from his un-accustomed physical exertion, he rolled over, slowly got to his feet, walked un-steadily over, and pulled the familiar looking ear 'screw' from the wood with one hand, while he held the letter with the other. He opened the door enough to reach in and flip on the porch light, and examined the envelope. He received hate mail from time to time, as powerful, and popular men often do, and he cautiously slid his finger under the flap, and removed the letter. Instantly, the all too familiar smell of 'Jungle Gardenia', rose to meet him, and flooded his memory banks with pictures of Wyvanelle's butter-soft body; images so strong that he started to swoon, as the blood that had only moments before been throbbing in his temples and legs, seemed to have been instantly diverted at the switchyard in his brain, and was now barreling toward his loins like a runaway train. As he read, he struggled to catch his breath. When he finished, he clasped the letter to his chest with both hands.

"Halleujah! Halleujah! I'm back in!"

He jerked up his arm to check the time, and it was then that he found out that his alligator strapped 'dress watch' had been smashed earlier in the evening.

"Shit!"

Dropping the letter, he charged through the door to the kitchen, where a big wall clock hung over a needle-point sampler that read, 'Will you be ready when your time comes'? He was panic stricken when he saw the time. Eleven thirty: and it was a long way to the motel. Without hesitation, and any thought of hygiene or appearance, he charged back through the house, and out the door. Not stopping to close it, or even to grab the letter as he blew past, he jumped off the porch, grabbed up the bicycle, and headed off in the direction of the motel. The muscles that had failed earlier, were now being controlled by the adren-aline injectors in his brain, and though they would eventu-ally un-ravel like the inside of a golf ball when the cover is cut away, as long as they got him to the motel, and that 'Monroe Class' body, he would gladly sacrifice his mobil-ity. The thought of a beautiful woman naked is what drives men to greatness. So it was in the beginning, so it shall be forever.

A scant twenty minutes later, the beat-up, rusty pick-up came creeping up the street, and shuddered to a stop in front of the parsonage. Datherd emerged, gun in hand, and strode purposefully toward the open door. As he climbed the steps, he spotted the letter lying at the thresh-hold, and surmising that it had something to do with the door being left open, he picked it up and read. As he dropped the letter, and it fluttered back to the porch, he pulled his pocket watch from the bib of his overalls and flipped it open.

"Gotcha' now purty' boy."

He snapped it shut, and headed back to the truck.

62

Steve was mesmerized by Wyvanelle, and he hung on her every word. Her life read like Erskine Caldwell, and her smoldering looks hinted at passions and pleasures that only come to men in dreams so salacious, that they jar you awake, for to dream one to the end, one would surely die in his sleep from pure ecstacy. It was the southern equivalent of being bitten by 'Dracula'. The bartender had called his name twice, very loudly, with no result, before the wet bar-towel had splattered his cheek, and shocked him out of his breast-induced coma.

"Phone for ya, Steve."

"What?"

"PHONE!"

"Who is it?"

"Ya' Mamma'!"

"My Mother?"

He made his way to the end of the bar, where the bar-keep was holding the phone in his out-stretched arm.

Wyvanelle, always distrustful of men, had stopped in mid-sentence and was eyeballing the pair with curiosity, watching for tell-tale expressions or baseball style ear pulling & nose tweaking, and straining to hear the open half of the conversation. Steve hesitantly accepted the phone and turned his back toward her, before timidly bringing it to his ear.

"Hello?"

"Hey boy, it's me, Doil. How's she goin' down nere'?"

The look that came across Steve's face was either relief or disgust, it was hard to distuinguish between the two. Either way, he turned and gave her a 'sorry for the needless intrusion' shrug, complete with the obligatory up-turned palm.

"Fine Mother, everything is just fine. Something wrong at home?"

"Naw, so far, so good. Jus' wonted' ta' check on ya', an' give ya' a little advice. You be careful. At' woman you with's a professional. She eats boys like you in batween' meals. She'll have ya' hangin' laundry & paintin' er' toe-nails fore' ya' know whas' hit ya'."

"Gee, I hope so Mother."

"Hope so hell! You wake up in Biloxie pullin' craws' an' workin' like a fiel' hand, you gon' wish you'da listened to ya' Unca' Doil."

"Well, thanks for calling mother."

"Awright, awright, jus' make damn sure she stays away from at' room. You on ya' own."

"Love you too! mean it!"

Wyvanelle's chatty affability faded somewhat, as she sipped her cocktail, and eyed him with suspicion.

"What wasat' all about?"

"Just my mother, wishing me a happy birthday. I'd forgotten about it."

"Really? When is it?"

"Today."

She immediately relaxed, and a seductive smile crossed her glistening, full lips.

"I don't have you a present."

"Just being with you is present enough for me."

"You're dangerously charmin', and quite a liar."

Steve felt his chest tighten, and he falteringly found the courage to speak.

"Why would you call me a liar?"

"Nobody's satisfied with conversation; not on their birthday."

She slid her tongue out of her mouth, and licked the rim of her glass very slowly.

His mesmerization became critical.

"Damn", he thought to himself.

"The gift that keeps on giving."

63

Betty-Fays' decades long head-full of holiness growth was hopelessly tangled and matted from the hundred mile-an-hour winds that had whipped and braided it into scores of knotty lanyards, and it shadowed her upper body like an umbrella. As she and Shirley made their way to the kitchen, she picked up a pair of scissors that lay by the sewing machine as they passed.

"Siddown' Shirley. I told ya' I'd tell ya' what happened if ya' brought me home. You wont' some coffee?"

"Naw hon', it makes me hafta' pee. Does it do at' ta' you? One cuppa'coffee an' I'll be up all night a-peein'."

"We'll skip tha'coffee. Makes me hafta' pee too.——- I made a fool o' myself tonite Shirley. Maybe ebm' wrecked my marriage."

Shirley looked shell-shocked, and for once, she kept her mouth shut and listened, without being told.

"I been havin' is' fantasy about tha' Preacher n' me joinin' up an' savin' is' little boy's soul, an' holdin' meetin',——- holdin' hands;——thinkin' everbody' ud' treat me like I'se sumpn' special, like they used to treat Wyvanelle. All tha' women whisperin' about what it must be like ta' be with a man so important that God chose im' personal like. I did'n care bout' who I hurt, cause Red taught me ta' believe they did'n matter no-way. If they was'nt followin' tha' path, his path, that they's goin' ta' hell anyway. Ebm' Doil: I treated him worst of all, an' he aint' ever been nothin' but good ta' me. I spent a lot o' years learnin' how ta' judge, an' believin' I could pray about them at' I judged un-worthy an' make em' go away,——-or worse. This aint' what God's about."

She raised the scissors, and holding a long, matted strand of her prized holiness mane at arms length, cut it away, and dropped it on the kitchen floor. Shirley was speechless, and sat with her hand over her mouth as Betty-Fay repeated the process, over and over, until the mound of matted hair in the floor was almost as tall as the chair.

"Aint' no turnin' back now Shirley."

She slid the scissors across the table to her. Shirley placed her hand on the scissors, but did'nt pick them up.

"I need a drink."

"In tha' shed."

Shirley dug in her rucksack sized purse and produced a bottle of muscadine wine.

"I got my own. You wanna' taste?"

"Might as well. Got nothin' ta' lose now. It aint' hurt tha' Catholics none."

"To tha' Catholics!"

Shirley turned up the bottle, bubbled it few times, and passed it over.

"Amen."

Betty-Fay took a dainty sip and sat the bottle to the side.

"Now, finish me up."

"I cut my brothers' hair. You want me ta' cut it like his?"

Betty-Fay broke into a broad smile.

"Does he look like Joey Heatherton?"

"A little bit."

"I guess at's close enough. Go to it."

Shirley snipped, and they laughed, and took turns nipping at the wine, like two high school girls getting ready for the prom. Layer after layer of religious callouses peeled away, and with each one, Betty-Fay became lighter, and even younger, and toward the bottom, she began to feel again, and the things that once would have made her angry, now made her laugh, and the laughter, whether she knew it or not, was healing her troubled soul.

"At's tha' best I can do. Ya' wanna' take a look?"

"No, I wont' ya' ta' put tha' proxide' in it. I don't wonta' see me till I'm somebody else. I aint' been too happy with tha' way I was."

Shirley led her to the kitchen sink, and although she had years of experience under her belt, she followed the directions on the box to the letter, still unable to confess her secret. They took their seats again to wait for the magical transformation. They talked and giggled, and even shared a forbidden cigarette. The minutes flew by, and when Shirley removed the cap, what was once a huge, dull pile of oppression, was now a gapped, spikey shock of honey blonde, that would do any runway in Paris proud, and looked as much like freedom as an American flag.

"God-a-mighty. You look like a movie star!"

Betty-Fay reluctantly ran her fingers through her still wet hair.

"Come on, les' rinse it out n' you can take a look."

She leaned over the sink, and Shirley rinsed and rinsed, applied the required solution, and patted it dry with a towel.

"Before I look, will you put some make-up on me?"

"Oh God yes. I always wanted ta' do that. I bleve' I could do make-up in Hollywood. Sometimes I paint up like at' Joan Crawford woman, with big eyebrows an' all. I been meanin' ta' go ova' to tha' funeral home an' see if they need somebody ta' paint tha' dead, jus' fa' practice an' all. You jus' siddown' an' let ol' Shirley work er' magic."

After several minutes of pain-staking daubin' and blanchin', Shirley pulled her from the chair and led her to the bathroom.

"Now close ya' eyes."

She pulled her in, and positioned her in front of the vanity mirror.

"Okay honey, you can opem' up now."

As she slowly raised her eyelids, she was met with an image that was as shocking as seeing a ghost, for she thought it long dead. Huge tears rolled down her cheeks, making ruts in the freshly applied cosmetic.

"Aw hon', whas' tha' matter? Don't ya' like it?"

"It's beautiful. I look jus' like Joey Heatherton."

"Ya' do honey. Ya' really do."

64

'A bicycle ride, a cool drink o'water, an' a piece o' tail ud' kill me about now.'

It was a saying as common to these parts as re-capped tires, and one whose basis in fact was about to narrow into sharp focus as the preacher came careening into the gravel lot at the 'Shady Lawn', oblivious to the patrol car that he almost struck. Lungs burning, legs so weak he could barely stand, he somehow managed to slide the bike across the concrete sidewalk and jump off, before it hit the motel wall. He grabbed hold of a porch pole and held himself up, as he struggled to clear the black spots from his vision, by swallowing enormous mouthfuls of air.

The last of the spots began to fade, and the look of utter exhaustion on his face morphed into a lecherous grin, as his eyes came into focus on darkened room thirteen, the door slightly ajar. Almost instantly, the last of his energy reserves were called up, like the Alabama National Guard on registration day, and he stood erect, and tip-toed toward his reward.

In the inky darkness, Arv lay on the spinning bed, the anticipation of having his fantasies concerning Seven fulfilled, having caused him to drain the remainder of the bottle to steady his nerves. He waited patiently, like a catfish, for a tempting odor to pass under his nose, and prompt him to suck her in like a chicken liver.

Red cautiously surveyed the parking lot for witnesses, slipped off his wing-tips, and held them in one hand, as he quickly opened the door and disappeared, silently closing it behind him.

As for me, the exitement of my 'Mission Impossible' assignment had faded considerably as I sat scrunched up in the blackness of the closet, and as the minutes ticked away, I had fallen fast asleep, with my chin resting on my chest.

65

In the bar, Steve was getting dangerously close to losing his perspective.

"Why doncha' get your buddy there to mix up a thermos fulla' martinis, and we'll go back to your room and blow out your candles."

"I don't have any candles. I don't even have a cake."

"Oooh, po' baby. Then we'll hafta' find somethin' else to blow."

Steve's resolve started to melt like a cone of ice cream in a hot station wagon. He was on the verge of capitulation, when Doil's voice, like a siren's song, came drifting back into his head, knocking at the door of his consciousness.

"An' remember, I got fim'onya'."

Steve's leaping man-spirit began to do battle with his sense of self-preservation.

"What's the penalty for accessory to kidnapping?" He wondered.

"Twenty five years? With good behavior, probably be out in fifteen. Might be worth it. My God, look at the body on this woman. I might not ever get a shot like this again. I might be gone tomorrow; hit by a bus; struck by lightning. The Russian's could attack."

He had opted for surrender, when way back in the dark recesses of his depravity, once more, he heard a tiny voice. It was Doil's.

"Remember, at' woman's a professional."

Whether it was the legendary Pettyjohn show bidness' acumen, or the last vestige of Steve's moral fibre, rising like a phoenix from his charred character, it's hard to say; but one thing was sure. He would get to spend the rest of his life as a free man, at least as far as his involvement this situation was concerned.

"Maybe we ought to stay here. The maids have'nt made up my room."

He knew the instant that it came out of his mouth, that he had blown his shot. Wyvanelle was indeed, a professional, and her radar, that had been turning slowly, trying to pick up signals, was now a bomb-sight, and he was lined up in the cross-hairs. Years of dealing with men had taught her what the 'Pavlovian' response should be when she rung the bell, and she knew instantly, when he hesitated, that something else was afoot.

"Really, and I so wanted to get outta' this ol' dress. It's so,—— confining."

Steve, as bright as he was, had exhausted his mental resources, and as he sat before her, defeated and demoralized, he racked his brain for a witticism, or a compliment that might salvage the situation, and land him even yet in the pastoral valley between her breasts.

"I'd love to see your tattoo."

Unfortunately for the cameraman, that was'nt it. Her alarms sounded, and that helpless, oppressive, 'feel like you're gonna' implode feeling that overcomes men when they're in the ire of an angry woman, blanketed him like a dry cleaning bag, and he started to suffocate.

"OH, YOU WOULD, WOULD YA'? AND JUS' HOW THE HELL WOULD YOU KNOW THAT I

HAD A TATTOO? BEEN TALKIN' TA' PETTYJOHN?"

She stood, her alabaster complexion tinged with crimson, tossed her martini in Steve's emotionless, depressed face, and stormed out of the bar, with Steve, very near blinded, and dripping with gin, hot on her heels.

He caught up with her on the sidewalk to the motel, and grabbed her arm in an attempt to stop her and apologize, but she wheeled around and slapped him so hard that snot flew out of his nose. They stood, face to face, as she blistered him with invective, and the snot and gin formed a 'snail trail' that creeped down his cheek.

So consumed were they, that neither even paid notice to the shadowy figure with the rabbit-eared shotgun that passed between them like a ghost, headed in the direction of room thirteen.

66

Doil, having set all the wheels in motion in this scripted train wreck, and satisfied that his casting instincts had been correct, locked the office, and headed for home, to put as much distance as possible between himself, and the drama that would be un-folding shortly at the motel. As he turned in and started up the drive, he met Nosy Shirley on her way out, and had to swerve off the drive into the yard to avoid being hit head-on.

"DAMMIT SHIRLEY, GETYA' HEAD OUTTA' YA' ASS!"

She never checked up, having finished off that bottle of muscadine wine, she just waved and yelled,

"Sorry unca' Doil," as she splintered the mail box post, and swerved off down the blacktop, with the mailbox sitting on the hood, the flag raised. Doil saluted it as she disappeared into the darkness.

"Goofy bitch." he mumbled, as he pulled back into the driveway and headed for the house.

Most of the lights were off, as was the custom when Betty-Fay retired for the evening, her self-absorption having not allowed her to consider that others might want, or require illumination after she took her leave. Doil fumbled around in the kitchen, and fixed himself a big bowl of raisin bran, as was his custom before retiring, as he said it kept all systems functioning properly, and capped it with a spoon-rattling belch, before attending to his 'toilette'. They had repeated this process every night for years. Doil in his boxer's, tip–toeing through the darkened bedroom, careful not to wake the sleeping pentinent who lay as far on the opposite side of the bed as space would permit, rolled up in the sexual security of her blankets and quilts like a big burrito. He slipped under the sheet, and lying on his back, locked his chubby fingers behind his head, just like always. It was Doil's time for quiet reflection, and meditation, in the minutes before he drifted off to dreamland.

"Is it my destiny to be poor? Have I struggled and sacrificed all these years in vain? Or has it taken this much time to prepare myself for greatness? Is this kid my Elvis? My 'chicken that lays the golden egg' as it were?"

As he pondered these cosmic questions, he noticed an un-accustomed warmth in the bed next to him. It had been so long since he had experienced close physical contact with another human, that he assumed that the dog had slipped into the bed. Suddenly, he felt a hand on his chest, and it scratched around in the sparse patch of pubic quality hair that nestled like a patch of moss between his man-boobs.

"She's dreamin' bout scratchin' tha dog. No wonder he sleeps in here."

"Doil?"

"Shit, she's awake." he thought.

"Yeah, you wont' me ta' put tha' dog out?"

"What dog, dear?"

Doil turned his head toward the sound of her voice.

She's gotta' be dreamin'. Callin' me dear?

"Tha' one in tha' bed," he said softly.

"There's not a dog in tha' bed."

"What tha' hell", he thought, and he reached over to feel for himself. To his shock, and amazement, what his hand came in contact with was not canine, but the unmistakable curves of a female form, and the heat from her body sent shock waves up his arm.

"Jesus", he thought. "One'a Shirley's ugly-ass' girlfriends has crawled in here drunk. Tha' ol' lady'll kill me for sure if she wakes up."

He leaned toward her and whispered,

"You gotta' get outta' here fore' you wake tha' wife up. She'll kill bofus'."

"She IS awake."

Now he was dumbfounded. The voice in the darkness sounded like Betty-Fay, but that was impossible, because human physical contact in the 'prone' position, is a mortal sin, or so he had been informed in no un-certain terms. Confused and curious, he leaned in the opposite direction, and felt his way up the bedside lamp to the switch and twisted it on. It took a moment for his eyes to adjust to the light, so he leaned on his elbow and waited. He felt the hand once again, as a finger slowly ran down the length of his spine.

"Now looky here", he said, as he rolled over.

"AAAAAAAAAAAAAAAAAAHHHHHHHHHHHH HHHHH!"

He jumped out of bed, caught his heel in the sheet, fell backwards over a chair, and crashed into the dresser, banging his head, and sending 'Avon Body Talc' flying in every direction. It settled on his face and chest like volcanic ash, making the patch of hair on his chest appear to be frosted, like snow on the trees in an alpine valley. Holding the knot on the back of his head, and spitting out clumps of powder, He made no effort to get up; just sat there, covered in talcum, staring in utter dis-belief, at the woman in his bed. A woman who looked for all the world, like Joey Heatherton. She was sitting upright, wearing one of Doil's striped dress shirts. It was un-buttoned, and though it revealed very little, it was obvious that it was all she was wearing. With her spikey blond hair, freshly manicured and painted nails, and coquettish' expression, she had the appearance of a 'Playboy' centerfold. She patted the mattress tenderly.

"Come on back to bed baby."

Doil rubbed the knot and shook his head.

"I musta' knocked mysef'out. This caint' be real."

He rubbed the powder from his eyes, blinked hard, and looked back toward the bed.

"It's real honey, it's me. You aint' dreamin'. Come get inna' bed."

Doil pinched himself hard, just to make sure, and when the image remained the same, he rose to his knees, clasped his hands together, and started to pray.

"Lord, I don' know what tha' hell happened here tonite, an' I really don't care. I know I aint' done much ta' deserve it, but if at' really is my wife in at' bed, an'you let me keep er', I won't ever do nothin' underhanded agin'. Swear ta' God!"

He slowly got up, and walked over to the bed. Betty-Fay held out her hand to him.

"I'm so sorry Doil."

"Sorry fa' what?"

"Everything."

"You aint' gotta' pologize' ta' me. I forgot how beautiful you are. You look just like at' Joey Heatherton."

"Get back in bed baby."

Doil reached for the lamp switch.

"Naw", she whispered. "Leave it on."

67

Datherd took on the appearance of a timberwolf as he approached room thirteen. He cast a furtive glance over his shoulder at the couple he had just passed between. They had not moved. She was still administering a tongue lashing to the down cast young man who stood, stoop-shouldered, in front of her, obviously not the tongue treatment that he was counting on.

"Poor bastard", thought Datherd as he reached to try the door knob. It was un-locked. He scanned the parking lot once, took a deep breath, opened the door very slowly, and stepped inside. It was pitch dark in the curtained room, the only illumination coming from the open door, and that being very little. His eyes were slow in adjusting, as he edged slowly toward the bed, gun in hand, tip-toeing to maintain the element of surprise.

The Preacher, who had slipped in just moments before, was positioned to his left, silently dis-robing, in preparation for his glorious re-union with his hot-blooded ex. He had heard the door open, and was holding his breath, for though there was very little light in the parking lot, there was enough to illuminate the two dark barrells that preceeded the sinister shadow into the room. An image that was all too familiar.

Still unable to see clearly, Datherd gently touched the mattress, feeling for signs of life. Finding nothing, he inched his way closer to the head of the bed and leaned over, trying to locate his target. Just as his hand made contact with flesh, two bony hands shot up out of the darkness, grabbed him around the neck, and yanked him down, as a long, lumpy tongue that tasted of 'Prince Albert' and 'Jack Daniels', forced it's way into his mouth, and halfway down his throat. Overcome with terror, Datherd dropped his shotgun, and one of the barrells fired, lighting up the room like a flame thrower, and blowing the light fixture through the acoustic tile ceiling. He was pushing with both hands, trying to extricate himself from the hellish creature that was attempting to swallow his tongue. Arv was sot drunk, and locked like a leech, onto what he thought in his stupor, to be Seven's enormous mouth.

The shotgun blast instantly jarred me awake, and I burst out of the closet, with floodlights beaming, and camera rolling. The Preacher, who had been too terrified to move, still standing over to the left of the bed, was blinded by the sudden, glaring hi-beams, which crippled him even further. My eyes too, were desperately trying to adjust to the overpowering glow, but I aimed the camera in the general direction of the action, and never took my finger off the trigger, just like Doil had instructed. Being on the back side of the lights, I gained vision quickly, but after gaining, I wondered if I might not go blind from the horribly grotesque tableaux that greeted me. There, on the bed, was Arvin Kilgore, world class chicken fighter, as nekkid' as a new-born, with his long, bony fingers locked behind the head of a pulp-wooder in a dirty flannel shirt, their mouths seemingly locked, making all manner of disgusting gagging, grunting, and gurgling noises. The pulp wooder was on all-fours, trying to push away, but Arv was locked fast, his unbelievably skinny legs wrapped around his waist, hanging on like a spider monkey, his ugly-ass feet locked tight. I had to choke back the urge to puke.

Practically everyone at the motel had heard the shotgun blast. Wyvanelle and Steve, who were only a few feet away, were there almost instantly. Wyvanelle charged into the room, just as Datherd tried to push away, and she stood, staring in utter dis-belief, as I filmed the horrific scene. Then she spotted Booger Red. He was standing in the middle of his discarded clothing, rubbing his eyes, trying to maintain his balance. He too was nekkid', that is, except for pair of electric blue, women's bikini panties.

"Are those my panties? ARE THOSE MY PANTIES, YOU SON-OF-A BITCH?"

In a fit of rage, she ran over, grabbed up the shotgun that was lying on the bed, wheeled around, aimed it directly at the Reverend, cocked and pulled the trigger on the barrel that had already fired, resulting in nothing more than a metallic 'click'. An outcome due no doubt, to the Preacher's celestial connections. It was at that instant, that the high sheriff marched into the room, and following the script to the letter, said

"What tha' Hell is goin' on in here?"

Wyvanelle immediatlely turned and pointed the gun straight at him, at which point he started to back-pedal, lost his footing, and fell backwards through the door, knocking down his deputy, who in turn, knocked down Steve, and they all started to crawl on their elbows toward the parking lot, and away from this magnificently endowed, heavily armed woman. The split second reprieve had allowed the preacher to regain his balance, AND his vision, and as she swung the gun back intending to finish him off, in the time it took for her to pull back the rabbit-ear, he dove through the window, sending shards of glass, and splinters tinkling over the hood of the truck that was parked outside. A milli-second later, she fired, taking out what little was left of the window, and blowing the porch-pole clean in two, causing a small section of the porch to fall, and land right on Cecil's 'puscle-gut'.

The stylishly pantied minister, who looked as though he'd been run through a cheese grater, scrambled to his feet, jumped on the bicycle, and tore out down the walkway that ran between the rooms and the office. Royce's resident 'cat in estrus', was on the walk, howling like a panther, and he screamed,

"Get outta' tha' way!" as he barreled toward her. This was not, however,'cat in heat' howling, but regular feeding time, feline 'vocalizing', and just as Red got up a full head of steam, Royce opened the screen door to feed 'pussy', and sent bicycle, rider, screen wire, feline, and electric blue bikini panties, tumbling in a big ball down the walkway. This, unfortunately, was not caught on film, but reported in detail later by Steve, who had crawled under the afore-mentioned truck during the melee' to gain a safe vantage point.

Back at room thirteen, Wyvanelle had turned her attention to Arv, who was still hanging like a baby possum under the belly of the struggling Datherd Dimond. She stepped to the foot of the bed, and using the empty shotgun as a pitchfork, poked the big steel barrells, as hard as she could, square in Arv's pitifully bony ass. He subsequently opened his eyes, intending to scream out in pain, but upon seeing that the mouth that he was exploring was not that of his dream date, it froze in his throat, and as he locked eye to eye with him, he felt Datherd's store-bought teeth clamp down hard on his probing tongue. He would surely have bitten it off, had not Wyvanelle backed up, and grasping the shotgun by the barrels, executed a round-house, full-arm swing, and whacked Datherd across the butt with the gun-stock, causing him to instantly release Arv's tongue, and the both of them to scream like two schoolgirls at their first horror movie.

The deputy had managed to clear the lumber off Cecil's 'puscle- gut', and helped him to his feet. He was peeping around the door facing with his hand on his weapon. Wyvanelle spotted him the instant his bald head appeared, and she grabbed up the lamp and sent it crashing into the wall, just inside the door, spraying the walkway with broken pieces of the house trailer quality fixture. The shade rolled to a stop next to Steve, hiding under the truck.

"Screw it", said Cecil, as he cocked his head toward the patrol car, and motioned the deputy away, following in a semi-crouch, hoping to avoid more flying debris.

Royce was desperately trying to free 'pussy' from the wadded-up' screen wire enclosure that she shared with the Preacher, before whoever took a shot at him came to finish the job. It was evident that pussy was not happy about her current circumstance, from the cacophonous howling and hissing, and the screams of the Preacher, as she tore out chunks of flesh and hair-do. The instant that Royce created a hole, she buried the claws on all four feet in Red's bare chest, and shot into the darkness like a roman candle.

The self-proclaimed county savior, bruised and bloodied, fought his way out of the twisted debris, and bounded off on his bare feet, the crack of his butt shining over the top of the electric blue panties, as he disappeared into the night.

Royce yelled out,

"Faggit" when he was sure that he was out of earshot. He looked around just in time to see Cecil and the deputy climbing into the cruiser.

"Hey! Where yall' goin'? Ain't ya' gon' do sumpn'? Who gon' pay for is' mess?"

Cecil rolled down the window as he drove out.

"Talk ta at' woman in room thirteen, She'll take care uv' ya'."

Royce looked toward the room, and saw Wyvanelle standing in the door glaring, so he ran in the office and hid behind the desk.

Datherd and Arv stood, looking down at the floor, each tenderly rubbing his respective ass, too overcome with guilt and shame to be angry. Both were speechless, and had the air of boys caught playing with themselves in the cloak-room. Arv held a pillow over his privates.

All of this transpired in a matter of seconds, and how I had managed to live this long is no small miracle in itself. I was still filming as Wyvanelle started toward me. There was, however, something much less threatening about her, and instead of the all-out thrashing that I deserved, she stopped, and started studying me thoughtfully, her innate business sense overcoming her 'IF IT'S GOT BALLS, KILL IT' sense of righteous indignation.

"Turn it off," she said, very calmly, but with intense sense of purpose.

Now I love Doil Pettyjohn, and there's almost nothing within reason that I would'nt do for him, but not being sure that I loved him enough to lose an eye, or possibly a testicle for him, I did as I was told, and shut it off. Immediately, we were plunged into darkness. At this point, I should have run. Maybe I was a little ashamed, and embarrassed too.

"Maybe you should leave tha' lights on an' jus' turn tha' camera off."

"Yes maam."

When I turned the light bar back on, Datherd had nervously edged a few inches toward the door, trying to somehow make a graceful exit, despite the circumstance. Wyvanelle accommodated him in no uncertain terms, by pointing her finger in his face and announcing,

"You; out! And don't forget your gun."

Datherd sheepishly stooped to pick up the firearm, never glancing at Wyvanelle, or myself, and slowly made his way to the door, stopping just before he stepped out, as though conflicted, struggling with his newly awakened inner feelings. He turned slowly to Arv.

"Will ya' call me?" he said quietly as he dropped his head and left the room. Arv did'nt speak, but timidly waved him good-bye.

Wyvanelle confronted me.

"I want that film!"

"It duddn' belong ta'me."

"I did'n ask ya' who it belongs to. I said I want it."

Now having grown up around Doil and Waddell, and coming from a long line of mule-traders and car dealers my-self, I had witnessed a fair amount of negotiation, and I sensed that now was my time to honor that noble tradition, and 'horse trade'.

"Whas' it worth to ya?"

"I don' know. What's yer' balls worth ta' YOU?"

My sense of self-preservation took precedent over any loyalties I felt still due Doil at this crucial, final stage of the negotiation, and secure in the knowledge that I'd upheld the family honor, I handed the camera to Wyvanelle.

"And take Steve with ya' when ya' go."

"Yes maam."

I made my way out through the debris, and quietly called out for the cameraman. He did'nt answer, just poked his hand out from under the running board on the truck. I squatted, lowered my head and peeked under. He appeared to be terrified.

"Is the shooting over?"

"Yeah, it's over, come on out."

"I'm afraid she'll kill me."

"Naw', she's cooled off now. She ain't gon' kill nobody."

Just to make sure, I raised up to see if she was listening.

"She's outta' ammo' anyway. Said ta' take you wim-me'."

Steve crawled out and nervously dusted himself off, never taking his eyes off the door. The flickering light from a candle was visible in the darkened room, and we could see movement in the shadows.

"Perfume candles, I seen em' when I snuck in tha' room. Probley' burns em' ta' cover up tha' smell uv' Arv's stinkin' ass."

We started walking toward my car. I glanced toward the office, and saw Royce behind the desk, motioning for me to come there. I half-heartedly shot him a bird and continued walking. I knew he would'nt come out. We sat down in the car and locked the doors. The security felt like home.

"What are you going to tell Doil about giving her the film?"

"I'll tell im' I had to; she pulled a knife on me."

"Did she?"

"Why hell no. But like Doil always says; if what ya' got ta' say won't produce tha' desired dramatic effect, LIE! At's what sho' bidness' is all about."

I cranked the car, and we slowly drove away.

68

Runt weaver was at the empty courthouse early, sitting on the ergonomically in-correct wooden church pew that served as the torture device for those seeking audience with the judge, pouring over his notes, and organizing his appeal on behalf of the Pettyjohns.

The judge, who had yet to arrive, was a former country lawyer, with wisdom garnered from advanced age, and an un-wavering belief in the judicial system. He knew all of the concerned parties, if not personally, by reputation, but he was considered a fair man, and not apt to cloud his decision with personal prejudice.

Doil rolled over and smacked his lips a couple of times in an attempt to reverse the effects of 'moose mate' snoring, which is so prevalent in men of girth, and which dries, and numbs the passages adjacent to, and just above the 'swaller' pipe. He managed to force one crusty eyelid open, and focused his bloodshot eye on the spikey, blonde 'rat nest', nestled un-characteristically close to him in the bed. He snuggled up tight, and the heat from her nakedness warmed him like seasoned hickory, burning in a fireplace. She was still sleeping peacefully, and as he leaned over to kiss her still-flushed cheek, that one 'gummy' eye fell on the wind-up alarm clock that squatted, ignored, and un-set, on the bed-side table.

"Shit, it's eight o'clock already! We gon' be late fa' tha' judge!"

Betty-Fay opened her eyes and smiled sweetly.

"We got time", she whispered, as she put her arms around his near nonexistent neck and pulled him down, to kiss him lovingly on his pudgy, parched lips. He offered no resistance.

Wyvanelle rose early. Arv was piled up in the tub like a dirty wash-rag, having been banished from the relative comfort of the bed, for his conspiratorial indiscretion. His nicotine crusted lungs made the forlorn sound of a rusty gate hinge blowing back and forth in the wind, as he slept. She stepped into the bathroom, and fastidiously applied her make-up. Up until her long lost Daddy's un-timely death, her looks had been her sole asset, and she maintained them with the same attention to detail that she employed in her business dealings. It was all a business to her. She gave herself a final once-over, and as emotionless as an executioner, she turned on the shower. The water was as cold as a whore's heart. Arv howled and sputtered as the freezing 'wake-up call' sent his alcohol fueled internal temperature plunging into the full body shiver zone. She left room thirteen quietly, and closed the door behind her, Doil's letter gently swinging on the 'ear–bob'. Scanning the parking lot, she spotted Steve's equipment truck, un'-moved, and empty.

"Dammit', you can't depend on nobody!", she mumbled under her breath as she stalked off toward the other end of the motel, and Seven's room.

She knocked, discreetly at first, but when she got no response she pounded harder and harder, finally banging the door with her fist and yelling for Seven to,

"Open this damn door!"

At last the door burst open, and standing before her, the bright morning sun illuminating him like a cherub in a classical painting, was Pee Wee. He was as naked as a 'skint' squirrel, bleary-eyed from the brandy, hair sticking out in every direction, and holding his 'fabled and storied' manhood with both hands. He threw his little head back, and 'crowed' like a rooster.

"AAAAAAAAHHHHHHHH!" she screamed.

Not the cry of one shocked and sickened by such a disgusting display, but the angry cry of a general whose battle plan has just been wrecked by a flank attack. She raised her fist high in the air, and brought it down with a resounding 'thud' on the top of Pee Wee's head.

"Cock-a-doodle-do' that, ya' little bastard!"

As Pee Wee dropped to his knees, she took off running toward room thirteen, stopping to remove her spike heeled shoes for speed, and yanking down the letter, as she stormed back in. She found Arv, still shivering in the bathroom. He was as blue as a corpse, and his chattering teeth echoing off the tile, made the place sound like an old timey' telegraph office.

"We been had!" she yelled, "Get dressed!"

But Arv was too cold to respond, and appeared to be on the verge of hypo-thermia.

"We gotta' get ta' tha' courthouse, snap out of it!"

There was still no response from Arv, who seemed to be half-conscious, and still drunk.

"I said get dressed!"

She reared back, and popped him on the cheek with the palm of her hand, and sent him tumbling backwards into the tub once again, banging himself up pretty badly as he crashed into the cold porcelain. Then, with all the compassion of a concentration camp guard, she reached in, and turned on the hot shower water, scalding him like a freshly plucked chicken, and shocking back to sobering reality, every freezing cell in his body. He screamed, and dove out of the tub, and onto the cooling relief of the tile floor. She threw a pair of pants and a shirt on top of his tortured, steaming head.

"And hurry up!"

Conway sat at the kitchen table, devouring a 'ho-cake' that was swimming in a plate full of sorghum syrup. Waddell appeared, fresh from a bath, dripping wet, wrapped in a beach towel decorated with brightly colored fish. His wet hair was slicked straight back, and stuck to his head.

"Sumpn' smells good in here, sides' me. Got another one o' them ho-cakes?"

Elsie dropped a big, flat one on a plate and sat it next to Conway.

"You don't mind if I join ya' do ya' boy? I know whatcha' thinkin'. You thinkin' is' guy puts me inna' mind uv' Clark Gable. An' you'd be right! Slide me at' canna' soggum' ova'here, if they's any left in it. Onliest' otha' boy I eva' seen eat at' much soggum' got sa' fat they had ta' wheel im' aroun' in a wheel barra', an' thas' a fact!"

Elsie sat down with a biscuit, shaking her head. She had poured them each a cup of steaming hot coffee, and Conway watched attentively as Waddell poured his into the saucer, and picked it up, with both his pinky fingers sticking daintily in the air. He rested his elbows on the table for balance, and placing the saucer next to his lips, he blew across it gently a few times, before slurping in a big mouthful, that made a sound like a hoover on a wet rug. Conway followed suit, making a point to try and slurp as loud as Waddell. Elsie continued to shake her head.

"It's purty' early. We probley' got time ta' wet a hook r' two fo' we gotta' be at tha' cawthouse', if you a'mind to."

Conway was out the door before it was completely out of Waddell's mouth.

"Lemmee' get my britches on!", he yelled after him.

Elsie gave him a sly smile.

"You gon' rurn' at' boy, Waddell."

"If teachin' a boy to fish'll rurn' im', consider him rurnt'."

At ten minutes to nine, the judge strode into the courthouse, accompanied by 'puscle-gutted' sheriff, Cecil Dowd. By this time, Runt was pacing the floor in front of his chambers, his butt having gone numb from time spent on the penitent's pew, and deeply concerned that he had not seen, or heard from Doil, whose was known to be as punctual as a train schedule.

"Counselor, where are the principles?"

"They'll be here any minute now your honor. You know Doil. You could set your watch by him."

"Uh huh; just don't set your wallet by im'. We start at nine sharp; with or without, if you know what I mean. I did'nt give up a Saturday mornin' of bird huntin' to be stood up."

"I understand completely."

'Puscle gut' Cecil, always awkward and intimidated by the educated, had said nothing, and followed the judge as he opened the door and entered his chambers. Runt caught him by the arm, startling him.

"Can I have a word with you sheriff?"

"I guess."

The counselor reached in, and gently closed the door behind the judge.

"Anything goin' on that I need to know about Cecil?"

The sheriff leaned over, and placed his ear close to the door to make sure the judge was busy, and could'nt overhear.

"They was a hell uva' row' at tha' motel las' night. Datherd Dimond tried ta' shoot Arv Kilgore an' Booger Red. At' big-knockered ex-ol' lady ov' tha' Preacher's Damn near shot me. Blowed tha' front offa' room thirteen."

"How did Datherd Dimond get involved in this?"

"Beats tha' hell outta' me."

"Did you try to stop em'?"

"Hell no I did'nt try ta' stop em'! Is' job don't pay enough ta' get killed. I did what what Doil told me, an I got tha' hell out from there."

"Wait a minute. You mean to tell me that Doil engineered all that?"

Suddenly Cecil realized that he was talking out of school, and dropped his head like an embarrassed school boy.

"He did'nt mean for there ta' be no shootin'. Datherd he—-"

Cecil stopped in mid-sentence at the sound of heels clicking on the hardwood floor of the courthouse. They both turned to see the preacher, battered and bruised, striding with a wide ambling gait, compliments of a sensible shoe, straight for them.

"Oh hell," they both said in unison.

The Preacher was in his glory, decked out in fresh sharkskin, wing-tips polished to a high sheen, and a matinee' idol hairdo that would make Charlton Heston appear a mere pretender to the throne. As he got closer, band-aids and bandages were visible on his face and hands, and there were claw marks evident through one eyebrow; mute testimony to 'pussy's influence on his overall appearance. He passed between them, never uttering a word, or acknowledging their presence, and disappeared into the judge's chambers, closing the door behind him.

"Guess she missed im'."

"Too bad."

The counselor looked at his watch.

"Two minutes to nine. Where the hell is Doil?"

Almost instantly, they heard the distinctive squeak of the courthouse doors, and two pairs of footsteps. They stared at each other intently, trying to discern from the echoes if it was in fact, Doil and Betty-Fay. One was the piercing clack of spike heels. The other was a slow, shuffling, as if a determined mother was dragging a reluctant toddler to his first day of school.

"That don't sound good."

"No shit."

Moments later, Wyvanelle and Arv rounded the corner. She was dressed impeccably in a business suit designed to make her appear less curvaceous and more corporate, but it failed miserably, and with every click of her heels, her voluptuous flesh tried to wiggle itself free from this bland and sexless prison. Arv, on the other hand, looked like an un-made bed. Clothes wrinkled, shoes un-tied, and a big, red hand print on his cheek. His shuffling gait bespoke the damage that a shotgun barrel does to the human rectal arena. As they approached the chambers, she reached into her purse. Fearing the worst, the sheriff ran inside, and took up a position beside the judge's desk. Much to the counselor's relief, she pulled the note from the desk clerk informing Arv of his required presence, and held it in his face as they passed him on their way in. They took seats on the opposite side of the room from the preacher. Cecil inched closer to the judge.

"Nine o'clock counselor, let's get this over with."

Runt nodded, and resigned himself to the fact that he was about to let Doil down, albeit by no fault of his own. As he slowly made his way in, he heard the front doors burst open yet again, and the staccato slap of running feet in the distant hallway. He poked his head out to see Doil, and what appeared to be Joey Heatherton, come round the corner at a dead run. The wooden floor was as slick as glass from the oily 'floor sweep' that the janitor spread liberally on the weekends, and as Runt watched, Doil's feet shot out from under him, and he crashed to the floor, the momentum of his bulk carrying him past the judges's door on his back.

"Was that Pettyjohn that just slid past?"

"It was, your honor."

"Well when he slides to a stop. Have him come in here. Is that his wife?"

"Not sure, your honor. A moment to confer?"

"You got two minutes; no more."

"Betty-Fay? Is that you?"

"Hello Samuel", she chirped as she hugged him hard, and kissed him on the cheek. He could hardly believe his eyes. This former dour, humorless pentinent, who had dressed like a kremlin chambermaid, was as pert and perky as Brenda Lee, and clad like a teenager in one of Doil's white shirts with a bold red stripe, the gold tassled 'cinch' cord off the living room curtains for a belt, ala' Scarlett o'Hara, with bobby socks, and a pair of tennis shoes. The counselor, though possessed of tremendous powers of reason, was speechless. Doil struggled to his feet, wheezing like a bellows.

"Ain't she sumpn' Runt? Ain't she sumpn'?"

He was as proud as a man with a new beagle.

"An' now we gon' have children. We gon' have it all! Colonel Parker ain't gon' have shit on me. An' Betty-Fay's as purty as Priscilla.—God-aw'-mighty, what a life!"

"Don't start celebratin' yet. The Preacher, his ex-wife, and Arvin Kilgore are all in there."

"What tha' heller' they doin' here? I figgered"—-

"You figured what?"

"Nothin, we'll deal with it."

Betty-Fay was crestfallen.

"Baby, don't you worry bout nothin'. Runt weaver is tha' best damn lawyer inna' country, and he gon' make sure you get at' girl an' er' baby. Ain't at' right Runt?"

Once again, the counselor was speechless. He knew that there was a snowball's chance in hell of this happening now, but he loved Doil Pettyjohn and Betty-Fay, and he would fight to his last breath not to disappoint them. He just smiled and nodded. Betty-Fay hugged his neck.

"I'm mighty proud of you Samuel."

"We better get in there, the judge is waiting. Where are Elsie and the boy?"

"You mean they ain't here? They're wi' Waddell. Ain't like im' ta' be late. They orta' be here any minute."

"If they're not here quick, were sunk."

Steve and myself had, since the fiasco at room thirteen, been attempting to purge our troubled souls through conversation, confession, and strong drink. A process that had taken all night, and produced several strong opinions about the current proceedings, the Pettyjohn supremacy, and the enormity of Wyvanelle's bosom, which we concluded that Steve would never be privy to. Though uninvited, our heightened powers of reason seemed to indicate that the situation at the courthouse would be better served by our presence, so off we went. Luckily, for us at least, the old courthouse, like most country courthouses at the time, was not air-conditioned, and we were able to take a strategic position outside the judge's open window, in case, God forbid, we were needed. The judge got straight down to business.

"This is an informal hearing to determine fitness and qualification for adoption of one Elsie Freeman, a young woman, and her child, one Conway Twitty Freeman, by Mr. And Mrs. Doil Willy Rufus Pettyjohn."

A snigger erupted in the chambers.

"Willy Rufus?" I whispered to Steve, who shrugged drunkenly.

"Where is the mother and child?"

"They'll be here any second your honor."

"Well, it's probably good that the boy does'nt hear everything. I'll hear from those present, pro and con, one at a time, in an orderly, and respectful fashion. Do we understand each other? Good; you." and he pointed to the Preacher, who stood up, and pulled his embroidered hanky from his suit-coat pocket.

"Ya' honor, I am the Reverend O.C. Dalrymple, representing tha' All mighty, and I am here ta'tell you that Doil Pettyjohn is"———-At that point, Betty Fay jumped to her feet, and pointed at the preacher.

"Yo' honor, that man is a damn scoundrel!"

"Hear, hear Miz' Pettyjohn, I said one at a time."

The judge had no more gotten that said , when Wyvanelle stood up.

"He's not only a damn scoundrel, he's a pervert! And I got tha' film ta' prove it!" and with that, she pulled the brownie-eight from her purse, and held it out to the judge.

Arv jumped up and grabbed the camera.

"You cain't show im' at' movie!"

"Shut up! ya' wormy bastard."

Wyvanelle's blood was up, and she lost all sense of reason. She pushed Arv back down into his chair. The Preacher lost control of his Burt Lancaster voice, and in a high pitched squeal cried,

"That film is a fake, cooked up in Hollywood by her and her lesbian lover to dis-credit me an' my ministry."

The judge was pounding on his desk.

"PEOPLE, PEOPLE, LES' EXERCISE SOME DAMN CONTROL HERE!"

Wyvanelle turned to face Doil, who was still seated;

"And you, ya' son-uv-a-bitch!"

Betty-Fay reached over and grabbed a handful of Wyvanelle's impeccably coiffed hair.

"Who you callin' a sov-a-bitch, ya' damn tramp?"

Arv grabbed Betty-Fay's arm, and was attempting to pull Wyvanelle free, when Doil back-handed him, turning him a flip backwards out of his chair.

Cecil was cowering behind the judge.

"SHERIFF, ARREST THESE DAMN FOOLS IF THEY CAN'T BEHAVE."

We were enjoying the show so much, that we did'nt even notice Waddell's truck as it bounced into the parking lot. Runt was pulling people apart, trying to restore some semblance of order, when the door opened, and in stepped Waddell and Elsie, each holding Conway by the hand.

The ruckus instantly stopped, everyone in the room transfixed by their presence. They were wearing matching white t-shirts that Waddell had purchased at the carnival. Airbrushed across the front of his, in bright red, and vivid blue, was the word 'STUPID'. Emblazoned on hers, in the same brilliant hues, was 'I'M WITH STUPID', and little Conway's bore a very colorful 'Me 2'. They looked positively angelic.

"Judge, me an' Elsie here wanna' jump tha' broom."

"Is that right maam'?"

"I reckon."

"Well that's the first sensible thing I've heard all mornin'. Gimme a few minutes to get my robe on, and all you people are gonna witness it, or you're all goin' to jail. Take your pick."

Waddell turned to Doil.

"Sorry bout is' partner. It jus' snuck up on me."

"Hell son, don't be sorry. I'm proud for ya'! Sides', tha' ol' lady's turned into a wildcat I'm tellin' ya, a damn wildcat! We liable ta' have a kid uv' our own fore' long. Heir to a show bidness' empire."

"She lookin' good Doil. Puts me inna' mind o' whas' er' name."

"Joey Heatherton?"

"Naw, at' woman onna' Brady bunch. Lissen' Doil; I sorta ' hate ta' ast' ya', after I screwed up ya' adoption an' all, but would ya' stand up fa' me as my best man?"

For the first time in his life, Doil was speechless, and from my vantage point in the window, I saw big horse tears roll down his chubby cheeks, and he threw his arms around Waddell's neck and gave him a big bear hug. He struggled to free himself from the embrace.

"Damn man, don't go all squirrelly on me now."

Betty-Fay had stooped down, and was gently adjusting Conway's 'comb' of red hair, talking to him quietly.

"Yall' gon' be fine, baby. Waddell's a good man. Little rough aroun' tha' edges, but he's got a big ol' heart, an' thas' what counts. He'll take good care uv' you an' ya' mamma."

Conway stared at her with wonder, rubbing his hand through her spikey blonde hair, and tracing her painted lips with his finger. A huge smile lit his face, and he threw his arms around her and held her close. She patted his back, and stood to face Elsie.

"You look wonderful honey."

"So da' you."

"Are ya' happy?"

"Yes maam, I'm tha' happiest I ever been."

"Be good ta' each other. This life ain't long enough ta' waste it bein' miserable. I oughta' know."

She took Elsie's cheeks in her hands and tenderly kissed her forehead.

"Les' get you married."

"Will you be my matron uv' honor?"

"You know I will honey, you know I will."

The judge, resplendent in his judicial robe, took his place before the happy couple. Little Conway stood in the middle, holding hands with his momma and Waddell. Doil took his place beside his partner, and Betty-Fay moved in to the right of Elsie and took her other hand. My perch outside the window proved to be the best seat in the house. Of all times not to have a camera, this was the most inopportune.

A scene worthy of 'Ripley's'. They say that all brides are beautiful, and I suppose on some level, they are, but this was certainly pushing the envelope.

The preacher, unable to witness his windfall evaporate, as well as the hundred bucks that he could charge for performing the ceremony, could'nt keep his big mouth shut.

"I must protest this un-holy union. To perform this un-sanctioned ceremony in front of a 'bona-fide' man of the cloth is an affront to every church wed couple in this county, and you are all goin' ta' hell."

"Sherriff, arrest this loud-mouthed son of a bitch!"

"On what charge ya' honor?"

"Interference with an officer of the court in the performance of his duty."

Cecil reluctantly moved toward the bristling Preacher, with all the authority of a puppy approaching an alpha male timberwolf. He gave Doil a pitiful, parting glance, and when their eyes met, Doil whispered,

"Buford Pusser"

The invocation caused Cecil to gain a full three inches in height. The transformation was startling; From Tim Conway, to Gary Cooper in 'High Noon'. He strode over, spun the reverend around, handcuffed him with the flourish and grace of a ninja, and pushed him, as he loudly denounced the gathering as a den of fornicators and bootleggers, out the door, down the hall, and ultimately, downstairs to the jail, and into a cell that was already occupied by Wormy. After he locked the cell door behind him, he informed him that if he heard a peep, he would stuff his purty' blue bikini panties down his throat. As Cecil left the jail, Wormy carefully un-folded the picture of the squirrell and presented it to Booger Red. Steve and I recalled afterward that we heard muffled screams emanating from an open window, but nothing short of barn-yard sodomy would have drawn us away from our ring-side seats at this production. The power of show bidness' was an amazing thing to witness.

The judge continued.

"If any body knows just cause that these two should not be wed, speak now, or forever keep your mouth shut."

Arv raised his hand, and opened his mouth to speak, but Wyvanelle, who had spent the last few minutes in deep reflection of her relationship history, and moved to tears by the genuine affection these people seemed to have for each other, planted her elbow between his third and fourth ribs, sending him to the floor gasping for breath, and clutching at her shapely ankle. She rolled her hand at the judge, symbolically bading him to continue.

"Who gives this woman to be married to this man?"

"I do."

A hush descended over the proceedings. Everyone, including myself, was dumb-struck, and when a couple of seconds passed with no one uttering a sound, he repeated,

"I do."

To everyone's utter amazement, it was little Conway. He placed his momma's hand in Waddell's, and turning to Runt Weaver, gave him a wink, and a thumbs up. The counselor broke into a broad smile. Conway stood under their joined hands as the judge asked,

"Do you Elsie?"

"I do:"

"Do you Waddell?"

"I guess:"

And as quickly as that, it was over. There was a lot of neck-hugging, and hand shaking, and a good deal of curiosity concerning the kid, who had not uttered another word.

In the trunk of my car, was my emergency rations Piggly-Wiggly sack, which I maintained in the event of sudden nuclear attack, or the sudden urge to lead a hunting expedition into the dense, hardwood forests of northeastern Alabama. It contained several packets of instant grits. Steve and I showered the wedding party with them in lieu of rice, as they exited the courthouse and stood on the front porch, continuing the rounds of congratulatory fellowship. Elsie took Betty-Fay by the hand, and led her away from the noisy throng.

"I need ta' tell ya' sumpn', but ya' gotta' promise me that you'll never tell a soul."

Elsie had a deadly serious look about her, and Betty-Fay, un-settled by her intense demeanor, answered very quietly,

"Of course honey. You're secret'll be our secret."

"Arv aint' Conway's daddy."

Betty-Fay was stunned.

"But who——-? I don't understand."

"Tha' preacher."

Betty-fays' mind was reeling, and she felt as though the porch was falling from under her.

"That son-ofa-bitch! That no-good son-ofa-bitch!"

"You cain't tell nobody! You promised!"

"But how? Does he know?"

"No, an' e' aint' ever gon' know! I had ta' get it off me. You tha' only one I can trust. At's tha' reason I went looney. Did'nt have nothin' ta' do with Arv. He'us just a freeloader. I got a new life now, wi' Waddell, an' I love im'. I don't wanna' ever let is' mess at' up."

"Will you do sumpn' for me?"

"Ya' know I will," answered Elsie.

"Will you call me your momma'?"

Elsie threw her arms around Betty-Fay's neck, and they hugged and cried, and held each other as if they would never get the chance again, and the adoption took place after all, in mind, if not on paper. Smiling and happy, arm in arm, they rejoined the celebration.

Parked over to the side, under the trees, unseen by the wedding party, was Datherd Dimond. I was apparently the only one who saw him.

"My God", I thought."He'll kill us all!"

He stepped from his truck, un-armed, and waved timidly. I saw Arv look down, and then back at Datherd. Everyone was busy with the second round of congratulations, and did'nt take much notice as Arv slipped off the courthouse steps, and walked to the truck. They climbed in, and slowly drove away. Wyvanelle watched, silently shaking her head, and then stepped over to Steve, who was bloodshot and rumpled from our long night of recovery.

"Ever been ta' Biloxie Mister Sanders?"

"No, but I've always wanted to go."

She took him by the hand, and they walked slowly down the street, in the general direction of the 'Shady Lawn'.

The wedding party was about to break up, when a big, black Lincoln came rolling very slowly down the street, headed west. As it slowed to a stop directly across from the steps, the driver's window came down, and a tiny fist came poking out, and as we watched in fascination, the middle finger rolled up, like the flag on Iwo Jima, and remained there, motionless. We had yet to see his face, but we knew it was Pee Wee. Draped over his shoulder, was a woman's hand, with long, red fingernails. The silhouette of her gigantic lips was plainly visible against the light through the opposite window.

"Let's go baby," we heard the woman say, and the Lincoln slowly moved off in the general direction of California, the arm remaining out, and the finger remaining as erect as a fence post as they disappeared over the horizon. We watched in silence till they were completely out of sight.

"Wonder where e' got at' car?" I asked Waddell.

"I magine' e' stole it."

"Reckon?"

We all stood around, scratching our feet on the wooden porch. There was really nothing left to say. Finally, Doil broke the un-comfortable silence.

"Now that, my friends, is show bidness'!"

LaVergne, TN USA
09 March 2011
219507LV00001B/1/P

9 781457 500305